THE
DEVIL AT TWO

RANDY STAN

NEWMAN SPRINGS PUBLISHING
320 Broad Street
Red Bank, NJ 07701

First originally published by Newman Springs Publishing 2022

ISBN 978-1-63881-691-1 (Paperback)
ISBN 978-1-63881-692-8 (Digital)

Printed in the United States of America

To Deb, who gave me strength and my path.

1

The full moon cast its light on the smooth body of the black widow. Its dark shape glistened in the illuminated night sky. Wings shot out from either side of its body, not the standard eight legs. There was a soft, faint yellowish glow from where the eyes should be. Instead of eyes, there were shields of glass. Blood or other bodily fluids didn't run through it. Instead, the lifeblood was made up of gasoline and hydraulic mixtures. This was no ordinary black widow. Not one made out of blood and tissue; no, this was one made of metal, wood, and fabric.

It was a Northrop P-61B Black Widow. A night fighter of lethal proportions. Built mainly to fly the night skies of World War II earth and wreak havoc on its enemies. It was in the employment of the United States Air Force. On this night in the late summer of 1944, it was on its mission of finding its enemies and hopefully sending them to a fiery death.

"I'm not picking up a gosh darn thing on this radar, Lieutenant! Not anything, zippo!"

"Relax, Gordy, we've only been in the air an hour. We'll find something to shoot at, trust me. And if not, we'll just enjoy a nice, relaxing flight," the pilot, Lieutenant Len Blackburn, responded.

"Yeah, but I wanted us to become aces tonight. We got four kills now and just need one more," Gordy Sloan, the radarman, answered back. His voice had a high tone to it, one of excitement. And it should, being that he was just nineteen and fresh out of flight school itself. He had enlisted in the air force straight out of school, ready to get into the thick of the fighting and give some payback to the old Axis powers.

"Don't let it trouble you, me boy. Stay calm. The old enemies will come to us. We won't have to go looking for them, you'll see," Glenn O'Shea, the copilot of the Widow, responded. Both he and Len were the older, more mature and experienced men of the three-man crew, if you called mature being in their midtwenties and experienced meaning they had been flying for about a year. But in this type of war, men died quickly; and yes, it made one fit the criteria.

"Like Len said, just sit back and enjoy the flight. My, the moon be really shinin' tonight, don't it though?" Glenn returned through his thick Irish brogue.

"Make sure the radar's working, Gordy. Don't need Adolf sneaking up on us and putting hot lead into our ass." Len spoke up. He had to, to be heard over the growl of the twin Pratt & Whitney radial engines. They were strong, powerful engines that sat on the wings on either side of the body of the plane. The engines had to be powerful to be able to do what was required of them. To be able to outclimb and outdive the enemy planes, that's what made the Black Widow such a formidable adversary. What also made it such a daunting foe was its newly equipped and revolutionary radar.

Before radar, planes just depended on eyesight to find and engage the enemy. With radar, you now could locate and find a plane or foe like a needle in a haystack. Another plane had only to be within range of the device, and bingo, it would show up on the radar screen as a blip or dot, thus giving one its location and proximity to you. You being the center point on the screen.

"Nope, the radar's working just fine. No blips on the screen at all."

"Good, just keep your little peepers on that screen, and we'll be fine," Len replied.

"Man, I can't wait to get this flight over with. We boys get the night off tomorrow. I can't wait to head back to town and get some ale in me gut." A smile broadened on Glenn's face.

"You and me both. We need a little cooldown time. We've been flying five nights in a row." Len blew a small sigh out of his mouth.

6

"Yes, sir, can't wait to walk into the Gooseneck Inn and see Shirlly. My, my, she sure is a fine-lookin' lassie." A laugh escaped from him.

Gordy chimed in, "You know, the last time we were in there, she told me if I gave her an extra dollar, she'd let me see her titties."

"Laddie, you're so young and wet behind the ears. For an extra dollar, she'd let me see 'em, touch 'em, and even suck on them." Glenn's laugh was a long, hearty one now.

"Gentlemen, I think if we all pooled our money together, we could get a lot more than just that from old Shirlly," Len declared, as he looked over at Glenn and winked.

This brought Gordy scrambling up to the cockpit, where the two pilots were sitting. The cockpit was not very spacious, just a little bigger across in the width than the front seat of a midsize car. The depth was about the same, with the instrumentation panel (holding all the controls) in front of the pilots, just like the dashboard of a car. There was barely enough room between the pilot and copilot chairs for anyone to maneuver. Now, with Gordy crammed in the slot, the three men were shoulder to shoulder.

"You really think so, Lieutenant? I mean, oh damn, that would be great. I mean, Shirlly is so hot. She's the cat's meow. I get a boner when I think about her."

"Calm down, lad. Getting this worked up right now, where we're at, is no good. Why, you'll want to start pulling on your pecker there; and the next thing you know, you'll have your manhood all over us and the plane." Glenn now returned the wink back to Len.

Gordy's face got red, his cheeks bubbling up in a blush. "I'd never do that here, not in front of you guys."

"I'm just having some fun with you, son." Glenn laughed as he put a hand on Gordy's shoulder.

"I know you are. It's just that…I mean…" Gordy's voice trailed away as his face remained a beet red.

Glenn leaned in close to Gordy, face-to-face. In the cramped quarters of the cockpit, this almost brought the two nose to nose. "Let me ask you this, lad, have you ever been with a woman?"

There was silence for a couple of seconds. Not that there was complete silence, the radial engines still roared. Then Gordy started stammering a reply. "Well...yeah...kinda...if you consider being with a woman...is what kinda...what Darla, my girlfriend, did for me?"

"And pray tell, what did she kinda do, laddie?"

"Well, I was getting ready to ship out for flight school... It was our last night together. Darla was crying that she might never see me again. That I wouldn't be back, only be back in a coffin. She was just a wreck, I tell you. Well...me...I was just so upset, knowing I wouldn't be seeing her for a long time. Not being able to feel her titties. She's got some real nice ones, so big and firm." Gordy's mind drifted as he spoke, grabbing his memories out of the air. "Wouldn't you know I had a big hard-on going on, wanting to burst out of my pants. Darla saw this...and she had always told me we wouldn't have intercourse until we were married, but..." Gordy stopped to compose himself.

"Come on, laddie, continue on. Don't just leave us poor souls hanging." Glenn's eyes were gleaming as he feverishly wanted to hear the rest of this very sexual story.

"Well...well...she said she would do this for me, only because I might never come back alive. She...she...unzipped my pants, took my dick out, and...and...did this thing with her hands. It was so good. When I...I...came, it shot all over her sweater. I thought she would explode, be mad, but she didn't. She said she loved me so much that it was okay."

"Lordy be, son, that was such a lovely story you just told us. You've got me all worked up. I bet those beautiful hands of hers were just so warm and firm, weren't they now? I hope she didn't have no calluses on them from jerkin' the cows fer milk, now, did she? That happened to me one time. This girl jerked me off. She was a big farm girl. Her hands were so callused and hard, I thought fer sure all the skin on me knob was being pulled off. Hope that didn't happen in yer case?" Glenn gave Gordy a laughing smirk.

"Hell no. Don't you even infer that about Darla. She's no heffer from the country. Her and I were raised in the city. Pittsburgh...

Pittsburgh, PA, fer sure, Glenn…so just…shut up! You shut up right now!"

"Easy, Gordy. Calm down. Glenn was just yanking yer chain. Right, Glenn, tell the boy you were just joking around. Com'on," Len said, trying to mediate the situation before it turned into something ugly. At the same time, his mind turned to Marrion, his wife. It brought back memories of their last time together before he shipped out. The fantastic sex they had had. Him tasting her, her devouring him, he could feel the slight arousal happening in his pants. He fought to turn the dial in his head back to off.

"Easy, me boy. I would just be spoofing with you. There was no harm intended," Glenn replied, trying quickly to defuse the situation that could get out of hand fast.

Gordy never got a chance to reply. His radar screen that sat on a latched drop table secured to the wall of the plane, six feet from the cockpit, gave out a loud bleep noise. This was the telltale sound given out by the machine when something entered the proximity of the radar. The big round screen of the radar unit had what could only be described as a clock hand that traveled around the circumference of the screen every six to seven seconds. When the clock hand came across an object that was within the range of the radar, it would make the bleep noise and give the location of said object in relation to the radar machine.

Gordy quickly made his way back to the instrument. By then it had already made two more rotations and two more bleeping noises. He hopped into his seat and studied the screen.

"What do we have, son?" Len yelled to him. He very seldom used the headset with the earphones and mic; he felt it was too impersonal for their close proximity.

A second later, Gordy replied, "Something moving fast. It came up at four, looks like, and moved past two and one and's almost at twelve o'clock now."

"You mean that it's almost directly above us?" Len barked, getting nervous quickly. Most planes they encountered, in their limited experience of using radar, never traveled that way in that short amount of time.

"That's what it's showing me, sir," Gordy responded. When his nerves started rumbling, he got very professional and regimental. No more first names; it was either sir or lieutenant.

Glenn leaned his head back and looked up through the clear glass canopy over his head. He craned his neck in several directions, surveying everything above them. "Don't see a damn thing yet. You'd think with the full moon I'd spot it just fine."

"Keep looking. The radar has never lied to us yet. If it says it's there, it's there," Len spat out.

"It's directly overhead, as close…almost on top of us!" Gordy shouted.

"How can that be? It can't have moved that fast and maneuvered that way. Glenn, make sure our 20 mms are locked in firing position. I'm diving this bitch, right now!" With that, Len pulled the control wheel of the Widow to the left sharply and hit the flaps, sending the plane dropping rapidly in that direction in a quick dive. The engines groaned, but they were strong engines and did what they were told. The Widow dropped two hundred feet, when Len brought it out of its dive and into a tight left circle, trying to survey what was chasing them.

"What do we see, boys? Be quick about it!"

"Nothing, Skip! I just don't see anything!" Glenn shot back.

"Gordy, what're you seeing on the screen?"

"He's there, Lieutenant! Hanging with us, right above us still!"

"That can't be, goddamn it! Gordy, go back to the back canopy and look, see if you can get eyes on him!" Len was yelling now.

"Got it, sir!" Gordy yelled as he put on his headset and moved toward the rear of the plane.

The main body of the Widow ran about thirty-five feet, with another clear glass canopy or cockpit section at the end of it. It was surrounded by two twin-tail sections on either side of it, running from the main wing and engine structure.

"What do you see, Gordy? Gordy, what do you see?" Len yelled frantically into the mic on his headset.

There was silence, for what seemed like an eternity. That kind of eternity could mean doom in the aerial warfare they were in. After seconds of quiet agony, Gordy's voice crashed into Len's headset. "I…I…don't know what the hell it is. It's just like a…" The headset went to static at the same moment the pilots heard the rear canopy explode into shattering glass and metal. They heard Gordy's voice scream in a bloodcurdling screech of pain and agony. It continued for several seconds, then faded into the distance, as if floating away from the plane on the wind currents. It clicked blazingly in Len's brain that it was not floating away but falling away. Gordy had fallen out of the plane.

"Get the hell back there and see what the fuck is going on!" Len feverishly screamed at Glenn.

Glenn yanked his headset off and stumbled out of his seat, trying to race to the rear of the craft. Len brought the plane out of its tight turn, leveling out into a straight path, straining his neck, searching the night sky for anything he could spot. There was no report of a machine gun or small cannon firing at them from another plane. His mind raced as he tried to come to terms with this crazy situation. What hit the rear of the plane? What happened to Gordy?

Glenn had only traversed three or four steps before he stopped in his tracks. "My god in heaven, no!" he yelled.

"What the hell is it? What the hell is it?" Len was screaming at Glenn.

One .45-caliber pistol shot exploded in the close quarters of the plane. It had the same effect as if standing next to a cannon when it is fired. Len could hear nothing but a large fuzzy bell being rung in his head. What he did see in the dark, moon-illuminated cockpit of the Black Widow were splatters of blood as they hit the front windshield and softly lit control panel. Not droplets, but goblets of thick hot blood ran down the glass onto the dashboard.

Len popped out of his seat and in the same motion pulled the .45 from his waist holster. He pointed it out in front of him as he turned from the chair. That's as far as he got.

Glenn's body lay sprawled against the starboard wall of the plane, his body all akimbo, as if he was trying to do a crazy dance. His midsection was splayed open from neck to waist, intestines spilling out to the floor of the compartment, blood pooling around them.

The face had a look of fear and bewilderment, all at the same time, the eyes telling the story.

He now looked upon the instrument of all the destruction and carnage inflicted on his crew and plane, on his Black Widow. What he saw made his blood go cold, his hand go trembling, the gun falling out of it. He never heard it hit the floor of the plane. He stood frozen as he gazed into hell's abyss. The fears and terrors of his subconscious stood in front of him. He wanted to look away but could not, transfixed as he was. He so wanted to close his eyes and go to a better place but could not.

That's when the grotesque creature standing three feet away from him did it for him. It plunged two long sharp, gnarled talons into his eyes and took his sight away forever.

2

The sky before them looked like a giant field of black mushrooms, some fading quickly, others springing to life instantly. The speed of their growing population was rapidly increasing. Inside of each new mushroom was a bright burst of life, a magnification of energy.

To the flock of B-17 bombers approaching, it meant death and destruction if a mushroom cloud touched any plane. From a distance, there was a low rumbling sound; but as the bombers got closer to the field, the sound became one of ominous thunder.

There were forty-eight heavy planes in this, the Thirty-Eighth Bomber Group, all from Molesworth Airfield out of England. World War II was in full bloom over the skies of Europe. Theirs was a late-afternoon, soon-to-be-evening, bombing run to the industrial city of Bremen, Germany.

"We're really walking into a goddamn wall of flak, aren't we?" Lieutenant Terry Graynor, the copilot of one of the bombers, called out.

"Yep, it's gonna be one big shitstorm." Captain Cullum Davis pressed his head mic button. "Heads-up, crew. Hold on to something. We'll be moving through heavy flak buildup in a sec."

All eight of his crew responded in unison, "Roger."

All the bombers were in their combat boxes. The boxes consisted of twelve planes. Of that, three were formed into separate triangle formations, with four of these per box.

Captain Davis's B-17 was the lead plane in the formation that was considered the low element. Respectively, one had the lead element, the high element, the low element, and the low-low element. The low-low element was the worst to be in. It was the closest to the ground and would be the first to be targeted by the guns on the ground, firing the flak shells up at them, causing the aforementioned mushroom fields.

Every plane in the group had a nickname given to it (thought of by the original crew christening it) with artwork painted on, depicting the name. The name attached to the bomber Davis and his crew were in was *Fallen Angel*. This was regaled on the port side of the plane, between the cockpit and the nose of the aircraft.

It showed the picture of an angel. Just not your normal type of cherub, but one of a more sensual, vengeful portrayal. It was a heavenly woman with blazing red hair, flowing back from the winds of heaven. She was in flight, her wings fully extended. Her attire was very risqué—a very wispy type of cameo adorned her lithe body, leaving very little to the imagination. Her ample breasts, barely concealed, showed pert nipples. The minute cameo came to just past her crotch, highlighting her long, slender legs. Her face was not one of peace and love, but more of anger and vengeance. In one hand, she grasped a mighty long broadsword, held high over her head, ready to strike. In the other was a bomb—the type of bomb that this B-17 carried and was now intent on dropping on the city of Bremen, to inflict death and destruction.

As the formation of bombers entered the flak field, they quickly started to be buffeted and bounced around by the shells exploding close to them. Those were the lucky ones if that's all it did to them.

The bomber to the port side of the *Fallen Angel* took a hit to its right wing. The explosion ignited the fuel lines to the two massive Wright radial engines. There was a second bright, fiery explosion, sending flames and debris out into the air. The *Fallen Angel* rocked and danced as the concussion hit her. The whole wing section attached to the body of the wounded plane broke free and fell away. The bomber, not able to compensate for the loss of weight and power, immediately tipped over on its left side and started spiraling toward the earth.

"Jesus Christ, they just got *Bengal Lancer*!" Bernie Mossberg, the port waist gunner, shouted over the radio.

"I see it. Watch, see if you see any parachutes coming out of it," Davis replied.

"Not one. The plane's spiraling too fast. They're all goners," Bernie shot back.

"Keep watching. Maybe someone will get out." Terry Graynor broke into the conversation.

"I'm watching too. Ain't no one getting out of there, Skip," the belly gunner, Lanzo Torrida, chimed in.

The sky above and to their port side erupted in a bright flash followed by the thick cloud of black. Shrapnel from the shell swept into the plane like a rain of heavy hail, pinging and dancing on the skin of the craft. A hole appeared in the *Fallen Angel* decal, her left breast obliterated. Another piece of shrapnel pierced the fabric just behind the side window of the cockpit, shooting into the compartment and bouncing off the opposite wall, landing on the floor between the two pilots, still sizzling as it lay there.

"You okay, Cull?" shouted Terry as the bomber bounced again from a nearby explosion.

"Yeah, I'm okay. Let's hope the old girl can handle it."

"Well, she's done it for seventeen missions so far. Let's hope eighteen ain't unlucky."

The B-17 had become a tough heavy bomber since they had been beefed up from their earlier version. Plating had been installed in key spots, protecting the plane from damage. But there were still many areas unprotected against bullets and shrapnel. The firepower was far superior to most anything in the sky. They were now equipped with a double-machine gun turret in the nose for the bomber. New turrets on the top, belly, and rear of the plane, all double .50-caliber machine guns, had been installed. Also added to it were single-gun waist openings on either side and one in the roof, by the tail section. It was now a sturdy, well-armed (as the nickname implied), flying fortress, carrying a heavy payload of bombs. What kept it in the air were the four Wright radial engines, two on each wing. Even when you lost one or possibly two engines, as long as they weren't on the same wing, they still had enough power to keep the plane in the air, of course minus the bomb load.

"Bombardier, Bombardier. Slade, can you hear me?" Cullum barked on his mic.

"Gotcha, Skip. Coming up on the drop target in five. Getting my sights lined up now," Slade Driscal, the bombardier, replied.

The bombardier became the most important man on the mission at this point. Once he lined up the target on the ground in his bomb sites, he was given control of the bomber, able to correct the course one way or another, giving him the precise point to drop the payload at that right moment, releasing the bombs on said target, hopefully obliterating it with deadly accuracy.

Their target today, in Bremen, was a plane factory, one that built fighter planes for the German Luftwaffe. The same planes that after they dropped their bombs and headed for home would be swarming all over them, like flies on shit.

Slade wondered why they hadn't hit the flight before the flak zone; most of the time they usually did. Today it was different. Maybe there was a snafu with them, and they were late getting into the air. Maybe they were employing a different tactic or method for shooting them out of the sky. He knew one way or another, the odds were high that they would now be attacked once they finished their bomb run.

"Jesus, my god. We lost another one," came the voice of Jessie Hildago, the top turret gunner.

Cullum and Terry stretched their necks and heads to look above them. Jessie, being the top gunner, had the best view from above; they had figured that's where he had seen it. Out ahead of them, to their right, they saw the flaming bomber as it plummeted past them, in a death throe, to the ground. Three parachutes opened up after the plane dropped past. Well, Cullum thought, at least three out of nine was better than zero out of nine.

Another heavy explosion rocked the plane, lifting the left wing high into the sky, taking them out of their level flight. As the bomber dropped back down, Cullum looked over to inspect the damage and saw there was trouble. The number 1 engine, the farthest engine out on the port side wing, was smoking. The propeller wasn't spinning quite right. In a couple of seconds, the smoke increased, leaving a long, thick, snaky black trail behind the bomber.

"Number 1 took a hit, Skip. We're leaving a big tail of smoke," radioed Lanzo Torrida, the belly gunner of the *Fallen Angel*.

16

"Copy that, Lanzo. I see it too. Watch it. Tell me if you see something I don't see. Over."

"I got a good eye on it too," Jessie Hildago chimed in.

The flak field was intense now. Black clouds were exploding all around them. A B-17 far up in the lead group took a hit in the nose and cockpit section, debris shot from the plane, hanging in the air long enough to collide with the *Fallen Angel's* flight path. It sounded and felt like large rocks peppering their craft. One piece smacked the windshield in front of Cullum, planting a painful wound and spidery crack in the glass.

"Number 1's starting to light up, Skip," Jessie radioed to Cullum.

"Roger that," Cullum answered as he looked over and saw sparks and flickers of flame starting to lick out from under the engine.

"Shit, that ain't good. Terry, cut off the fuel to number 1."

"Aye, aye," Terry replied as he reached over to the dashboard in front of them and flipped the toggle switch marked engine 1 fuel to the off position.

The engine would keep running, prop still turning, but without fuel, basically the engine now was feathering out the flame. Within seconds, the flame and smoke had stopped.

"Okay, that takes care of the fire. Might as well kill the engine. Do it, Terry."

"Got you covered, Cull," answered Terry as he flipped another switch.

It took another thirty seconds for the propeller to end its somewhat catty wampus rotation and come to a stop.

"Can't we go up a little to get out of the flak? We're getting killed here." Terry worriedly looked over at Cullum. He knew the answer before his captain even said it.

"We're supposed to stay at twenty-eight thousand feet. We go up much higher, the ceiling will have too much cloud coverage, and we won't be able to see our target. It's just our crummy luck."

"I know, I know. Just had to get it out. It's so crazy. We're like sitting ducks."

"Yep. I agree." He gave Terry a pained grin. "Slade, come in. How much farther to the target, over?" As Cullum keyed his mic, a slight shake came to his fingers. He quickly brought his hand back down to conceal it from Terry.

"About sixty seconds, sir. You can switch over the plane control and open the bomb bay doors anytime, over," returned Slade Driscal, as he sat over his bomb site, lining everything up.

When it came time to drop the payload (bombs), the pilot's primary job was to open the bomber's bomb bay doors; racks of highly explosive bombs sat over it. Once the bombardier maneuvered the plane over the target, he was the one to press the release button, sending the load of falling death down onto the location.

"It's all yours, Slade. Good hunting," Cullum chirped nervously as he finished the transmission.

Slade peered through the periscope-type sight, tweaking his steering controller slightly to his right. The plane bounced as another shell exploded close by.

"Damn you, Fritz," he muttered as the scope popped him in the eye, from the turbulence. Beads of sweat were forming on his forehead, just below his flight headgear. No matter how many times he had done this before, it still tore him up when it came time to push the button. It wasn't just the process, of lining the target up and dropping the bombs; it was what the bombs eventually did, what they accomplished. Yes, it would destroy valuable equipment and material that the Germans needed for their war effort. But it also snuffed out lives. Human lives of men and women, even children, that would be in the way of this deadly payload. Innocent people who probably didn't care one iota about killing Americans or Allied soldiers. They just wanted to live their lives normally, without all this bullshit. To laugh and love with one another, not having the worry about death coming their way. This war was so goddamn stupid, he thought.

He now saw his target through the flak clouds. It looked just like it did when he and all his fellow bombardiers had looked at the reconnaissance photos in their preflight briefing. He saw the forty or so warehouse-type buildings below. Some lay out perpendicular to him, some horizontal.

His finger hesitated for a millisecond, gently quivered, and then pressed the release button. He touched his mic. "Bombs away."

Cullum looked out at the exact same moment and saw all the remaining bombers release their payload of bombs from the belly of their planes, through two open doors. It was always a sight watching thirty or forty bombs drop two at a time from the undersides of these massive machines.

Terry Graynor looked out and down from his side window in the cockpit. Twenty seconds later, he saw massive explosions engulf the earth below. Huge geysers of dirt and debris flew up into the air. The big warehouse buildings of the airplane factory weren't as big and intact anymore.

"They're doing their job. Target engaged and hit, Cull."

"I figured that. Now let's get the hell out of here." As he flipped the switch back to regain his control of the bomber, the speaker on his dash came alive with a voice.

"*Rattlesnake* to group. Prepare to make turn, over."

Cullum reached and grabbed a larger mic piece from the dashboard. "*Rattlesnake 1, Rattlesnake 1*. This is *Fallen Angel*, making my turn now, over."

"Roger that." The voice that replied was garbled in static and interference, due to other bombers sending messages. *Rattlesnake 1* was the lead bomber in their element; all other bombers followed its lead.

Almost at the same moment, all the bombers in the flight made a slow turn to port. It gave one the image of a flight of ducks heading home for the winter. It took about forty seconds to make the complete turn, but when it was done, the whole flight was turned and headed west to England. To Molesworth Airfield and safety. But to everyone on the *Fallen Angel*, they knew they weren't safe yet.

3

"Okay, boys, we're going up to thirty-five thousand feet to get away from any more flak. Get your oxygen masks on now, over." Cullum Davis spoke to his crew.

Almost to a man they replied, "Roger."

"Be ready. We're not out of the woods yet. Be on the lookout for bandits," Cullum said this to his crew, knowing if they hadn't encountered enemy aircraft before the bomb run, they sure would now.

The big bomber labored a little to get to thirty-five thousand feet, with only three running engines, but it did. Once the whole flight was back in formation, Terry Graynor took a quick count of the planes. "Damn, they got a bunch of us." Cullum just shook his head in regret.

Two minutes later, Jessie Hildago cried out, his voice crackling through the headsets. "Bandits coming in at one o'clock."

Cullum looked up and out. He counted quickly; it looked to be about fifteen or twenty fighter planes, probably ME 109s (Messerschmitt 109 fighter planes). These were deadly craft. Quick bastards that had not only 13 mm machine guns but also cannons. Always two 20 or 30 mm cannons, and sometimes two more under each wing.

"Fire when they bear. Make your bullets count, boys," signaled out Cullum.

The first pass of fighters came in, all gun blasting away. Pinging and thumping sounds reverberated throughout the bomber, like hail hitting and bouncing off a metal shed roof. Only these shells weren't bouncing; they were penetrating. All the .50 calibers opened up on the fortress, a deafening roar, but quickly dissipated in the vast open sky. The first wave flew past and under the formation, the gunners keeping their sights and fingers on the triggers till they flew out of range.

Now the dogfight broke down to fighters picking out wounded or disabled bombers, ones showing signs of weakness (burning or smoking). It was the pack and herd mentality. The fighters were the pack of wolves, looking for prey, while the bombers were the herd, just looking for safety.

Terry cried out on the radio, "Fighter at three o'clock, starboard, dammit, starboard!"

The ME 109 was leveled off coming straight at the starboard side center of the fortress, its machine guns and cannons spitting flame and sending lead toward them. The top turret, bottom turret, and waist side gunner all trained their guns on it and let loose.

Holes opened all along the side of the *Angel*. The number 3 engine, closest to the side of the bomber itself, ignited in flames. The bullets were taking a toll on the massive fortress, but at the same time, the fighter was being inflicted with major pain from the bomber. Pieces of the fighter started to break apart and come off in chunks, the whole body being ripped asunder. It flew past, over the top of the *Fallen Angel*, in a state of rolling smoke and flames, the burning oil and gas quickly enveloping the craft. It made it about fifty yards from the bomber and then fell into a death spiral toward the earth.

Dentiel Reed, the starboard waist gunner, yelled to his counterpart on the port side, "Did we get him? Did we get him?"

"Sure did, boy! He's a goner!" screamed Bernie Mossberg, as he fired a few rounds into the burning wreck.

There was no time for cheering in all the chaos. "Bandit coming up at five o'clock stern!" Lanzo Torrida yelled from the bottom (belly gunner) turret. He opened up on it as Dentiel swung his machine gun down and blazed away at it, empty shell casings falling from his .50 to the floor of the bomber. They bounced and clinked against each other, giving off a sound of many glasses being brought together for a large toast.

The bullets from the ME centered all on the waist and starboard side of the bomber. Pieces of material, torn away, from the skin of the plane fluttered all around Dentiel in a mad snow globe dance as he feverishly kept his sights on the fighter. He squeezed the trigger of the .50 with both hands in a choke-like grip.

A bolt of immense light and pain wrapped his body as he lost all vision. The next thing he knew, he was lying on the floor of the bomber, Bernie Mossberg looking down at him. "You okay, you okay? Christ, you ain't, dammit!" he screamed, as he fired his gun at fighters, then gave a glance back at Dentiel.

The ME 109 shot past the bomber's starboard wing, all its guns firing. The engine closest to the body of the plane erupted in a ball of sparks and flame, sending metallic debris spewing into the air. The enemy fighter continued its path of destruction toward another bomber.

Cullum Davis instantly flipped off the fuel feed to the number 3 engine. "Fuck, they got another one!" he shouted at Terry.

"And it's burning pretty good! Wing's on fire!" Terry shouted back.

"Hit it with fire control!"

Terry reached out and flipped a button marked fire control 3. Each engine had one of these, a small container situated by them that had an antifire foam solution in it. Most of the time the foam wouldn't help against a raging fire, but if you caught it before it got of hand, it could do the trick.

Most of the flames went out as white foamy gel encased the burning engine, trying to choke out the burn. Cullum switched off the engine. "How's it look?"

"I think that got it under control. Hopefully, without fuel to it, the rest of the fire will go out," Terry replied, a little relieved.

The dogfight raged for another twenty minutes, fighters diving and flashing through the formation. One bomber, all engines smoking or blazing with flames, slowly drifted from the formation, headed for the ground. A group of bodies exited the plane, their chutes opening immediately. One chute opened too close to the flames wafting off the doomed bomber, instantly igniting it. The chute quickly melted away to nothing, leaving the man attached, plummeting to the earth and inevitable death.

"Rotten fucking luck, I tell you," said Terry as he shook his head.

"That was *Lucky Lou*, wasn't it?" asked Cullum.

"I think so. How ironic, no luck there. Poor bastard, I'd hate to die that way."

"Looks like the fighters are starting to peel off. Probably out of ammo," Davis quipped, viewing the retreat of the MEs. One by one they broke away from the B-17s and headed east.

Within five minutes, the formation, what was left of it, were the only planes in the sky. The *Fallen Angel* was slowly drifting and falling back from the group.

"The engines took a beating. The two we have left can't keep up with the rest of the flight. Hopefully we can limp home. Don't want to have to bail out over enemy territory. Everyone, keep your fingers crossed," Cullum said to the crew over his mic.

"You and me both, especially now that it's starting to get dark. Don't want to have to chute down on some trees or buildings in the black. Man, I hate these late-afternoon missions." Terry fumed, looking toward the western sky, as the sun slowly approached the horizon. It seemed to take the energy or life of the stricken bomber with it as it started to fade from view.

"This is *Fallen Angel* to *Rattlesnake 1*, over." Cullum now had the mic for ship-to-ship communication in his hand. He could feel their situation turning for the bad. The two remaining engines were starting to chug and cough at different intervals, as if trying to tell him and the crew that soon they would be spent.

"Go ahead, *Fallen Angel*," *Rattlesnake 1* replied.

"Can't keep up with the formation. Lost two engines. The others are in bad shape. Will try to get home best I can, over."

"Tough luck, Davis. Will let base know the situation. Stay on this course. If you go down, it'll be easier to find you. Good sailing and Godspeed, over and out." Those were the last words heard from *Rattlesnake 1*. It and the rest of the formation continued on their journey home, while the *Fallen Angel* limped along like a three-legged dog.

"Captain to crew. Keep eyes peeled for night fighters. Fritz might have them up tonight," Cullum said over his headset.

"Shit, I didn't even think about that." Terry's tone was agitated.

"Hell, I wouldn't worry too much, Terry. We'll probably be bailed out and on the ground before the *Heinkels* [German night fighters] find us."

"Hey, Cap." This was Lane Arnold calling Cullum over the headset. He was the extra top gunner for the bomber. His glassed opening was small, mounted toward the rear of the bomber, holding a single .50-caliber gun. The opening gave him sight of just above the plane and to the rear or stern of it. He wouldn't be able to inflict much damage on any fighter unless it was diving straight down on them or coming at a forty-five-degree angle from the stern. But in this type of bomber and its mission, the air force figured anything added couldn't hurt but help. An extra gun was an extra gun; it could help protect the plane.

Besides being a gunner, he was also their medical man. He had taken the prescribed courses the air force had given him for first aid and minor surgical assistance.

"You want to come back here. Dentiel's been hurt."

Cullum looked over at Terry, an expression of "Oh, not this too" came over his face. "Shit, was hoping we got through the scrape without a scratch. Don't look like we did."

"Aw nuts. It had to be Dentiel too, didn't it?" Terry responded back.

Dentiel Reed wasn't supposed to be their waist gunner on this flight. He was their ground mechanic for the bomber. The man who helped keep it in shape to fly. The one who repaired or replaced engines and put new pieces or sections on when they either got shot up or blown away. He wasn't supposed to set one foot on the bomber when it was in the air. The United States Air Force said so; it was their rule and law. Dentiel Reed was a black American. In 1943, black Americans were not allowed to be involved in any combat actions of any type. Racial discriminations were at their zenith. All a black man could or was allowed to do was be a mechanic, supply man, or cook, period. In another year, things would change in a most different way

THE DEVIL AT TWO

and have a different outlook for the black man and his service to his country. But as of right now, it was total taboo to have a black man flying on a B-17, over war-torn Europe.

Their assigned waist gunner was Johnny Gyrinich. Two hours before the mission, while the ordnance crew was loading ammo and bombs to the flying fortress, Johnny had climbed into the plane to check his .50-caliber gun. Make sure it was in working order. He had already been credited with two kills, meaning he had shot down two enemy fighters. He wanted to make sure his gun was ready to get at least another one.

On his way out of the bomber, he was exiting through the trap door on the belly of the plane. He wasn't paying much attention as he swung his legs out and pushed off; the load of 200 lb. bombs was right there on the tarmac, by the door. The munitions crew had set the pallet there, waiting for the bomb bay doors to open so as to load them in the racks, like they had done so many times before. Johnny caught one of the heavy metallic bombs just right with his left foot and, bingo bammo, snapped his ankle.

Lying there on the tarmac, he said to his crew, in tears of pain, "Boy, I really fucked this one up, didn't I?"

"Don't worry, we'll get someone else to take your spot, you dickhead," said Bernie Mossberg, his fellow waist gunner and best friend.

Only there wasn't anyone else. At this time of the war, they were very shorthanded. A replacement gunner would take at least a day or two to get; that's just the way it was.

Dentiel had been there with the rest of the crew, making final inspections. When Captain Davis looked at the crew and said, "We'll just have to fly shorthanded," he responded, "Please, Skip, let me go in his place. I sure know I can cover it. I won't be no trouble."

A couple of the crew members looked pensively at him, their racial hairs rearing up on their necks. This included Johnny's buddy Bernie.

"No offense, boy. But I don't know if I want you up in the air next to me."

Dentiel felt his ire start to rage. He could feel the heat in his face and cheeks. "You ain't got to worry, Bernie. My black won't rub off on you."

"Screw you, nigger. I just don't want you there, that's all." The tendons in Bernie's neck tightened. His fists clenched together as he moved toward Dentiel in a racial rage.

"Stop your shit right now, Mossberg. I'll not stand for none of that stuff happening here. We got a war going on, and it's up to all of us to win it." Cullum got between both men, looking hard at Bernie. "Look, you either let him fly with us and man the gun, or you don't, and then there's no one protecting your back and the starboard side of the ship. What's it gonna be?" Cullum was looking at Bernie, eye to eye.

The Jewish store clerk from Queens, New York, lowered his head and responded in a low voice, "Okay."

Cullum didn't give anyone else time to respond. He spun around and looked Dentiel dead in the eye. "Son, I'm giving you this chance. Don't screw it up. If there's a major problem that comes out of this, it'll be my ass in the fire, not yours, got it?"

"Yes, sir, I understand. There won't be any problem." Dentiel was calming down but still on edge.

Skipper Davis was taking a big chance with him. Dentiel knew if the brass found out, it could even lead to a court martial for the skipper.

Davis looked at the rest of the crew that was formed around Johnny Gyrinich. "That goes for the rest of you, swingin' dicks. If this gets out about Dentiel, I'll shoot you myself, got it!"

Everyone murmured acceptance of the situation in unison. They liked Dentiel for what he did for their bomber; but as far as flying in it, that brought up other feelings, some good, some bad. But they all liked and respected Captain Davis. They would go to hell and back for him.

Cullum, feeling the situation over, looked back at Dentiel and put a hand on his shoulder. "Just don't get hurt." Dentiel nodded in agreement. "Okay now, Dentiel, you and the rest of these clowns, get Johnny to the hospital and get right back."

4

Cullum got out of his seat and walked through the cockpit door. He took a couple of steps and patted the dangling legs of the top turret gunner, Jessie Hildago. "You okay, Jess?" he yelled up to the jovial Mexican.

Jessie sat in a padded fabric seat harness that was attached to the turret gun on top of the B-17. The turret was operated by hydraulics and controlled by the gunner. As he rotated the turret around, the seat rotated in unison with it. Jessie could do a full 360-degree view of the sky.

"I'm doing okay, my good man. You know we got us another fighter today. That makes seven so far."

"I know. Good job, to you and the guys. Keep an eye out though. Not out of the woods yet. Could run into some night fighters in a bit, once the sun is completely down."

"I agree. Those Fritzy Heinkels are one mean killing machine. But we've got a lot of firepower too." Jessie tapped his twin .50s with a wry grin.

Cullum made his way around the bomb racks, sitting in the center aisle of the plane. They were all empty now, having accomplished their mission, delivering death and destruction to Nazi Germany.

To his left sat Lieutenant Don Lanier, his navigator and radioman. In front of Don was his desktop, hinged and bolted to the wall. A big radio unit sat on it, buzzing and glowing with a yellowish life. To one side sat his codebook, for sending and receiving messages. On his right was another walled partition, separating the compartment from the rest of the bomber. On that wall sat a shelf, holding folders that comprised all the navigational charts. Charts he needed to get them anywhere they wanted or had to go. He was an important cog to the operation of this bomber.

"Send our position and situation out to base. Just in case *Rattlesnake 1* didn't radio it."

"Got it, Skip." Don had a protractor and pencil in his hands, fumbling with them while looking over a chart. "Lane's back in the waist with Dentiel."

"I figured as much. Anyone else hurt?"

"Not that I know of."

"Well, go ahead and do a head count. Let me know if they are."

"Will do." Don gave Cullum a short snapped informal salute, as he put his headset on to talk.

Cullum stepped through the doorway into the next compartment; he could hear his crew talking. The two engines operating were still spitting out life, creating a loud coughing drone, but nowhere as loud as when all four were running and functioning properly. He sidestepped the hatch for the belly gunner turret and now could distinguish whose voices he heard.

"I knew you shouldn't have come on this mission. Your black ass put a jinx on us, I tell you. Don't think we're gonna get back to base, probably be jumping our butts out over occupied territory. And at night no less. Oh boy." Bernie Mossberg sat on a little stool, across from Dentiel and Lane Arnold.

Dentiel was lying, half sitting over on the starboard side hull of the plane, by his gunport. His left hand was pushing on his rib area; his flight jacket and shirt had been removed. Medical gauze was wrapped completely around his bare midsection, now turning a pink, reddish color, from the blood oozing out of a bullet wound. He grimaced as he spoke.

"Listen, you stupid Jew. If I hadn't been here, we might have been in worst shape. No gunner on this." He motioned with his head toward the .50 sitting in the gunport opening. "Your ass would have really been fried from that fighter."

"Yeah, yeah, that's what you think. You're just bad karma, that's all," Bernie replied, shooting a finger in his direction.

"I agree with Dentiel, you asshole. You would have been taking shells up your keister, if he hadn't been on that gun. So let it go!" Lane yelled, sitting back on his legs and feet, in a kneeling position over Dentiel. A hypodermic needle was in one hand. He squinted an eye as he looked intently into the syringe, trying to figure out if he had the right dosage dispensed for Dentiel's wound.

"I can't believe you're on his side, Arnold. I mean, taking the side of this black monkey bastard. I...I...*oy vey!*"

Cullum interceded himself into the heated dispute. "You want to shut your stupid trap, Bernie. If not, I'll throw you out of this plane without a goddamn chute. Got it!" He bent down and said this to Bernie with the tips of their noses inches apart.

Bernie quickly lowered his head and looked at the floor of the craft. "Okay, okay."

Cullum turned and knelt by Dentiel and Lane. "Well, what's the story, boys?" He smiled as he looked at Dentiel, trying to ease the man's temper and fears, knowing it wouldn't.

"Two shells got him. One just grazed his shoulder. I think it almost cauterized it on contact. Hardly any bleeding at all, almost dried up now. The other one is the bad one. Got him here off the ribs." Lane pointed down at the growing, colored gauze. "Probably broke a couple of them. Went in and came out his back, clean. Don't know what damage it did internally, but at least it came out. Got it plugged and wrapped, but he's still bleeding pretty good. Gonna give him a shot of morphine for the pain."

"That's the whole story in a nutshell?" Cullum asked.

"That's all for now. Told him to keep the pressure on the wound, might help to keep the bleeding down," Lane said, grim faced, as he looked back and forth between the two men.

"I'm sorry, Skip. Didn't want this kinda shit to happen, no way." Dentiel's face had a pained look, but a smile quickly formed. "At least I got that 109 bastard."

"You sure did, didn't you? All I can say is hang in there. I'm gonna really try to get us home. Hopefully soon. You and me both are gonna say our prayers about that, okay?" Cullum smiled, as he gave Dentiel a thumbs-up.

Cullum looked over at Lane. "Give him the shot and then come see me." He motioned with his head toward the front of the bomber.

"Sure thing, Cap," Lane replied, looking at Cullum and then with disgust toward Bernie Mossberg.

Cullum headed back to the cockpit. "You get that message off, Don?" he asked as he got back to the radio panel.

"I did. Got back a reply. They said, 'Good luck. Hope you have good winds.'" Cullum watched as Don gave him a pessimistic grin when he finished. He knew it was going to be tough, the engines laboring the way they were. As long as nothing else got put in their path to hinder them, they had a slim chance.

Cullum plopped into his seat and looked over at Terry in the growing gloom of approaching twilight. "Dentiel's shot up pretty bad. Couldn't count all the bullet holes back there in the waist section. There's just so many of them. And on top of that, the two remaining engines sound like shit."

Terry took his officer's hat off and rubbed his forehead with the back of his arm, blowing out a long sigh. "We're really in a shit bag, aren't we? At least we've got a nice sunset to look at."

The sun was a promising, glowing ball of energy as it was slowly sinking, halfway below the horizon. It gave Cullum the feeling of peace. A feeling of calm and happiness, despite everything that was going on now, and for everything that happened to him in the past. But in the fringes of approaching dark, he felt an unease, an anxiety of tension, as if the night was bringing a dread to him and his crew.

Zack Prettner, the rear tail gunner, brought him out of his thoughts when his voice came slicing through his headset. "Hey, Skip. Can you hear me, over?"

Cullum woke, as if from a faraway dream. His eyes had spots and flashes zipping around in front of them. He hadn't realized he had been staring into the sun for that long of a time. He felt Terry looking at him as if saying, "Well, you going to answer him, or should I?"

He keyed his mic. "Yeah, I got you, Zack. What's up?"

"I see something or should I say things off our stern, at about two o'clock."

"What are they doing in relation to us?"

"It looks like they're following us, over."

"How many are there, over?"

"Can't quite make that out, but there's a flock of them."

"What do you mean a flock, Zack? Are they birds?" Cullum's mind did an abrupt stop as he pondered the information.

Zack didn't reply right away. There was dead air over the plane's radio for a short span, then he responded, "All I can say right now is they got wings, big flapping wings."

Cullum looked at his altitude gauge. They were flying at sixteen thousand feet. Zack continued on with his assumptions. "They might be eagles or condors, maybe."

"At this height, it can't be anything else," Cullum replied. He knew the air and its currents. At this height, it didn't allow too many other birds to travel in it.

"Guess so, Skip. Just weird, that's all I can say."

"Well, just keep those good eyes on them. Let me know when you finally get a good confirmed visual on them, roger."

"Roger out, Skip." Zack ended his transmission as he peered out into the darkening eastern sky.

The things he was looking at sure weren't planes, like he told the captain; they had wings. And these wings were flapping pretty good. He could now make out that they were closing the distance between the ship and them. He started counting. It looked like at least ten of these things. Other people would never or could never see things at this distance. It was too great. But he could; he always had good sight. As far back as he could remember, his eyesight was always spot-on. He could pick out a bird in a tree, or a squirrel in a field, from way over a hundred yards. He had won contests because of his sight. Had trophies sitting on the fireplace mantel to prove it.

He watched these, whatever they were, birds approaching, their wings flapping up and down in a rhythmic motion, an almost hypnotic motion. He remembered the big hawks back home, how they would flap their wings like this and soar high in the air. He could spot them from a long distance. That's how good his eyesight was, and still was.

The big birds were closer now, wings beating into the purplish sky, beating in Zack's head. His eyes pulsated to their metronome-like motion. He became one with their movement. Time around him faded. He now was one with them. As they continued their approach, Zack's eyes glazed over.

5

The rabbit came out of the woods into the wide prairie field in slow bouncing hops. After several hops, it would stop, motionless, and seem to listen. It raised its head to smell the air. The nose twitched in nervous pinches. Seeming satisfied with its position and situation, it made several more jerky hops and landed alongside some flowering growths. It again sat and made its inspection of the surroundings. When feeling content, it started nibbling one of the flowers.

Zack Prettner looked through the V-sight on his .22 rifle. Even though he was roughly eighty yards from the rabbit, he made it out clear as day. He saw its light brown-white fur, and the ears (that had perked up now, standing tall) were a pinkish white on the inside of them. He had no scope on the rifle, to zoom in. Just his eyes and the mechanical grove on the gun. He took a breath, deep in his lungs, feeling his heart beating, not hard and fast, but slow and steady. He put his finger slowly to the trigger of the rifle. At the same moment he exhaled his breath slowly out through his nose and mouth, he gently squeezed the trigger. The rifle burped out a semi-loud pop sound. A .22-caliber shell didn't have the same power as a .38 or .45, nowhere near the power of a .30-30 rifle; but on a small creature like a rabbit, the effect was fatal. Within a second of firing, the bullet traveled the eighty-yard span and hit the rabbit. It threw the rabbit up into the air, where it did an acrobatic somersault and landed back on the earth, dead.

"Nice shot, son! Looks like you got him right in the head! Destroyed all his brain matter!" his buddy, Drew Larson, yelled as he peered through a pair of binoculars.

Zack's heart started beating hard, as if letting go of the pent-up and restrained energy. "Yep, got him dead-on, didn't I?"

"Well, that's number 4 for the day. All I got is a measly one. And not much of one either."

"Like I said, you can't use that big old .30-30 Winchester. Not hunting little things. It tears 'em up too bad," Zack said, as they both stood up from their kneeling position in the tall grass and brushed themselves off.

It was an early autumn day in 1941 Kentucky. They hadn't had a frost yet, so the grass and ground were dry in the early morning hours. They slung their respective rifles over their shoulders and started walking out into the field toward their newest kill.

"Man, you sure are fucking good with that rifle. I ain't never seen no one better," exclaimed Drew.

"We're both young, my friend. We haven't been around and able to see all the great shooters. There's plenty better than me," Zack came back, as the pair carefully proceeded through the big expanse of the field, carefully avoiding all the gopher and rabbit holes.

"Yeah, I know. But you've won a couple tournaments already. I sure as hell know your name is being thrown around."

"But they've been small, local ones. When you start winning big state ones, that's when you get the limelight," Zack said as he patted Drew's shoulder.

They made their way and finally arrived at the site of their prize bag. Blood was sprayed on some of the tall grass, droplets running down the stems to the ground. The rabbit lay several feet from where it had been eating, on its side, a pool of blood around what was left of the head. The bullet had traveled through one eye and out the other, destroying what brain it had. Zack knew it was an instant kill.

"Hell, the one I shot, there was nothing left of the head, neck, or shoulders. Yours looks like it wasn't even hit," exclaimed Drew, shaking his head.

"Like I said, too big a caliber gun will do that. If you want to have something to eat after you shoot it, it's gotta be a small caliber." Zack flipped his knife open as he knelt down beside the rabbit. He laid it over on its back and started digging the blade into the soft white underbelly.

"I know. But I like my Winchester. I feel like an old frontier cowboy with it. Just like in the movies."

"Yeah, but here in Kentucky, you want to be Davy Crockett, not Hopalong Cassidy. You need to be able to take food back to the family." Zack had sliced open the belly of the rabbit and started pulling the guts and internal organs out onto the ground. They all felt warm and alive to the feel, but he knew the creature was way past alive.

"Give me the sack." Zack stuck out his hand toward Drew. Drew pulled open the drawstring on the burlap pouch he was carrying and held it open. Zack held up the rabbit, letting any remaining blood spill out, inspecting the carcass for parts of the innards he might have left in it. When he was sure he had done a good gutting, he dropped the rabbit into the sack.

"Okay, Drew. Let's call it quits for today. I wanna get home, give this to my mom so she can make a stew."

"You sure? I still feel like killin' me some more things, anything," Drew replied, as a maniacal grin came across his face.

Zack looked at Drew and knew that look. They had been friends since they were little boys. Drew had always had a coldhearted, mean streak in him. There were many times Zack would come across him torturing and killing small animals for no reason. The only reason he gathered was that Drew got immense pleasure out of doing that. When he would ask Drew why he did what he did, he would always answer back that he got such a good feeling watching a helpless thing struggle for life. Knowing that he held that power over the life of the creature gave him a feeling of energy that one couldn't imagine. The satisfaction he got of killing, snuffing the thing's life out, was incredible. As they got older—they were both seventeen now—Drew was able to channel it better. His killing wasn't as blatant, but it was still there, always ready to pop up at any time.

He still remembered the incident a couple of years back with Darrell Headley's dog. The dog never liked Drew. It seemed like the animal knew his character or smelled it on him. It would always bark and snarl at Drew. One day Drew just simply let go, kinda snapped, and took a baseball bat to the dog, bludgeoning it to death, in front of Zack. With every swing of the bat, Drew's grin got wider and wider, his eyes glazed over in delight.

Darrell, who was a big man, came out of his house, wanting to kill Drew on the spot. Zack had gotten between them and stopped what could have been a fatal fight. In the end, Drew's dad had to compensate Darrell for the loss of his dog. No one ever knew the amount of compensation, but it was some type of a monetary amount. For a low-class family in rural Kentucky, it hurt Drew's family to a good degree, let alone their reputation. Drew's dad took it out of him physically, beating him badly, leaving him with scores of bruises and a black eye.

Besides the sadistic streak, Drew also had a possession issue. This one didn't come from childhood but grew over time. Anything he truly liked or cherished, he thought it should be or become his. That it should become his sole possession, added to his collection of things. He would then lord over it, till the time came when he grew tired of it. Then he would simply toss it to the side and move on, without a second thought. There were many times Zack had something that Drew truly wanted. Drew would pester and persist to Zack until he finally would give in and hand it over to him. Many a time it would come down to a trade, Zack knowing how much Drew aspired for said item and using that to his advantage. Zack would walk away from the trade, with a way better reward, compared to what Drew got out of the deal.

"Nope, let's go. Sara Lynn will be waiting for me." Zack and Drew turned and walked back into the woods for home.

Sara Lynn Baisden was Zack's sweetheart, his girl. She was a thin, long-legged country girl of fifteen but had a down-home prettiness that in ten years she would be a beauty. It was that way with some girls or women. They started out scrawny and homely, but as time marched on, so did their looks and body. They turned into diaphanous creatures of sensual looks and desires.

Her long brown hair had been straight her whole early life, but in the past year, it had started to get a natural curl to it. That's what had first attracted Zack to her. No one else had paid her any mind. There was just that something that drew Zack to her. Once he got over his shyness to talk, he found out they had the same likes and dislikes. She was so sweet and loving to him. He fell for her hard.

Some talked about him being too old for her. In a month, he would be eighteen, her just turning fifteen. But in the backwoods of Kentucky, most people still got married at fifteen or sixteen. It was common for that to happen.

"She's always waitin' for you, you lucky stiff. Wish I could have a girl like that," exclaimed Drew.

"Hold on, you've had a lot of girlfriends. I could count them all out for you right now," Zack replied, as they walked.

"None of 'em weren't that good. Not like Sara Lynn, she treats you like a king. She's a keeper, my friend."

"I don't know, Helen was some kinda great girl." A little chuckle escaped from Zack.

"Yeah, I know, but she had to be in control of everything. What I did, where I went, even what I was to wear. I mean, at first, she was great, did a lot of things for me, to me. But once she put her old mouth to my tadpole, that was it. She thought she was the boss. I didn't like that one bit."

"What, her bossin' you or her lickin' your lollipop?" Zack laughed a little harder.

"Well, of course the bossin' around. I couldn't beat the lickin'. Now look at you. You probably don't mind Sara bossin' you around as long as she keeps pulling yer pole. Am I right?"

Zack's face got a reddish look to his cheeks as he sheepishly put his head down and responded, "She's never done that to me. Not yet anyways."

"You've got to be kidding, boy. Has she at least used her hand on you?" Drew proceeded to close his fist and do an up-and-down motion.

"Nope. We decided to wait till we're married for all of that stuff. Once I turn eighteen, I can get a good job at the sawmill. I've got some money saved up from the shooting contests. We'll buy us a little tract of land. Maybe start a farm, have some kids."

"Son, I think if you're gonna get hitched, you had better try some of the milk before buyin' the cow. You might not like the milk, if you know what I mean." Drew was now doing the chuckling as he talked.

"Don't worry, Drew. I can wait. I know it'll be good once we're married. I love her so much. When we kiss and hug, later, you know, I kinda take care of myself." Zack spoke softly, his head looking directly at the ground.

"Well, if she was mine, I know she would be taking care of me, that's all I dare to say. She'd be yankin' my pecker for sure."

The pair now saw Zack's house as they came out of the thicket. Standing on the porch was Sara Lynn, waving enthusiastically toward them. As they got closer, she hopped off the porch and ran toward them. She threw herself into Zack's arms, as he pulled her into his embrace. She kissed his lips hard, then proceeded to kiss every inch of his face.

"Whoa, girl. Settle down. Looks like you want to eat the man. Calm down," cried Drew, looking at the two entwined together.

"He's my man, that's all. I wanna let him know that," Sara replied, looking with disdain at Drew.

"Easy, girl, calm down. I was just makin' an observation," Drew shot back.

"Well, keep your comments to yourself about me and Zack, that's all." There was a little tone of disdain in her voice.

"Hey, Zack, you wanna rein your woman in a little," Drew replied. The veins in his neck bulged with anger.

"Both of you just calm down. Close the damper on the stove. She was just showing me a little affection, and you were just kiddin' her about it. Right, Drew?" Zack now looked at Drew as if to say, "What are you trying to start? Stop it."

Drew caught the look and replied, "That's all I was doing. Honest, Sara, just jokin' around."

Sara Lynn looked from Drew to Zack and now gave him a more passionate kiss on the lips. When they finished, Zack stuck his arm out to Drew. "Give me the bag."

Drew gave the satchel of dead rabbits to Zack. He opened the bag, mulled around inside it, and pulled three limp carcasses out, handing them to Sara. "Take these to my mom so she can start cookin' 'em, okay?"

"Sure, Zack, anything you say." She turned and ran toward the house, swinging the dead bunnies in the air as she skipped.

Zack and Drew watched her run, her cute little hips and ass swishing back and forth. "Man, if she was my girl, I'd be tearin' into that, let me tell you," Drew whispered to Zack as he leaned in.

"Remember she's my girl. She's not yours." Zack turned and looked at Drew, handing back the sack. "I gave you one of the rabbits to go with the one you blasted to hell. Your mom should be able to make a meal out of the two."

"Thanks a bunch, Zack. That should be enough for my brother, me, and Mom. Dad's gone to Tennessee to see his brother. He's real sick." Drew nodded as he grabbed the sack and turned to go. He looked one last time at Sara, who had just reached her way to the porch, hopped the steps, and bounded into the house. "You know, that is one fine girl. Zack, you're a lucky man, let me tell you. A lucky man indeed," he said as he started walking away.

Zack caught a glimpse of Drew's face and was puzzled with the expression he saw. It was one of jealousy. He had seen it many times before when they were still boys. Drew turned and looked back at Zack, his eyes quickly traveling back to the house where Sara was. He caught Zack looking at him, nervously gave him a thumbs-up, and waved goodbye.

Zack turned and walked to the house. He just shook his head. That was ol Drew, wanting something he couldn't have.

*****

Zack's heart was beating hard in his chest as he ran home from the general store. He got to his house and cleared all the steps to the porch in one leap. He flung open the door and shouted. His mom, Claire, came running from the kitchen where she was making lunch.

"My god, son, what is it?" she exclaimed, her face in a panic.

At the same instant, his dad and younger brother came through the back door of the kitchen. They had also heard him yell. "What in tarnation is goin' on, Zack? I heard you scream all the way from the pump," his dad extoled.

"I got it! I got it!" he yelled, a big grin exploding on his face. His hand was holding an opened letter.

"Got what?" his brother Silas now asked, looking at Zack's shaking hand.

"For the state tourney. The big shoot-out. The one in Frankfort. The invitation finally came!" Zack was giddy as he spoke. The family had known about it. It was the big state firearms tournament, held once a year in May. It was a personal invitation tournament, allowed for only a select few. A person entering the affair had to have some considerable credentials. Zack had sent all the paperwork, along with the entrance form, of all the local tourneys he had won. The state board must have looked it over well enough to agree that he was indeed qualified to be entered in this year's shoot.

"Hot dog! The prize this year is a thousand dollars for first. Second is five hundred. Third is three hundred. Ain't that somethin'?"

"It sure is, son. That could really buy you a nice piece of land for you and Sara Lynn to start out on. Couldn't it, Ma?" Zack's dad, Les, exclaimed.

"It'd be wonderful. Whether it'd be first, second, or third, it sure would be more than enough to start a life and family with Sara Lynn." Claire was beaming as she spoke.

"You tell her yet?" Silas asked. His smile said it all to Zack, goofy and yet heartfelt all the same.

"Nope. That's where I'm headed now, after I told you all. She told me she'd be headin' this way, after she got all her chores done. Maybe I'll catch her on the way here, or maybe still at her house, if I hurry," Zack blurted, trying to catch his breath.

"Well, don't pass out before you even get going. Sit down, relax," his mom playfully scolded.

"I'll be all right, don't worry," he exclaimed as he ran out the front door, hopping to the ground in a quick walk.

As he walked, thoughts ran through his head like flashes of lightning. *I know I can win this thing. Even if not first, I know I can win some money. Sara and I can get hitched, right away. Her parents would definitely say okay. We could buy that section of land past the O'hern house that they got for sale. That's good land to grow things on.*

Zack decided to take the shortcut to the Baisden house, through the woods. That would bring him to the back of the property. Sara and he always used this path. It was way quicker than using the main road.

Thoughts of having kids came to him now. He wanted four for sure, two boys, two girls. They could all help with the farming. It would be way better than it was with him and his brother. With just two, it was a hell of a lot more work.

The thought of sex with Sara sparked in his brain. To finally be able to touch and caress her in certain ways, to be able to lick and kiss her beautiful body, to enter her with his manhood would be fantastic.

Zack got to the out shed of the Baisden property. A little shack used for storage and shelter when out hunting and the weather got bad. Sara and he met there many a time, to talk, kiss, and dream about their future life together.

As he walked past the door of the shed, his eyes saw it. It was Drew's Winchester, leaning on the wall, by the doorway. He thought to himself, *Why would Drew leave his prize gun out here? The stupid boy, what was he thinking? He must not have been thinking at all.*

That's when he heard sound. The sound of voices, or a voice. The sound of activity, a commotion going on in the shed. He stopped, then slowly crept toward the building. Why he crept, he didn't know why, only that he needed to know what was going on in that little shack of a building. He stopped at the door and listened. His hearing was as good as his eyesight. He heard the small table that was inside, cracking and creaking, bumping against the far wall. Now, he picked out Drew's voice, and his voice alone.

"Tell me, tell me how much you like it. You love it, don't you!" Drew's voice got stronger, louder, with each passing second. "Com'on, tell me, bitch! Tell me you love it!" he yelled.

Zack's mind raced. Thoughts of all things unimaginable bounced through his brain. At the center of all his thoughts was Sara. His Sara, involved in God knows what with Drew. It couldn't be her. She couldn't be in the shed with Drew, could she? His heart was beating like a steam engine as he pushed open the rickety door.

As the door slammed open, his world exploded in front of his eyes. On the small table lay Sara. She was skewed at an angle across the corner of the table closest to Zack. He observed everything in that moment as if he were standing, watching for minutes. Her bare legs hung over the table, spread apart. She had on her white and brown saddle shoes. The frilly white socks she always wore with those shoes still adorned her feet. Her legs bobbled and bounced, below her knees, to the motion they were put in. Her white panties lay on the dirt floor, now stained by the dirt and mud as if they had been trampled on. The pink dress, the one Zack loved when she wore it, was pushed up, exposing her waist and lower body.

All Zack could see of Drew was from behind. From the waist down he was naked. His pants were down by his ankles. His feet were doing a herky-jerky sort of dance step. Puffs of dirt floated in the air around them. He could see some of Drew's penis; it was rock hard. He watched as it slammed into Sara's exposed, tender young patch of pubic hair, pulled out, then slammed in again. Traces of blood were on her inner thighs, splattered, declaring that her one-time virginity was now destroyed.

Drew's arms were stretched out, to their furthest limit, the hands on each tightly grasped Sara's neck. The nails on his fingers were digging in on her tender young throat, digging in so hard and feverishly tight, puncturing the skin, producing droplets of blood. The droplets ran slowly down her neck from the wounds.

Zack looked at the face he so dearly loved and knew it was over. She was gone. The once-healthy face of a vibrant fifteen-year-old girl was now a shade of reddish blue, the color a face gets when deprived of oxygen for far too long of a time. Veins bulged in stress, from the strangulation, on her dead young face.

Drew turned his head toward Zack at the sound of the door slamming against the wall. His face had a look of maniacal, feverish glee; but it quickly turned to one of panic, as the thought of the whole situation imploded back on him. He let go of Sara's neck.

It dropped away at an extreme angle, bouncing when it reached its utmost limit, hanging at a most bizarre slant, lifeless.

He took in breath and gulped rapidly, blinking his eyes, seeming to come out of his crazed, trancelike state. "I…I…" were the only sounds that came out of Drew's dry, crack-lipped mouth.

Zack's movements were a blur, as he ran and grabbed Drew, slamming him into the wall of the shed. "What have you done! What the hell have you done!" he screamed, as tears welled up in his eyes.

"I…I wanted her so bad. I told her that. But…she said no. All…I…wanted was just a little piece of her, just a little…you know that…don't you?" Drew's eyes were frantic and bulging as he looked at Zack, trying to speak. "She just had to…slap me. I…I don't like that. I told her that. But…she had…just had to fight me. That made it…worse. I just wanted her even more."

Zack let go of Drew, as he kept stammering his contemptuous story. He crossed over and knelt down beside Sara's face, softly lifting her head to look at her. Her eyes were opened, staring off into the distance, not registering. The once-pure, creamy-textured white face was still there, now lifeless.

"What…what are we gonna do, Zack? We can…a…we can tell everybody we found her this way." Drew's mind was working hard, trying to form a story, a story to save himself. "Tell people it might've been a traveling hobo did…did it. Yeah, yeah, that's it. That's what we'll tell them." Drew now, more under control, his senses returning back to normalcy, pulled his pants up and zipped them as he talked.

Tears were rolling down Zack's cheeks and dropping to the dirt floor as he gently lifted Sara's head and shoulders and repositioned it back unto the table. He turned and faced Drew, instantly feeling the rage bubble and well up in him. "You're gonna answer for this, you bastard. You killed her, you killed the only person I truly loved. Just like with everything else in your life that you want. Anything that you think you should have or want, you take it. No matter what the consequences, you grab it. Now…now this time you're gonna answer for it!"

Drew looked at Zack, then at Sara's dead body. The wheels turned in his head as he stepped toward Zack. Gone now was the scared, panic look. It was replaced with the look of the sly fox, planning its next move. His eyes had the look of a devious predator. "Fuck that. You killed her! I caught you strangling her! I'll tell everybody it was you that did it! You went crazy and killed her!"

With that, he jumped at Zack, swinging his right fist as he did. The punch caught Zack on the side of his face, sending him sprawling to the ground. Drew followed the punch by jumping on Zack, straddling him and trying to rain another blow down on him. Zack brought his left arm up and deflected the swing. With his right hand, he shot a punch up and into Drew's jaw. The punch connected with a crunch and sent Drew falling backward. Zack rolled to his knees and crawled toward Drew, who was lying in the doorway of the shed, resting on his elbows, trying to get his senses back. Zack was almost on him. As Drew realized this, he grabbed a handful of dirt and threw it into Zack's face and eyes. Zack threw his hand up to protect himself, but it was too late to stop it all. Blinded, his eyes stinging, he rubbed at them, his vision gone.

Drew was up standing over him. He reared his right leg back and brought it forward, slamming into the side of Zack's ribs. All the air in his lungs escaped from him, as he fell over to the ground.

As he sucked in new air, he could hear the footsteps. Drew was running now, away from the shed. Zack was still rubbing his eyes as he got to his feet. He staggered to the doorway, vision starting to clear. He could make out Drew, running down the path, the path that he and Sara had walked and made over time. This path led to the Baisden house. He rubbed his eyes hard now, trying to get back full vision. With his other hand, he steadied himself in the doorway. His hand felt the coarse wood of the doorway frame and cold steel. He instantly looked down. It was Drew's Winchester lying against the shed. Drew had totally forgotten it in his haste to run. Zack brought the rifle up and pulled the big lever forward on the trigger, locking a shell in the chamber. He knew Drew always kept bullets in it, ready for action.

He knelt down on one knee and brought the rifle up to his shoulder. "Stop, Drew, I'm telling you to stop! I'll shoot!" he screamed.

Drew was now about fifty yards away, running in a staggering fashion, not looking back.

"I said stop! Dammit, Drew!" Tears again formed in his eyes. This was his friend, his childhood buddy. He didn't want to shoot him. In fact, he thought, why was he going to shoot him? His mind was in turmoil.

Then the sight of him raping and choking Sara to death flashed before him. The vision of it burned his brain, seared it with pain. The callousness, evilness of it filled his mind. Rage swelled back up like a giant wave, forming up, racing to crash into the rocks on the shoreline. He cleared his eyes with the sleeve of his shirt and looked back into the sight of the gun, nestling his cheek on the smooth wooden stock.

Drew was almost eighty yards away, legs pumping now in a steadied gallop. Zack looked intently into the V-section of the sight and took aim. He gently squeezed the trigger, as he had done hundreds of times before. When he had squeezed the trigger before, it was always at some type of animal or inanimate target, not a human being. This was something he was taught by his father never to do, never to take a human life. His heart ached with pain. But now the hatred raged. It was too great; it could not be quelled. The pain he felt was swept away as the wave crashed into it.

The Winchester recoiled with a loud, zipping crack. Zack followed the trail of the bullet through the sight. A second later, the left side of Drew's head exploded in fragments. Chunks of bone and brain flew out into the late morning air. Drew's arms flung up toward the sky as if praising the glorious day, then fell forward into the Kentucky soil.

Zack let the rifle drop out of his grasp, to the ground. He collapsed on the dirt, next to it. Tears ran like a river from his eyes as he looked to the heavens. He cursed the eyesight that the Lord had bestowed upon him. Because with that eyesight, he had taken a life and had watched a loved one's life taken from him.

6

"Tail gunner. Tail gunner. Come in, over. Zack, Zack, can you hear me? Over." The inquiry came over the headset, but it seemed like it was being yelled from a mountaintop. The distance seemed so far away as the words faintly came to him. Where was he at? Wasn't this the shed back in Kentucky? The rifle, he must have dropped it; it was now lost in the deep earth. He turned to look in the doorway of the shed. He needed to see Sara Lynn, even if she was dead. He needed to look at her, to hold her sweet, beautiful face in his hands, to feel her lips against his. He spun around in every direction. Everything seemed as if in a heavy mist; only now the mist was dissipating, fading rapidly.

Zack knew where he was now, in the rear gunner compartment of the *Fallen Angel*. He heard the thump-thump sound of the .50s opening up. The sound was above and behind him. It had to be Jessie Hildago in the top turret. At first, it seemed the firing of the guns was so far away; but the more the guns spoke in their short staccato bursts, the more pronounced, clear, and defined they became.

"Zack, Zack. Tail gunner come in, over." The words were blasting in his ears now. He knew exactly where he was, but what had been happening? What had he been looking at? There was something, but what was it? Some kind of flying birds, big birds, that much he remembered.

A heavy thud impacted the left side of the tail section, close to his canopy. It brought all his faculties and senses back home. Kentucky and Sara had been a long time ago. He was in a darkened sky, in a bomber, over Germany in 1944. Another heavy thud shook his canopy glass. His neck swiveled from left to right, peering out into the darkening gloom, eyes searching. Something with large wings flew past him, on the right, slightly above him. It was one of those things he had spotted approaching the ship.

Another burst of the .50s erupted, sending tracers flashing past him from below his cubicle. It was the belly turret, shooting shells into the dark. He watched as the red of the tracers dimmed into the distance and were gone.

The hairs on the back of his neck raised as he felt an eeriness come over him; a dread consumed him. He slowly turned his head back to the left and came face-to-face with a living nightmare. He thought it was some type of man at first. But it couldn't be, not outside the plane, sitting, and the plane flying at twenty some thousand feet in the sky. But yet it had all the features of a man, a man thing.

The face and head had a polished reddish-ebony look to it. A smooth, almost-porcelain texture, but yet it gave the appearance of a hardened diamond. Yet a diamond that had been weathered by the harsh winds and elements of the sky and heavens, over a long period. The hair, if that's what it was, atop the head was long, black, and straight. It was tapered or combed back behind the head in a type of naturally oiled texture; an almost greasy sheen adorned it. This must have been what kept it in place. It never moved once in the strong currents of wind billowing around it. To Zack, it reminded him of the hair of a horse's mane, the ones he used to ride back home.

The eyes of the creature froze his blood as he looked into them. Dark, black marbles, in the center was a small reddish-orange pupil that looked back at him. When the creature blinked and the lid opened back up, the small orangish pupil pulsated more brightly, radiating untold energy.

Zack reached for his mic button but never depressed it. He sat transfixed, staring at the thing.

"Zack, Zack. Answer me!" came the command from Cullum over his headphones on his skullcap. His mouth opened, but nothing came out. He was hypnotized by the eyes, the eyes from hell. His body started to tremble as fear coursed through his veins.

The creature, in response to Zack opening his mouth, now opened its mouth. It revealed a set of sharp, rigid teeth. They had the appearance of saw blade teeth, sharp, not too big, but tough enough to rip and tear and to bite into anything it needed to. Blackish saliva dripped from the top fangs and were windblown onto the glass of Zack's canopy. The glass immediately started to sizzle in the spots where the fluid splattered on it.

Zack gulped hard, regaining some composure, enough composure to speak his last words ever as he queued his mic. "Skipper, I…"

The creature raised a left arm up and brought it down into Zack's canopy. The three fingers on its hand were long and sharp talons of death. The glass framework shattered into dozens of fragments. Flying glass cut and stuck into Zack's face. The only thing saving his eyes were his flight goggles, which he still had on. It gave him the respite to gaze upon the pointed talons, as they tore into his throat, ripping it open and yanking his jugular out. The creature held it high above it, inspecting and examining it, then stuffing it into its mouth and devouring it. When it had accomplished this, it looked back in at him. Zack never looked back. His head had fallen back over the headrest of his seat, exposing the entirety of his ruptured throat, spraying blood. The tendons and muscles that normally supported the head were now destroyed. The creature leaned in and began feasting on the bloodied mess.

7

Jessie Hildago sat in the top turret on the *Fallen Angel*, looking intently back east from where they had come. The sky had turned completely black. Stars peeked out every so often through the cloud formations above. He had heard Zack on the radio. Damn, that country boy had good vision. As for him, he couldn't see shit. Once the light left the sky, he was a blind man.

He kept looking at two o'clock in the sky behind them. That's where Zack said he saw those things. Since Skipper had told him to keep an out for them, he hadn't heard any more chatter on the radio.

He blew into his cupped hands; they were starting to get cold. At this altitude, no sun, it got pretty chilly at night. These late-afternoon missions were for the birds. He could always put on his leather gloves, it would help, but then he would lose his feel for the guns. Other guys didn't mind the gloves. In fact, they liked them better when they were in action, firing away. It was just a preference thing; that's what Jessie always told the other crew members. If it was night back in his hometown of Tucson, he wouldn't even have to worry about gloves. In the fall, it was always a balmy sixty or seventy degrees after the sun went down. Even in the dead of winter, the evenings never dipped below fifty.

His mind snapped back to the now as he saw movement to the northeast of the ship, almost in a parallel line with it at three o'clock. "Hey, Skipper. This is Jessie. I saw some movement off our starboard rear. Over," he radioed as he leaned forward, straining to see.

"What does it look like?" Cullum answered back.

"Must be some kind of bird. Maybe a group of them. Looks like they're closing in on us." He thought that odd. How could a flock of birds, even big birds, keep up with a fortress bomber? Yes, it was down to two serviceable engines now, but still moving at a decent clip. It would be hard for flying fowl to keep pace with.

"Don't need them to screw with us. Don't let them get any closer. Wouldn't want them flying into our good props and losing another engine. Fire a warning burst to keep them off us. Over."

"Roger that." Jessie watched intently. The moon was starting to rise in view. Its translucent opaque light rays together with the stars gave Jessie a better sight line now. These birds were big, way bigger than eagles or loon cranes. He had seen enough of them in his day to know that; plus these wings were really different. They didn't have what seemed to be any feathers on them. They were more like a bat's wing. He could make out the crescent curves on them, at least three, where tapered feathers should be.

His heart skipped a beat. These birds had what appeared to be arms, separate from the wings, and legs. What the hell were they?

No matter, he didn't want them close to the ship. "Skip, Skip. These aren't birds!" His head felt like it got hit with a hot hammer, and something heavy dropped in his stomach. His old grandmother, who had more Indian in her than Spanish, used to tell him tales of the occult. Old tales of days gone by, when the devil still walked in this world, snatching souls to take back to hell. She would set him down in front of the fireplace back home at her old house. Late at night with nary a light on, just the glow coming off the fire, he would listen to her yarns. Some would make him tremble and want to pee his pants. Most would send him to bed with nightmares.

One of these tales dealt with these flying man birds. They were the devil's little helpers she would say, sent out by Satan to cause grief and destruction on man. They could rip a man limb from limb, thirst on his blood, and eat his heart. Or take the man, whole, back to hell to live in eternal damnation, because of the sins he had wrought in his life. These things or creatures, she said they were called a harpy. Is this what these things were? Jessie contemplated. Was his grandmother correct? Were these the harpies, the devil's helpers?

Jessie didn't have time to ponder. Instead of flying parallel to the bomber, they now made a sharp, quick beeline for the tail section. Jessie grabbed the triggers for his twin .50s and fired a long burst.

He didn't anticipate their agility and quickness. The red tracers shot harmlessly into the night sky behind them.

"*Madre de Dios!* They are harpies!" he screamed into his mic, as he lost sight of them. They had flown behind the tail section and just under the sight of his guns. "Skipper…they're behind us. By the tail and rear gunner! By Zack!" he cried, as he strained intently into the black sky, hoping, hoping beyond all things heavenly, that the light of the moon, now rising higher, would help him see when they came at him, which he knew they would, God help him. All the time his stomach churned violently, and the daggers of pain stabbed in his chest. He knew these feelings all too well. They had happened to him long ago.

8

The summer night was stifling this time of year. His shirt stuck to him, sticky wet, long after the sun had set from the heat of the day. It was always this way in late August in Arizona, but this summer had been exceptionally hot and dry. Days like this just sucked the bodily fluids out of one very rapidly.

Or maybe, he thought, the intense sweating was also due to the current situation. He was here at the US-Mexican border to help his cousin and wife cross from Mexico to the United States.

He had fought intensely with his family over this. He was staunchly opposed to it, while the family, as a whole, was thoroughly behind the attempt. He really thought, go through the proper channels and procedures; it may take a while and some money, but it could be done. They could come across under a visitor's visa, as temporary citizens, and then gain their true citizenship.

But now things had changed. Time was of the essence. Luis and his wife, Simi, were now expecting. A new one was on the way. It was now or never, to come to the United States, for a better life, for them and the baby. Jessie's family had come years ago, way before he was born. His father had gotten his papers and citizenship, then married his mom and brought her here. They had raised their family of two girls and him quite comfortably and well. It was tough early on, but his father and mother worked hard and diligently at it and pulled through to a good life.

Now his mother and father thought it was time for a cousin to try life here. But it had to be done quickly. This was the only option right now at this moment. The baby coming had thrown a monkey wrench into doing it the right way. Everyone had concurred that it was better to have the baby born in the States, making it a citizen, rather than trying to bring a young one across and then trying to obtain citizenship. They all said that that could and would get a might messy.

Jessie had argued that being caught by the border patrol could get quite messy too. He had heard the different stories, some bad, and some really bad. All border guards weren't as nice and sympathetic as others. Some would catch immigrants crossing over, lock them up, and send them back. Others would beat and hurt the people, sometimes killing them and burying the bodies in the expanse of the desert, never to be heard of again.

His mother and father thought long and hard. In the end, that's why they sent Jessie out to help with this ordeal. He and his family lived in Tucson. His cousin was crossing the border one hundred miles away, down by the border town of San Miguel, Arizona.

San Miguel was not quite on the border, maybe five or six miles north of it. After many letters and correspondence, it was decided Jessie would drive his truck down to San Miguel, leave it there, trek to the border on foot, wait for them to cross, and then bring them back to Tucson.

On paper, it sounded easy. In real life, Jessie knew it wouldn't be. The heat and landscape would be brutal. The desert in August was intimidating. Now that Simi was pregnant, it would be even more arduous. She was roughly four months along, tough; but if she was eight months in, he would have strongly opposed it. But Jessie was a good son; he would go along with the wishes of his mother and father.

The plan was for Luis and Simi to cross over the border on the night of the twentieth of August. They would come across through the area of the Rhyo Valley. The hope was it was in an area that the border patrol didn't frequent as often. Being that it was such a barren and desolate region, why would any sane person try to cross there?

Jessie made his way down to San Miguel on the eighteenth, looking for good spots to leave his truck in town, and not being too conspicuous. He found a small Mexican-owned grocery store, on the west side of town, talked to the owner, said he needed to leave it for several days, and made up a story about hiking with friends to Papago

Farms. These farms and town were on the Indian reservation roughly thirty miles away. It was a nice scenic area Jessie had been to years ago. The shop owner had looked at him a little dubiously, telling him it was not a good time of year to do this, what with the intense heat. But he also stated it was Jessie's funeral and that he couldn't pass up selling Jessie the provisions needed for the trek. Money was money.

Jessie bought more than he needed, sticking with the story of making the journey with friends. It fell right into his plan. He needed the extra water and food for Luis and Simi.

He started out of San Miguel on the morning of the nineteenth. He headed west toward Papago Farms, giving any indication to anyone watching that that was where he was heading to meet up with friends and make their sojourn.

Several miles outside of town, alongside the seldom-used road, he knelt beside a group of desert bushes and began to dig. He didn't have to dig too long and deep before he found what he had buried there the day before. It was an item in a long piece of burlap material. Before talking to the shop owner, he had driven out here and found this spot, thinking it was good enough for placing his item there, for safety. He didn't need anyone to see him with what he had in his possession now.

He unwrapped the burlap, hoping it would still be in working order. Sand can do bad things to this type of equipment. Inside the material was an Enfield rifle (M1917), from the First World War. His dad had had it for several years; he acquired it in a poker game. He taught Jessie how to use it and treat it with respect. They had shot it for practice in the desert areas around Tucson. A small grin came to his face. The rifle looked to be in good order. He had wrapped it tight to keep the dreaded sand out. He prayed he wouldn't have to need or use it at all, as he pulled the bolt back and dry fired it. He loaded the detachable clip with five bullets and slammed it back in place. As he looked up into the rising, intense desert sun, he reached into his back pocket of his pants, pulling out his folded Chicago Cubs baseball hat. He put it on his head, knowing he would need it for this journey.

Jessie turned south toward the Rhyo canyon. The terrain was rough and ragged as he walked. South of the road, the sandy desert complexion turned into more of a rocky texture. Boulders and stony craigs dotted the desert surroundings. He passed several dried riverbeds, extinct of water for years. A few cacti, tuffs of dried grass, maybe a Joshua tree every so often; but otherwise, it was a barren world. He marched on and got to the canyon a couple of hours before sunset. It took him longer to travel this distance just for the fact of being careful. He inspected the area for recent tire tracks or footfalls, probably made by the border patrol. He found none. He speculated which paths would be easier going when he brought Luis and Simi back through.

Looking out over the canyon, he realized why not many people came here. It was a barren, desolate, wind-ravaged hellhole. The canyon sat in a salt flat. He could taste it on his fingers and smell it in the air. Nothing would grow in this area except rock and misshaped boulders. He realized it would be a treacherous place to traverse, especially at night.

Jessie found a place on the northern rim face of the canyon. A group of boulders and rocks sat about twenty yards down from the lip of the canyon. It made a perfect spot to set up camp. There were three big boulders situated around each other, giving him a somewhat comfortable spot to squeeze into and be out of sight of anyone passing behind him, on the ridge ledge. The middle boulder had a slight overhang shape to it, giving him shade from most of the sun. The morning sun and when it set in the evening would still fry him good, but the intense midday rays would be kept off him. He ate some dried meat and fruit, drank a little water, and hunkered in for the night.

Soon after dark, the coyotes started talking. Their howling and wails chilled him inside. He laid the loaded Enfield on the smaller rock sitting in front of him, ready to shoot at whatever came his way, wanting to cause him harm. He finally fell asleep to their constant talking, snuggled up against the rocky nook he was in.

The new rays of the rising sun hit his face and woke him the next morning. He looked out on his new environment, no movement anywhere. He got up to relieve himself. Standing on the east side of the rocks, he stood urinating into the sand, viewing the south side of the canyon. He figured it had to be at least three-quarters of a mile across and roughly two miles long. When Luis and Simi made their trek across it in the dark, the chances of them running smack-dab into him would be slim. That's why he chose his location to sit and wait for them in the middle of this canyon. He patted himself on the back for thinking of and bringing along a flashlight. Short bursts of it in the on position would help pinpoint his location for his cousin. Luis had written that he would also have a light for signaling, hopefully not attracting the wrong attention.

As Jessie zipped his pants up, he heard noise to the west, traveling along the lip of the canyon. It increased steadily. Something was coming, a vehicle. He carefully looked around the boulders, keeping out of sight of said vehicle. Dust plumes were rising in the air, kicked up by the tires. He slid quickly back into his little nook in the boulders, making sure he was out of sight. His heart caught in his throat; he saw the Enfield sitting on the small rock in front of him, in plain sight for anyone to see. His hand shot out, grabbing the butt of the rifle and pulled it toward him. The car or truck was almost to him now. Sweat instantly started to form and slid from his temples and back of his neck. His mind raced. What would he say if confronted by anyone, let alone the border police? He had his driver's license to prove he was a citizen. The only plausible story was that he was out hunting rabbits or other small prey of the desert. He knew it would be a weak story at that, though. What was he doing hunting all the way down here, when he lived up by Tucson? He could hunt up there just as easy.

The vehicle traveling along the lip came to a stop. To Jessie, it seemed like it was right behind the boulder, where he sat. His fingers were trembling as he tried to hold the rifle and not drop it. He counted with his thumping heartbeat the amount of time it sat there. To anyone else, it would have been thirty seconds; but to Jessie, with his heart pounding double time, it was way over several minutes. He could hear voices over the idling engine. It sounded like at least two different people. After another long thirty seconds, he heard the clutch engage and the gears grind as the vehicle was put into first point. It slowly moved away, traveling east from him. He waited a good amount of time before inching his head around the boulder to have a look.

It was a jeep, an old-style one, probably from the First World War. Kicking up dust, it continued east along the rim of the canyon. Two people, men he thought, were in it. To him it definitely looked like the border patrol. A second later, it was confirmed: he saw the blue circle with the white star in the middle, two white stripes on either side, depicting the United States government. He lay back against his large rock and blew out a big sigh of air and relief. They hadn't spotted him. He waited a good half hour before getting back up to relieve himself again. This was due to the buildup of all his nerves over the current situation. He moved very tentatively, wanting to make sure the jeep was long gone.

He sat the rest of the long hot day sweating and thinking. He pulled the binoculars out of the backpack he had brought along. Scanning the far lip of the canyon and the surrounding horizons, for any vehicle or human movement, he found none. He didn't want to be caught off guard again.

He drank some more water and ate at midday. He watched his consumption of fluid, knowing he had to save a good portion of it for their trek back to San Miguel. Luis and Simi would be spent after their journey, and considering her condition, she would really need it. He hoped they had prepared well for the ordeal and packed enough supplies, but one never knew. Like his father had always told him, be prepared for the unexpected.

Midday was the hardest part of the sit. The rock he was under kept the sun off his face and shoulder but left the rest of his body exposed. The sun quickly roasted his lower torso. He had worn shorts, not knowing if that was a good or bad move; but in this situation, he found it to be to the negative. He had brought along a light jacket, in case the night got too cold. He now used it to cover his legs, keeping the powerful hot rays of the big orb off them. The sweat ran from him like a river, soaking every inch of his clothes.

As he watched the sun move across the sky heading for the western horizon, he pondered. Could he do what his cousin Luis was trying to do, especially with a pregnant woman at his side, across an unforgiving desert? At this time of year, border police all around, hoping upon hope that your other cousin would be waiting for you, to take you the rest of the way? Could he? What if something had happened to the cousin and he wasn't there? What would he do then? Jessie wondered if he had the same type of balls to try such a thing. If he had the spark in him to want a better life, in a different country, not knowing the language, the people, all the baggage that came with it. The United States was all Jessie had ever known. He was born here. How bad was it somewhere else? He didn't know. He realized it had to be bad, if Luis was willing to do this now, this arduous journey. To put his wife and unborn child at risk, to accomplish this task, he had to have some big balls.

The sun was going down now, shadows starting to form in the valley. He peered with the binoculars, looking south, hoping upon hope to see the couple approaching through the gloom. He dreaded spending the night watching and listening for them. It would be risky shining the flashlight on and off. Light traveled far in the dark desert. Yelling out would be bad also. Sound carried very well in this open expanse.

He started fifteen minutes after the sun was completely gone and darkness had descended. One short burst of the flashlight toward the south wall of the canyon. Then he would sit and listen for any sort of reply, waiting for a flash of light from that end of the canyon.

What there was of a moon came up. It was a small sliver in the sky, giving hardly any light to the landscape. It was a cloudless sky; the stars twinkled in abundance.

Two hours into the night, Jessie flashed his light and watched. Off in the southern distance, a light appeared and then quickly went out. Were his eyes playing tricks, wanting him to see a light that wasn't there? He rubbed his eyes hard and looked, nothing. He tried his light again. Seconds later, a light flickered in response. His heart skipped a beat, with joy and anxiety. It had to be them. He did his light again. The other light responded in kind, closer to him now. They were moving toward him. It seemed that maybe they were halfway across the valley. He stared into the darkness for minutes. He could make nothing out, no light, no movement.

A minute later, a light flashed, this time close, very close. He responded back with his flashlight. They were maybe a hundred yards away, almost to him. Only a couple more minutes and they would be with each other.

All at once a spotlight erupted from the ridge of the canyon, fifty yards to Jessie's right. A voice came booming from the same direction. "Stop where you are. This is the United States Border Patrol. You are in violation of entering the country illegally."

How could this be? Jessie said to himself. He didn't hear any vehicles pull up. He should have heard it if it did. The only answer that raced through his mind was his preoccupation with his cousin and his wife. He had focused entirely on them coming across the valley, he had forgotten to pay attention to his surroundings. The vehicle and patrol had slipped in quietly, once they saw the flashes of the lights, coming from the valley. It was their bad misfortune they were on patrol so close by.

Now Luis and Simi were in a dilemma. He watched as the spotlight panned out into the valley, closer to the northern ridge. It searched for several seconds till it found them. It was a man and woman, both wearing baseball hats and backpacks, Simi and Luis. They were about sixty yards from Jessie's perch of boulders. They began running as the light focused on them, not away from it but toward Jessie.

"Stop where you are or you will be shot!" the voice boomed again. Jessie was now sure it was coming from a megaphone, next to the spotlight. Silhouettes of two individuals ran in front of the spotlight, moving down from the ridge lip, toward the couple.

Jessie quickly moved out from the rocks, bringing the Enfield up to his shoulder as he knelt on one knee and took aim. He had to take out the spotlight and give the runners darkness; that was their only chance. He fired at the light. The Enfield felt comfortable as it recoiled, but Jessie hadn't shot it in a long time. His aim was off. The bullet hit what appeared to be the metal of the jeep, creating a spark of light and a loud pinging sound as it struck the side of the vehicle. He readjusted and fired again. The bullet was dead on this time. The light exploded in a quick burst of brilliancy and dust. Darkness fell back over the landscape.

The blackout was short lived. Two flashlights now came on, searching for the pair of runners. The beams of light moved up and down the slope till they found them. Luis and Simi were running up the slope to Jessie, only twenty yards away.

"Odelay! Odelay!" yelled Luis to Simi. Jessie heard her crying now, in fear and panic.

The border police had run a little below them in their haste and were moving back up the slope, behind them. Their flashlights framed the immigrant pair in front of Jessie.

"Stop! Goddammit!" yelled one of the officers. Luis and Simi paid no mind and kept running, inching closer to Jessie.

Jessie laid himself down behind the small rock he had earlier laid his rifle on. He could sight and shoot better using the rock as a rest; plus it gave him cover, he thought.

His body jumped as the first shot rang out, fired by one of the officers. It hit the dirt next to Luis, spitting up pebbles and sand. The pair struggled in the sand, slipping and lurching, trying to keep their footholds. Luis held Simi's hand firmly, trying to bring her along with him.

"Stop!" he cried. Jessie didn't know why he said it, maybe to the guard to stop shooting or maybe for the whole ordeal and insanity to just end.

Jessie could see Luis's and Simi's faces in the flashlight silhouette. For a split second their eyes made contact. A feeling of desperation and dread filled up in Jessie; his heart thundered. A second shot rang out. Instantly, the material on the front of Luis's shirt exploded, material ripping and shredding as blood erupted from his chest, in a fine spray. His arms flew up as he fell forward to the ground.

"You bastards!" Jessie screamed as he aimed the rifle at the flashlight that came into view, now that Luis had crumpled to the earth. He swung the gunsight over a little from where the flashlight beam was being held, making a guess that the man was holding the light in his left hand and shooting with his right. He fired between the assumed positions of the two hands. The Enfield recoiled hard, into his shoulder, as he slammed the bolt back and forward, loading another shell.

The flashlight of the man Jessie had shot at flipped into the air, making several cartwheels, the beam of light searching the ground and sky in crazed revolutions, before falling to the ground. Jessie trained the rifle toward the other beam of light but couldn't get a good line of sight to fire. Simi was in the way. She had grabbed hold of Luis's one arm and was pulling, trying to drag him along. Luis was not obliging to help her at all. He lay in a pile on the ground. She let out a scream of grief and despair at the now-motionless body in the dirt and sand.

Jessie heard the other patrolman yell loudly over her screaming, "Dammit, you fucking wetbacks, look what you did!" His gun fired twice, in quick succession.

Whether both bullets hit her, Jessie couldn't tell; all he knew was that one did for sure. It hit her and spun her around like a rag doll. She pirouetted once and collapsed to the ground.

Jessie now had an unobstructed target; he squeezed the trigger on his rifle. The shot went straight and true. The flashlight flew backward, as if thrown hard, landing on the ground with its light still working, shining on the horrific scene that had just transpired.

The echo of the last shot faded in the distance, and now just silence permeated the landscape. Jessie watched as the dust settled around the bodies of his relatives, lying motionless. He instinctively pulled the bolt of the Enfield back and rechambered another shell. No movement anywhere, just silence, and the feel of a slight breeze that had just started up.

Jessie lay there still, motionless, peering out into the faintly lit darkness. He held his breath as his heart pounded in his chest and temples. He surmised that there must have been just two patrolmen. If there had been more, they would have been on him by now. He lay there for several seconds before getting up and walking over to the bodies. He held his rifle in one hand and his flashlight in the other as he gazed down at the gruesome visage.

Simi lay half on top of Luis's body, staring up at the starry sky. Her eyes made no blinking or movement of any kind; they were lifeless. An area of dark red was quickly forming on the left side of her chest, soaking through the material of her torn and tattered shirt. Jessie saw where the bullet had exited, leaving a horrific hole of shattered bone and flesh. Below her, facedown, lay Luis, lifeless also. He saw where the bullet had entered the small of his back, tore through his heart, and of course knew where it exited.

Jessie turned and looked back down the slope, training his light toward the ground. He discovered the two officers' bodies, also motionless, crumpled in the sand. He figured they were dead too. But now hatred rose in him like a fiery hot stove. A hatred, so blazing, for what they had done to his cousin and pregnant wife. Why did they have to shoot them, to kill them, instead of just shooting to wound? This pair of immigrants weren't murder-crazed lunatics. They hadn't hurt or done anything to anyone. All they wanted was a better life for them and their child, to live a happy life.

Jessie walked down the slope to the officers. He looked them over. They were wearing border patrol uniforms, one lying on his back, the other on his side. He spit on both of them for what they had just done. Jessie picked up one of their handguns. It still permeated with the warmth of being held. The warm human feel of a person who didn't give a damn about the precious life of another human being, just about the laws and politics of the land.

He took the handgun and fired a shot into each of their heads. As the last blast echoed away into the open vastness, he threw the pistol down and walked back to Luis and Simi. He needed to take their belongings and any kind of identifications off them. There could be no tracing back to his family at all. They could not be implicated. As he took Luis's wallet out of his back pocket, pictures fell out. They were pictures of family members, some he knew, some he didn't. That's when it all hit him, like a storm buffeting a house with torrents of rain. Only the rain now were his tears; the sobbing came all at once.

Two hours later, it was all done. Jessie had found a shovel in the jeep of the border patrol officers. A shovel they probably would have used on Luis and Simi also, if they had accomplished their task and not got killed themselves. He had dragged his cousin and wife a good distance from the site of the killings, out into the desert. The ground wasn't as hard as he thought it would be. It was very loose once he got past the top crust. Jessie dug the hole deep. It had to hold both their bodies. In life as in death, he thought to himself. He again burst into tears when he was done, thinking he could never put up any markers in remembrance, just a few large stones rolled atop the newly dug graves to hide its freshness.

As he left the valley, never to return, he looked up at the immense night sky and spoke. "God, please watch over their souls. Do not let the devil's helpers get them."

9

Lanzo Torrida listened to all the chatter coming over his headset. He was bone tired. Sitting in this turret in the belly of this goddamn bomber made a person so tense, it could fry your brain noodles, he thought.

There were several things that contributed to it. One thing for sure was you were sitting in a cramped ball turret, with two big hot .50-caliber machine guns. The other was your ass was exposed to the whole world. A person was basically sitting on the glass of the turret, nothing else. After that, it was just the open sky and eighteen thousand feet to the earth. Yes, he had straps attached, holding him to the plane's structure. When you thought longer, you realized it was just those fiber straps, that was it. No parachute. There was no room in the turret for it. It was big enough for just a man, the guns, and the ammo.

A person had to be of a small stature to be a belly gunner, and Lanzo was basically small. He was the runt of the family, standing at 5'4" and weighing roughly 145 pounds; he definitely was the smallest. His brother and sister were a little taller, maybe two or three inches, but Italians in general weren't a tall people. All the relatives he knew, including Mom and Dad, were small.

No one on the crew ever made fun of his size. They were thankful to have him sitting in that turret and protecting their underside. He knew for a fact he was solely responsible for shooting down two enemy fighters. The Krauts always thought they could tear up a B-17 from the undercarriage. Not once did they think about that rotating turret spitting hot lead at them as they came up on it. At least two Krauts didn't.

Sometimes his legs would fall asleep, being crammed slightly above him in the bubbled glass. He had just the slightest amount of room to flex and move them up or down, to get the pins and needles to go away. He was doing just that thing when Jessie yelled over his headset, "*Madre de Dios!* They are harpies!"

Everything percolated back to life in him, no more aching in the haunches or fogging of the brain. It was all on full alert. Visions of winged demons, out of the books of mythology, he had read in school, came to him. Creatures with bat-like wings, devil tales, fanged teeth, and sharp talons. He saw them in illustrations, flying on the currents of the air.

This couldn't be, he thought. It was just pure lunacy. Jessie was just tired, exhausted from the day's turmoil. He was just seeing birds. Big birds, like Zack had said, that's all.

Then the twin .50s opened up over his head. That got him rethinking the whole conversation. Skipper Davis came shouting in his ears, "Everybody be ready! We got something coming at us!"

Lanzo had his turret facing forward, toward the front of the plane. All radio traffic said the things were coming from the stern at them. He hit his controls, and the hydraulics kicked in, humming. The turret spun around, facing the rear. There was enough light from the moon and stars to give him some vision. He could just make out the stationary wheel sitting at the tail end of the bomber, under the rear gun, where Zack was sitting. He swung his head from left to right, searching the night sky in front of him.

Then he saw it, as the skipper kept yelling in his ears for Zack to answer. The shape slowly crawled from the tail gun section to the under carriage of the bomber. It definitely had a distinct resemblance to the harpy creature he had read about and seen in the drawings on this mythical Greek devil. It had a darkish red tint to its body. The wings had the telltale bat shape. They were huge, but they quickly folded to its body, like a bird's wing would do when not in flight. He figured it had flapped the wings to gain air advantage when it moved from the stern to the undercarriage. It seemed to examine the new terrain it was on, the head moving up and down, back and forth, in a rather jerky motion. The head came to a complete stop, becoming motionless, as its gaze spied Lanzo. He saw two small glowing orang-ish dots, peering straight at him. In an instant, it started hopping toward him. The hops were short, only a foot or two at a time, but increased in speed as it moved. He saw the talons on its hands and feet dig into the frame of the plane, holding it secure to the bomber as it moved.

He heard his voice, as if from a great distance, very weak, almost inaudible. As the creature neared, the volume increased in volume and pitch. "No…no…no…NO!"

Lanzo looked through his sights for the .50s. The whole body of the harpy was framed in it. He pulled the lever by his head, the trigger for the machine guns. The bark of the .50s was heavy in his head, a staccato *chug-chug-chug* reverberated in the turret. His eyes stayed glued to the gunsights as the shells impacted the creature. At a distance of only eight feet, the results were dramatic. The entire body of the harpy was ripped apart simultaneously. Shards and chunks of flesh and bone erupted into the night air and were carried away by the swift wind currents.

The only thing left to show that there had ever been a harpy on the belly of the bomber was part of a lone foot of the creature. A sem-blance of an ankle and three talons still hung to the undercarriage, impaled in the fabric.

Lanzo trembled as he released his grip on the trigger lever and in the same breath screamed, "Not today, fuckhead! Not today!"

10

The blow caught him on the left side of the face with a meaty splat. He fell to the smooth, cool floor of the boys' restroom, sliding across the surface and ending up against the wall.

"Hit 'em again, Geanie! Hit 'em again!" yelled Emery Bradsford, the second accomplice in the incident.

"Naw, don't want to hurt his purty face any more than I have to," returned Gean, a tall massively sturdy black boy. "Okay, Lanzo, give me the money or I really will fuck up your face."

The stars were quickly clearing from Lanzo's head as he looked up at the hulking boy, standing over him. He didn't want to be hurt any further. He dug into his pocket and pulled out the money, two dollar singles. He licked his lip at the corner of his mouth, tasting the blood that was starting to form there.

Gean Turnbury saw this as he grabbed the bills out of Lanzo's hand. "Yeah, man, you sure do have a purty face and a purty mouth. I think I might like to put my dick in it and let you suck on it fer a while." He grabbed his crotch and held on to it tightly, all the time looking directly at Lanzo.

"What's going on in here?" said the man standing in the door-way of the restroom, holding the door open.

"Nothing, Mr. Dunderling," said Emery sheepishly, backing away from the other two boys.

The tall lanky white man surveyed the boy on the floor and the one standing over him, holding the dollar bills. "Well, what do you say about it, Gean?"

"Ise just getting my money back from him. That's all." He pointed down at Lanzo, holding out the other hand with the dollar bills.

"Are you saying he stole it from you? Is that what you mean?" Mr. Dunderling looked down intently at Lanzo.

"Yes, sir. That's what he did all right. Yes…sir," Gean stammered.

"What do you say about that, Lanzo?" Bill Dunderling now let his gaze linger on Gean as he asked Lanzo the question.

"I did not. That's my money. He took it from me." Lanzo looked gravely at the man, as Bill gave the same stare back to him.

"Well, well. We have a dilemma here, don't we?" The teacher now put a hand to his jaw, squeezing it with his thumb and index finger. He looked around the restroom and back at all three boys. "Get up, Lanzo. You, Gean, and Emery follow me. Let's head to the principal's office." He turned, opened the door, and started walking down the hallway.

As Lanzo got to his feet, the other two boys crowded up against him, pinning him to the wall. "Listen, you little white wop. Don't be sayin' anything to get us in trouble, or you're gonna have hell payin' fer it," Gean spat out at him. An ugly, vile grin came to his face, exposing teeth, some on the verge of rotting away.

"Yeah. You, white cracker, we'll mess you up bad," Emery added, putting a finger in Lanzo's face.

"Now get goin'. Remember what I just said." Gean grabbed the collar of Lanzo's shirt and pulled and pushed him toward the door.

Bill Dunderling was waiting halfway down the hall, when the boys appeared from the restroom. He motioned for them to catch up with a quick flip of his finger. The bell rang loudly in the empty hall, announcing the start of the next class.

It was somewhat comical looking at the three boys walking down the hall. They all walked abreast of each other. Gean stood at a good six-foot height, Emery a couple of inches shorter, and then Lanzo, who stood at way below five feet tall. It reminded one of an evolutionary chart with the short man ape at one end of the line, then evolving in stages to the tall fully grown man. All the boys were supposed to be eleven years old, and in the fifth grade, but Gean had the looks and stature of being very much older. It had been said that his parents had lost his birth certificate; and when they got a new copy, they sorta fudged his age, when they enrolled him in this school after moving up from the south. Gean could easily be assumed to be eighteen years old with no hesitation.

The boys caught up with Bill and proceeded down through different halls till they got to an office door. Stenciled on the glass window of the door in bold letters was "Principal—Leonard Pittinger." Bill opened the door and ushered the boys in. A secretary's desk sat in the left-hand corner of a small room, with several chairs on the right wall. Sitting at the desk was a heavier-set white woman, in her mid-fifties, her hair pulled up high on her head in a tight knot. The nameplate sitting on the desk read June Sternvill. One look at her and one knew she could be trouble if her stove was turned up too high.

"What can I do for you, Mr. Dunderling?" she asked, looking past him at the trio of boys, sizing them up. A shade of disgust crept up on her hardened face.

"I need to talk to Mr. Pittinger. We have a little matter to discuss over with these gentlemen. Is he in?"

"Yes, he is. Go on in. Just knock before you do, all right?" she replied, motioning with her head toward the door in the right corner of the office.

"Thank you. You boys have a seat, while I go in." Bill pointed to the chairs adorning the wall. The boys quickly jockeyed for position and sat down. He then knocked lightly on the door and slowly cracked it open. "Len, it's Bill. Can I talk to you for a moment?" As if from a short distance came a reply. Bill Dunderling opened the door the rest of the way and went in, closing it behind him. One could hear a conversation going on, but at a muted tone.

Lanzo and his family had moved to Detroit, Michigan, going on four years now. His father had lost his job back in New York. Everyone told him to go to Detroit and get into the auto industry. The whole area was booming right now. It would be a cinch to get work. So Lanzo and his family pulled up stakes and went to the northwest. He was seven at the time. He thought it would be fun moving like that. Going to someplace totally different would be fun.

It soon all became a bad dream. First off, his family didn't have the fiscal appropriations to afford good housing, so they were relegated to move to the more lower-income homes in the city area. They ended up in what was called Patesville, a seedy, slum-type apartment complex in the vast metropolis. His dad had told them all that this was just a temporary thing. In a year or so they would be out. He had gotten a low entry-level job at Ford Motor Company. The pay was just adequate enough to afford this three-bedroom apartment in one of the Patesville buildings, but he promised them that in no time he would move up to a better job, and so would they. In the three years since, Lanzo and his family of five never saw it materialize.

Then there was the schooling for him and his sisters. Because of their location in Detroit, they were required to attend Adams High School and the subsequent middle and grade schools. Lanzo was at Jackson Grade School, while his sisters went to Adams. The schools and community had a predominantly black population. Lanzo's Italian heritage was considered close to the black culture, but nevertheless, they weren't truly accepted by them. They would always be considered low-end whites, but still white.

The black kids were tough on him and his sisters. They were constantly harassed physically and mentally. Lanzo now understood what the black populace experienced, in terms of the racial hatred shown to them from the white society. It was reverse discrimination toward him and his family. He and his group were at the bottom end of the shit ladder, and it was being heaped on them with a vengeance.

Every day at school, he was either beat on or verbally talked down to. Things were always stolen or taken from him. A prime example was this case in point. His mother had given him a dollar; that was to take care of lunch meals and bus rides to and from school for a month. Sometimes he would not eat one day or not take the bus home but just walk, giving him added money he could save for himself. It took him a while to accumulate some extra funds. Over the span of several months, he had put aside a dollar in savings.

Today, that dollar plus the dollar his mother had just given to him for the month had been taken from him by Gean and Emery. They were considered the two biggest bullies of the sixth grade. They would always find younger, smaller prey to pick on. Today was Lanzo's turn in the barrel. Somehow they had spied Lanzo's little treasure of money and decided it should be theirs.

Most of the teachers at Jackson Grade School were white, including Mr. Dunderling and Principal Pittinger. In the early 1930s, one didn't find too many teachers teaching who weren't predominantly white. They were all strict disciplinarians. No matter if a child was black, white, or Hispanic, punishment was still dealt out to all equally. Lanzo figured today was going to be the same as all the rest. Swats for everybody, whether guilty or innocent, and told not to let this type of incident happen again.

The door to Mr. Pittinger's office opened, and Bill Dunderling stepped out. "Okay, boys, enter. The principal will see you now." He motioned with hand to enter the office, like a maître d' would do seating someone at a restaurant table.

As Lanzo passed by Mr. Dunderling, a hand from the teacher was laid on his shoulder and a little squeeze delivered. Lanzo looked up at him and discovered a look of compassion had come across the man's face and eyes. He returned a slight apprehensive smile back to him.

Bill Dunderling closed the door and stood behind the boys. All three were in a single line, Lanzo at the far-right end. Leonard Pittinger sat behind his desk, hands folded together, resting on the paper date pad in front of him. He was an older man, in his midsixties. White hair adorned the sides of his head, but the top was totally bald. His face was starting to wrinkle and exude a prune-like complexion.

"Well, gentlemen, what do we have here?" He waited several seconds for a reply, but none came. "Well, somebody needs to start. It better be quick or else."

"It was him, Mr. Pittinger." Gean spoke up, pointing at Lanzo. "He took my money. Ain't that right, Emery?"

"Yep...sure is," Emery echoed back.

Leonard sat for a minute looking at the three boys, then spoke. "So you're telling me, Gean, Lanzo here took the money from you? How'd he do it?"

"He...he...just took it from me," Gean stammered, nerves starting to get the better of him.

"How did he do it? I'm just asking. Did he reach into your pocket and take it? Or did he threaten you to get it? What is it?"

Gean thought for a second. "He just yelled at me to give it to him. Said...he...was gonna hurt me bad. He...he"—Gean thought through the story as he stammered—"pulled a knife on me, he did. Sures he did. Right, Emery?"

It startled Emery to respond as Gean gave him a little nudge with his hand. "Yeah...yeah... He sure did."

Leonard Pittinger now eased back in his chair, putting both hands behind his head, cradling it. He slowly turned, looked out the window, onto the bright spring day, and then slowly returned his gaze back to the boys. "A knife? Well, now that's really bad, isn't it?" He looked directly at Lanzo. "Do you have a knife, son?"

"No, I don't, Mr. Pittinger," Lanzo responded. His father had always told him to answer back quick and respectfully to anyone in authority, especially teachers.

"Well, if you're lying, we'll find out now. Empty your pockets, son."

Lanzo quickly stuffed his hands down both pockets, pulling them back out, inside out, revealing what he had. It amounted to two pennies (which looked utterly dismal for wear and tear) and a blue crystal marble. The marble was his prize possession. He won it fair and square in a game of marbles with Tommy Bretton, one of the other few white kids at the school.

"I don't see any knife, Gean. Do you?"

The boy put his head down, thinking hard. "He...he...musta threw it away." His head snapped back up when he responded. He looked intently at Lanzo with a sneer quickly forming on his face.

"Is this true, Lanzo? Did you throw the knife away?"

"No, sir. I never had a knife at all. He punched me and told me to give him all my money." He motioned toward Gean with his head.

"He's lyin'! That white boy's a lyin'!" yelled Gean, now pointing his finger back at Lanzo.

Leonard Pittinger looked back out the window and spoke. The words came out in a slow and precise manner of tone. "Well, if he had the knife and just threw it away, how'd you get the money back?

Wouldn't he have stuck you with the knife when you tried to get your money back?"

Gean looked nervous, eyes darting from place to place, his mind whirling in panic. "I…I…" was all he could get out.

"Listen, son. I've seen you do this with other kids. You're a big bully. You and Emery are both just that." Leonard Pittinger now turned from gazing out at the world and looked at the boys. "I want you to give Lanzo his money back, right now." He motioned with his hand, flipping a finger from Gean toward Lanzo.

Gean held tightly to the money, still resting in his hand all this time, reluctant to do it.

"I said give it to him now!" Mr. Pittinger's voice rose considerably when he said it, his face taking on a snarling wolf look. A look that said, "Do as I say or I will rip off your face and eat it."

Gean reached over and opened his hand to Lanzo. Lanzo snatched the dollars quickly, stuffing them back into his pocket with his pennies and marble.

"I won't or don't want this to happen again. Do you boys understand?" Mr. Pittinger now stood up from behind his desk. "Lanzo, you can go back to class now. You other two gentlemen can stay here another second, and we'll discuss this a little more." Leonard Pittinger reached down, opening a side drawer, and pulled out a paddle. The paddle was made of wood, about eighteen inches long, an inch thick, with holes drilled in it toward its end. Lanzo knew, as well as Gean and Emery, that this added pain to the swing when the paddle was applied.

Bill Dunderling opened the door to the office. "Go on, Lanzo, go back to class." He motioned with a nod of his head.

Lanzo moved spiritedly out of the office as the door quickly closed behind him. He did a very gingerly and mannered walk past June Stanville and opened the door that led out into the main hallway.

"You go straight to class. No lollygaggin' anywhere. You do understand that?" she said with a mean smirk.

He nodded back in compliance, as he closed the door and stepped out. As his hand came away from the door handle, he heard the first splat of the paddle on one of the boys' ass. He kept walking as he heard another swat being administered. He knew for him this was not the end of it.

*****

Tommy Bretton caught Lanzo in the hallway by his locker, an hour before school was to be let out for the day. "Don't know the whole story, but I do know you're in big trouble," he said as he leaned his head in close to Lanzo and the open locker.

"Let me guess, Gean Turnbury," Lanzo replied as his head snapped out of the locker and searched the hallway in both directions.

"What'd you do to him?"

"He caught me in the john. Him and Emery Bransford took my money, those rotten assholes. Gave me this." Lanzo rubbed his jaw and lip, which was now swollen up pretty good. "Mr. Dunderling walked in on it. We ended up in Principal Pittinger's office. They had to give the money back. Plus Pittinger cracked the board on them, I think big-time."

"Well, he sure is pissed. Told people he's gonna get you after school."

"Shit! Thanks, just wonderful. What'll I do?" Lanzo felt his heart starting to skip beats.

"My thought is run. Get your ass home. I'll walk you to the north door, make sure they're not there, then you take off through Miller Field and go the back way to home. Got it?" Tommy looked up and down the hallway as he walked away from Lanzo. "Just make sure you meet me at my locker as soon as class is done, okay?" Lanzo shook his head in agreement, closed his locker, and headed for last class.

Time moved fast for him. His stomach was doing flip-flops as the clock hands got closer to 3:30 p.m. He figured he wouldn't head back to his locker. They might be there, waiting for him. He would go straight to Tommy's locker and hand off his book and folders to him. A black girl, Joan Harris, sitting next to him, leaned over at 3:28 p.m. and whispered in a low voice, "Youse are so fucked, white boy. You best say your last prayers right now."

Those words chilled Lanzo but also ignited a little madness and meanness in him, a little primal spark. "You can just go to hell, Joan!" he whispered back.

She shook her head from side to side and replied in an uppity voice, "Hmmmmm."

Lanzo was up and out of his seat in social studies class ten seconds before the bell rang. The teacher, Ms. Davis, started to say something; but he never heard her. He pushed the door open and was gone.

The bell rang as he flew down the hall, made a turn, and saw Tommy's locker. Tommy was there, waiting. Lanzo ran past him and yelled, "Com'on, let's go!" Tommy immediately joined in this mock hundred-yard dash, as they headed for the north door.

At the end of the school day, mostly teachers went out the north door. The parking lot and their cars were back behind the school, nothing else, unless one was looking for a shortcut home. No one was at the doors as they pushed them open and stopped. Tommy leaned out from the building and looked east and west.

"Nothing. Go, go!" he shouted. Lanzo jammed the book and folders into Tommy's stomach, not caring if he had hold of them or if they fell to the cement. He jumped the four stairs to ground, landed a perfect leap, and landed on the terra firma running.

Lanzo was halfway through Miller Field when he heard Gean's voice, shouting from a distance, "Hey, Torrida, I'm gonna get your ass!" He looked back over his shoulder and caught a glimpse of Gean and Emery coming down the stairs. Tommy was sprawled out on the concrete. He was not sure if they had pushed him or just plain punched his lights out.

Lanzo ran another fifty yards and was at the edge of the woods. Left was home; right was toward the train tracks and Lansing River. At one time, Lansing River was really a big waterway. Now with all the industries moving in, it had receded down to a long, forgotten stream.

Lanzo's mind raced. His pursuers might know a better route to his house than him, beat him there, and lie in wait, to pummel him when he approached. Right toward the river might really throw them off, and he could lose them and make it home before they figured it out.

Being young and in a panic, the mind does not think right. All his pursuers would have had to do was just go to his apartment and wait for him. Eventually he would have to go home. Fear intercedes in the most dire of times, completely wiping out clear and logical thought. Lanzo turned right toward the river.

This section of woods was full of trees with low-hanging branches and thickets of weeds and bushes. He fought his way through them, pushing the branches aside, causing great gashes and scratches on his arms and hands. He pushed whatever pain he felt out of his mind. Survival was more important. He heard the two boys enter the woods and continue their chase for him.

"I see you, you little wop! Your white ass is mines!" Gean shouted as the duo started to slowly gain on Lanzo's lead. He was doing all the heavy lifting. He was clearing out the arduous path, and the pair following had easy sailing. Even if they lost sight of him, all they had to do was follow the trampled undergrowth and all the broken branches lying before them.

The river was dead ahead now. The B&L train tracks were in his sight. They ran over the river in this section. Lanzo had been down here many a time, sometimes with Tommy, but most of the time by himself, just exploring. To the right of the river on the embankment for the tracks was an old sewer entry. It had once belonged to a big sawmill that had been there years before. Now, time and the economy had passed the mill by, leaving just the sewer, a remnant, as evidence of another era.

Lanzo hit the river in full stride, water splashing up and around him. The river, or now stream, was only a few feet deep, just up to his upper thigh. He strode through the gentle current using his hands as paddles to aid in his progress. He made it to the sewer ledge and pulled himself up. At one time, the ledge would never have been seen. The mighty Lansing would have risen above it. Now, he looked down on the slowly moving waterway. He turned and looked into the mouth of the entry to the sewer. He could only see about ten feet in; the rest was in complete darkness. Tommy and he had been here before but never ventured in. Their childhood nightmares and fears had gotten the better of them. The stench of something rotten and dead brought the hairs up on the back of their necks. They gladly passed it by.

Lanzo knew Gean and Emery were close. He could hear their grunts and groans as they fought their way toward him. He felt the sweat trickle down his neck and soak into his shirt. He knew he had to lose them or that sweat would soon be his own blood spilling and washing down over him. He made a quick decision and entered the old sewer. The archway was about six feet high and in bad disrepair. Sections of the brickwork had already let loose and lay crumpled in the entry. He made his way over them as the dreaded duo broke out of the woods. The world darkened around him as he got several feet in. The only light available was the daylight from the entrance. He was in what was termed the main spillway, a large room with a high ceiling of ten feet. He could make out two more sewer ways branching off on his left and right, at forty-five-degree angles, from the main trough. They were in complete blackness, as was the main trough in front of him. The aroma he had smelled long before hit his nose like a brick wall. The pungent smell of earthy dampness mixed with an odor of rot and decay overpowered him.

Lanzo heard the splashing of water outside. He turned to see Gean and Emery pulling themselves up onto the sewer ledge. His heart sank as his temples throbbed. They had seen where he had gone; the jig was up. He stumbled backward, paying no attention to the putrid water splashing up on him. Wild panic had set in. Should he keep running into the center sewer trough or take one of the other openings? There was no light in them whatsoever, so he would be moving blindly into God knows what. At this point, it didn't matter what was in the infernal black. It would be better than getting pummeled to death by the two Neanderthals.

"We know you're in there, boy! It's time to make you pay! Make you feel some pain too, and fer sure it's gonna be the last thing you feel!" Gean yelled as he and Emery stood in the archway, peering in.

"Yeah, youse white cracker, youse done for now." Emery's fist slammed into his palm with a heavy, meaty thump.

Lanzo, in a world of distress, lost his balance, falling into the archway behind him. Pieces of brick and earth rained down on his body. He felt no pain, as adrenaline flowed through his body. He put his hands behind him to push away from the crumbling archway, when he felt metal. It was cold, slimy, rusty metal but still could be a weapon, he thought. He put both hands around it and pulled. It moved some but not enough. He quickly put a foot up against the collapsing wall and pulled with all his strength. This time it broke free and came out, his exertion sending him into the rancid water. The liquid was in his eyes and mouth, the taste making him gag. He spit the foul fluid out of his mouth as he got to his feet, rubbing his eyes clear with one hand. In the other, he firmly held what he fought to exude from the debris. It was a piece of rebar, roughly four foot long, the ends of it jagged and gnarly.

"You done messin', boy." Lanzo turned to see Gean standing in the middle of the chamber, watching him. Emery slowly inched around to the left of him, squinting, getting his eyes adjusted to the semidarkness.

Lanzo held the rebar out in front of him, holding it like a spear, pointing at Gean. "I swear I'll stab you with this." He thrust it forward to show Gean and Emery what he had.

"Youse can do all the swearin' youse want. Youse ain't gonna do no such thang. Youse don't have the balls to do it. But when I'm done with youse, you're gonna have some balls, my balls, in your mouth. Got it!" Gean inched closer as he talked. Emery had just about made his way to the side of Lanzo, close to the sewer opening on his right.

Lanzo thrust the bar out at Emery and then back at Gean, waving it wildly. "None of you come any closer. I...I...will stick you."

"Boy, boy. It's done. It's over. Put that thang down, and just get what's comin' to ya." Gean now stood about three feet from Lanzo.

All the boys heard the noise at the same time. It was a low throaty growl. One that started to reverberate as it got louder, seemingly closer, with each passing second. It was coming from the blackened archway to Lanzo's right, where Emery was standing. Everyone's head and eyes turned toward that area and peered into the inky dark.

Two glowing reddish eyes, low to the water, appeared out of the blackness. Soon the head and front legs became apparent as it slowly slunk out of the tunnel. It was a German shepherd dog from what Lanzo could make out. But this dog had seen better days. It was a mangy-looking creature. The fur was all matted and dirty, large sections missing fur at all. In those areas, the skin, normally a healthy pink, was now red, splotchy, and infected. There was a rotted black look beneath the blistered skin, now oozing a pus type of fluid. The lips of the canine now pulled back, revealing its large gnarled teeth. The dog seemed to be in a rabid state. Large amounts of foamy, lathered spittle ran from its mouth dropping to the water. The dog kept emitting its incensed growl as it cleared the opening.

Emery staggered back several steps. "What the fuck is that—" was all he got out as he stumbled and fell into the water with a mighty splash.

The maddened dog took this as a show of aggression; a loud yelp-bark came out of its mouth as it made its leap. Emery tried to get up out of the water but made it only halfway as the dog flew through the air, hitting him full force, sending the pair sliding through the trough, in an explosion of splashes.

Emery's arms began flailing wildly, trying to deliver blows to the animal. All the while the snarling, growling, rabid dog kept snapping and biting at its intended victim. Its fangs found the side of Emery's cheek, tearing a large splay of flesh and tendon from it. His fist found the head of the dog and connected with a heavy thud. The creature's mouth shot out and seized the wrist, between its jaws, and clamped down. Tissue and veins erupted in a spray of blood. Emery jerked the arm free and swung again, blood spitting out from his wounds, covering parts of the dog's body. The crazed animal now went for the kill. Its snout shot in for the throat, clamping hold and biting down.

Emery's blows found the dog but became less effective. His energy was quickly fading. The dog let loose its grip and tore into another section of neck. The intended result was instantaneous. The wild, flying arms stopped. Emery's whole body seemed to go into a spasm, shaking and jerking, spiraling toward its death knell. Within seconds, his body went limp. Emery was dead. The rabid canine realized this and released its hold on the body, its attention now taking in Gean.

All this time Gean stood frozen in place, watching the gruesome spectacle that played out before him. If he had wanted to help Emery, fear had gripped him so hard, it wouldn't let him do it. Now self-preservation kicked in; he knew he was the next victim of this animal. He reached down into the shallow water and picked up a large chunk of concrete. He brought it high over his head, as the menacing thing moved toward him, snapping and snarling, spitting foam and blood from its mouth. It was intent on another victim.

All in the same motion, Gean threw the chunk of concrete at the animal and turned to run for safety, or God knows, just to get away from the hellish ordeal. His prior thoughts had evaporated from his mind. Lanzo and the rebar were totally forgotten from his consciousness. But in the real world, they were still very much there, ready for defense. Gean's turn was but two quick steps, but the two steps were right at Lanzo. The rusty rebar caught him midchest, impaling him. His mouth opened, forcing air out his lungs in one big gasp of pain and astonishment. His eyes opened wide to the unexpected realization of what had just happened.

Lanzo saw the energy in Gean's eyes fade and diminish rapidly; his body quickly went limp. In the last remaining seconds of Gean Turnbury's life, Lanzo spoke to him. "Not today, fucker, not today."

Gean's massive body became a literal deadweight, as it collapsed to the water, pulling the bar out of Lanzo's hands, still impaled on it. The body hit the water, sending a large splash into the air. Gean lay on his back, the rebar standing tall in the trough, a marker for his watery grave.

Lanzo was now defenseless against the rabid fury of the animal. He stood motionless, waiting to see the shape of the German shepherd emerge out of the gloom, its jaws snapping for his neck. As some sense of quiet settled in the sewer chamber, he heard the dog. It seemed to be having its own set of problems. He took a step forward. Looking several feet past Gean's body, he saw the dog lying in the tepid water trough. It was attempting to get to its feet, but with no luck. The once-disease-ridden, snapping fanged head was in ruins. The chunk of mortar and stone, like a missile, had found its target when Gean had thrown it. The skull of the creature was split open, exposing what oozing brain matter it had left. The long snout had been snapped (broken) and was pushed to one side, at an almost right angle. An eye dangled out of its socket, held only by a fine tendril of vein. It was spasming and jerking like Emery had, trying to gain an upright position, but collapsing back on its haunches.

Lanzo knew it would be dead shortly. He calmed his beating heart the best he could. His hands were still trembling, his legs shaky. He slowly and hesitantly moved around Gean's dead body, giving the dying dog a wide berth. In his head, he saw the dog making a futile last lunge toward him, grabbing hold with those jagged fangs. He made it past the beast without incident.

As he gained the entrance of the sewer, he turned and looked back. Quiet had settled over the chamber. Everything that was in there was now motionless and dead. Lanzo turned back toward the vibrant sunlight and sweet-smelling breeze. He felt life again.

11

The harpy came out of the night sky to Jessie's starboard side of the plane. Hugging the side of the bomber, its wings unfurled, flapping in unison, in rapid strokes. Jessie swung the turret around and fired. This time he led the creature, the way he was taught to lead and fire at approaching fighters. The harpy flew right into the fiery tracers, standing it up and pushing it away from the bomber. A section of one of its wings tore apart and blew away on the wind. The shells pinpointed the center of the harpy's body, ripping it to shreds. It fell out of his sight in bloodied ruins.

From the corner of his eye, Jessie saw more movement. He swung the turret back around as another harpy flew at him. An instant before he pulled his lever to fire, the creature was knocked out of the sky by a flurry of shells. It took a sharp nosedive and hit the bomber roof, ten feet from him, with a heavy thud. It was Lane Arnold firing his .50 from the small gunport, located between him and the tail section. *Good for old Lane*, he thought. The thing slowly slid down the port side of the craft. Jessie figured it was dead, ready to blow off the bomber, and be carried away on the wind. But good reasoning doesn't always come to pass. A clawed hand sprang to life and dug its talons into the bomber's fabric. Jessie could barely see the creature's face, but enough to see the small eyes open and a devilish orange glow radiate in them. His fingers fumbled for his firing lever, but it was too late. The harpy's mighty wings propelled it straight up into the air. He fired, his shots flying at a now-empty space. He quickly recovered, raising the guns to follow the harpy's ascent. To his own chagrin, he realized the guns only raised to a seventy-five-degree angle, a deficiency of engineering by the aircraft company, and a critical error to him.

The harpy now directly overhead came down hard on the turret glass. It shattered, exposing Jessie to the elements and the creature. Razor-sharp talons dug into his shoulders. The pain intense, he screamed in agony. The next instant, the harpy's strong hands gripped his head and twisted sharply, ripping it away from his body. Blood pulsed into the wind and was carried away on its currents. The creature feasted on what remained.

12

Lanzo Torrida saw the thing-creature crawling along the port side of the bomber. It wasn't low enough to be in his gunsights, just low enough to see the nightmarish monster. It was somewhat bigger than a man in its frame, but the whole girth of the body was lanky. The wings made it look enormous. The slender body was well muscled and defined, sleek, but formidable.

He fired several bursts at it in vain, missing by a good six feet. He was hoping to startle it, to make it move closer to him, so he could have a better aim. Instead, the creature moved up toward the side gunner opening where Bernie Mossberg was. "Bernie, Bernie!" he screamed on his mic. "Side gunner, over! For god's sake, Bernie, it's coming at you!"

To his left, there was quick movement. It was another of these things, running rapidly on all fours, tearing its talons into the structure as it came for him. He swung the turret around and fired. In that same moment, the harpy stopped the travel of the guns by grabbing the left .50-gun barrel. The hot firing barrel seared into the creature's palm, as it screamed in pain, a shrill, birdlike screech. The harpy jerked its hand and arm in a downward motion, snapping the barrel off. A shell, caught in the barrel, exploded in a bright flash and intense concussion, taking Lanzo's sight away. The creature's hand was blown away at the wrist. Blackish goo coursed out of the emaciated stump, as the thing howled in pain.

Stars of intense brilliance danced in front of Lanzo's eyes as he tried to regain vision. Pieces of metal fragments had penetrated through the glass shielding in the turret and now were embedded in his cheeks and nose. Blood ran down his face, landing on his flight jacket. As he got some semblance of sight back, he could make out the creature examining its wounded stump of a hand, the gooey blood still pumping out into the wind.

It turned its head back to Lanzo, the orangish pupils glowing, now igniting with anger, its mouth, in a screech of rage, sharp teeth, foaming with a reddish-black gore. The other still-functional hand shot out, shattering the turret glass, grabbing Lanzo's head in its clutch. He felt an instant hot pain, searing into his brain as the thing tightened its grip. His body's thermometer boiled to its extreme; his head burst like a grape being pinched. Brain matter splattered all over the remaining turret glass.

13

The sun was gone now, just a lingering glow on the western horizon. Lane Arnold popped his head into the cockpit of the massive B-17. For all its impressive girth, the cabin for the pilot and copilot was small. It would be hard pressed to fit three bodies in there. Lane Arnold might have gotten away fitting into it with the other two. He was tall and lanky, six foot and maybe pushing 150 lbs. He leaned in closer so as to be heard over the engines' roar.

"He might bleed out on us, Skip." He shook his head, supporting a pessimistic look. "Ain't much more I can do. Could try stitching him up. I never did do very good with that back at the classes. I mean, what'd they give us, four classes of hands-on and a couple for the dispensing of medicine? Com'on, I say."

"He's really that bad? I'm just saying this, 'cause to me, it looked like you were getting it under control," Cullum asked, looking over his shoulder at Lane.

"If he stays still, he'll be kinda okay. But when he starts moving, like he does when he's in pain, he really starts leaking. I gave him the morphine, but I think there's more problems inside. That bullet tore his insides up pretty good. I'm sure there's internal bleeding going on."

"Aw shit! I've seen that happen before. Once you start bleeding inside, you're screwed. Unless we get him to a doctor or hospital right away, forget it," Terry Graynor chimed in, looking at the other two.

"Well, that ain't gonna happen for at least another hour, hour and a half. And the way this bus's engines are doing, maybe longer, or maybe not at all. We lose another engine, we're done. We're going down." Cullum heard the number 2 engine sputter and gulp, as if in response, having its own type of spasm. In a few seconds it righted itself and smoothed back to a roaring hum. "See what I mean?" He motioned his head toward the port side engine, so both men caught the drift of the conversation.

That's when Jessie Hildago came over the plane's radio. "Hey, Skipper. This is Jessie. I saw some motion off our starboard rear. Over."

Cullum responded back, "What does it look like?"

"Must be some kind of bird. Maybe a group of them. Looks like they're closing in on us."

"Don't need them to screw with us. Don't let them get any closer. Don't want them flying into our good props and losing another engine. Fire a warning shot burst to keep them off us. Over." Cullum looked questionably at Terry, who in turn looked out his side window, straining to see what Jessie was looking at.

"Hell, don't see them yet. They're out of my view," Terry shot back.

"Roger that," Jessie answered back on the headset.

"I figured Zack would have been keeping an eye on them. Haven't heard a peep out of him for a while. Probably should talk to him." Cullum went to key his mic when Jessie came over the radio. "Skip! Skip! These aren't birds!" All three men looked at each other, now puzzled and all feeling a bit of trepidation growing in their thoughts.

The overhead twin .50s from Jessie's turret opened up. "*Madre de Dios!* They are harpies!" Jessie screamed over the mic.

"What the hell does that mean? I ain't never heard any German plane called that!" Terry shouted, straining his neck even harder to look out behind his side of the bomber.

"There ain't no Jerry planes even nicknamed that," added Lane.

Jessie came over the radio very clear now. "Skipper, they're behind us, by the tail and rear gunner."

Cullum quickly keyed his mic. "Tail gunner. Tail gunner. Come in, over. Zack. Zack, can you hear me? Over."

Cullum swung around looking at Lane. "Get back there. See what the hell's going on!"

14

"Runners, take your mark." Lane Arnold was a wealth of nerves as he looked on either side of him, eyeing the runners as they got into position on the blocks. Two were on his left, three on his right. He was smack-dab in the middle for this race. He had run this one-hundred-yard dash so many times before, it was old hat; then why was he so damn nervous? Maybe because it was the last qualifying heat. After this one, it would be the finals. He had to finish first or second to qualify for the championship sprint.

He got down on one knee, slowly settling his feet into the starting blocks. The fingers on both hands gently touched the clayish brown earth of the track, just behind the starting line. The chalked line ran across the breath of all six runners, blazing a brilliant white color in the afternoon sky. Lane's body trembled slightly, not in fear, no, more in anticipation of the outcome. Each runner on those blocks was there for the same thing: to win, to hear their name exalted in triumph before their peers and the crowd.

"Runners, get ready" came the commands from the official starter. He stood to the runners' left, decked out in a black outfit, with white stripes running across the shirt. In his hand, he held a small pistol, the starter pistol.

The attendance for this whole event was huge. The stadium it was in was packed to the brim. Lane estimated a good eight to ten thousand people were assembled today. Their resounding talk and yelling sounded like an angry field of bees to him. As the crowd saw the starter raise the pistol in the air, the clamorous buzzing came to an abrupt halt.

"On your mark." Lane steadied himself on the blocks, getting a good feel, one that would allow him to push off from them with force. His mind talked to him. It said block everything else out, the stadium, the people, the sky, the whole environment. Just let it be him, the track in front of him, and the finish line tape at the end of his run.

"Get set." Lane lifted his knee off the clay, putting weight on the wood blocks, tensing his body, coiling it up for a springlike action. He was now in a semicrotched state, fingers pressed into the ground, firm but yet not firmly, waiting, just waiting for the blast of the pistol. An agonizing second passed, him thinking was this man going to fire the pistol or not? He and the other runners couldn't remain like this for not very much longer.

The gun fired. It was a shrill, sharp, blank blast. He had heard it many times before, but it had always startled him somewhat. He had always told himself to block it out, but one can't, not when everything depended on one hearing it. For the firing of it meant go, time to run your heart out.

Lane's body shot off the blocks in a low, resistance-free spring. After three yards, his body was upright, legs pumping, arms slashing from in front to behind him, helping propel him down the track. He saw the finish-line tape across the track, so far, yet so very close. He could feel his heart pounding loudly in his head, the world around him bouncing up and down. He could hear the loud buzzing of the bees in the stadium, roaring in unison now. The finish line was close, very close. *Put it all in high gear*, he said to himself. His legs burned with intense energy, as if they were on fire.

He could really see the tape now, very clearly. On it was the word "finish" in between the yellow and black stripes. His mind yelled, *Don't reach out and grab it! Don't do that! Hit it with your chest!* Every time he ran, his mind would always play games with him, telling him to just grab the tape, to touch it, which he knew was wrong. He would just tell himself to push that thought away, push it to the back of the room and into the sealed box.

The next instant he felt the paper tape touch and wrap around his body. The race was over; he could stop running. He trotted to a stop, yards from the finish line. The whole stadium was roaring. He could feel the energy from them coursing through his body, giving him a euphoric high. The din of the people bees was astounding, seemingly ready to attack and smother him into oblivion.

Hands clapped him on his back. "Good race, great run!" one person, close by, yelled at him. The faces blurred around him, as he stood sucking in air, hands on his hips. He looked down and saw the finish ribbon falling off him, floating the rest of the way to the ground. He had won. He was in the finals.

Another arm and hand circled his shoulders. Close to his ear he heard the words, "You won this time. Tomorrow is my time, you asshole." This snapped Lane back to clarity. He looked at the out-of-breath runner, speaking to him. It was Chet Cockburn. He had been running in the outside lane, to his right. They had run against each other several times, at different track events. They had become rivals or, as Chet often remarked, fierce adversaries. He didn't like him much, and he knew Chet felt the same. There was a jealousy of speed between them. Chet was so sure he could outrun Lane but just quite never did. This time was no exception; he was told he had beat him by just half a stride.

He looked at Chet and nodded. "Whatever, buddy, try your best."

People crowded around him, pushing Chet out of the picture. His mom and dad appeared in front of him, shaking his hand and hugging him. Tom and Helen Arnold were proud of their boy. He had won many races and garnered many trophies and ribbons for first place, but this was the Indiana state finals. This was the big-time.

"You did it, son, you did it!" his dad said to him.

His mom beamed with a smile and put her head on his chest. "I knew you could do it. I just knew it."

As they walked back to the school bus that would take Lane back to the hotel for the night, the three family members walked arm in arm.

"You sure you don't want to go out for dinner tonight?" his mom asked Lane.

Tom spoke up emphatically. "No, no, no, Helen. He needs to rest up, concentrate for the race tomorrow. His coach and team will

THE DEVIL AT TWO

have dinner tonight and breakfast tomorrow with him. He needs to focus on what is at hand, not on us."

"You sure? It's just one little meal."

"Nope, Dad's right. I'll just take it easy at the hotel tonight. Be ready for tomorrow," Lane replied.

"Okay, honey. Go on with your team. We'll be there tomorrow. Yours is the first race of the morning, but we'll be there to watch you. You're going to win," his mom said as she hugged him tightly.

"I hope I win. It's going to be tough. Lots of good runners from all across the state."

"Son." Tom put his hands on Lane's shoulders and looked directly into his face. "It's all about focus. See the finish line, run for it. I've always told you, put your eye on an object, focus, and run for it as hard as you can. God's given you the ability to do this. To run like the wind. Tomorrow, pick out that object, and run like there's nothing else but you and it. Okay?"

"Sure thing, Dad. You know I will."

*****

The runners got into position. The sky was dark; intense black clouds approached from the north. They rumbled as they crept closer and closer. Lightning streaked through them in ragged shards, menacingly threatening pain and terror. It would be storming soon. Lane could smell the ozone and moisture in the air.

He looked at the runners on either side of him. That's all this race had, just three entrants. Where were all the participants? Lane wondered. To his left was Chet Cockburn, the boy who truly hated him. On his right was Bruce Stellanin, another nemesis of several races.

Lane nervously got into position, chancing another glance at Chet. To his disbelief, he watched as his hated foe's body dissolved away, doing a waxy melt, pieces of skin, bone, and hair dropping away, splattering on the dry clay. The running outfit remained, hanging in space. Something else, now, morphed into it, something hideous and nightmarish. It was a werewolf-like creature. A big gargantuan-type beast that towered over him. He could see muscles rippling underneath the mangy, furry hair. It looked down at him with sickly yellowish eyes and grinned, showing teeth that were sharp and ragged. Pieces of meat and skin hung from them. As if it had just finished devouring someone or thing and wanted him as the next meal. It raised a sharp talon to its mouth and picked out a piece of debris from the teeth. To Lane, it looked like a piece of intestine. The wolf examined it and greedily dropped it back in its mouth, chewing viscously and swallowing it.

Lane shook his head to clear this nightmare and looked to his right. Bruce Stellanin had evolved into a lizard beast. Not just a normal-looking reptile, but something way more terrifying. Its black marbled eyes studied him intently. It stood upright on two heavily muscled legs. Its arms were shorter, adorned with sharp, clawed fingers on its gnarled hands. The points on the ends of these talons dripped with a greenish goo. As the fluid hit the ground, the clay surface began to boil, bubble up, from the acidic liquid. The lizard creature opened its mouth; the long forked tongue slithered out and reached toward Lane. It curled over and gently flicked against Lane's cheek. The pain was instant and intense. His whole body burned in agony. The tongue quickly returned to its mouth as a smile formed on the lizard's face.

The starter with the pistol yelled, "Runners, get ready to die!" Lane's head snapped around to look at him. The person was in some type of hooded, shroud-like form of a cloak. It ran from his head to the ground. It had a dull brownish color, tattered, and threadbare, giving one the impression that it had been worn by this person for eons untold. Lane peered intently into the blackness of the hood. He couldn't pick any feature out. He saw no face or form, just complete Bible black exuded from it. Then in the next moment, two blazing red eyes opened and peered back at him. He felt a sense of evil and chilling coldness flow over him.

"On your mark." A hand raised out of the cloak, a skeletal arm, holding an ancient blunderbuss of a gun. One that ancient pirates or soldiers used from times long past. The dry, bony fingers cracked as they held the gun tightly.

"Get set." Lane awkwardly put his fingers to the now-blackened earth. The texture of the soil had a rubbery, spongy feel to it. The tips of his fingers sank into the porous mass. He pulled them back out and examined them. None of the strange soil was on them. He tried placing them back down, but with the same result happening. He tried to lightly touch the earth, but the tips of his fingers still sunk in.

The sky was a purple black; the storm was upon them. A jagged bolt of lightning arced out of the swirling sky, hitting the ground off to his right, sending blazing currents of flame back into the air. The storm bellowed and boomed, creating a deafening roar, in the completely empty stadium. It was the only sound accompanying this hellish event.

The gun erupted in an earsplitting bang. For a split second, Lane thought it was just another boom of thunder. When his two opponents took off, he knew otherwise. He went to pull his fingers from the ground and found they were held tightly in place by the tarlike mess. He pulled back hard, popping them free, leaving the skin of his fingertips in the goo. He sprinted like the wind and soon gained back the lead his adversaries had on him. In another several strides, he was neck and neck with them. The wolf thing looked over at him, snarled, and swung its clawed hand at him, one of them finding skin and tearing a chunk of flesh out of Lane's bare shoulder. He screamed in agony as the lizard creature spat a wad of its greenish venom at him. It struck the thigh of Lane, closest to it. The skin bubbled and dissolved down to the bone.

The pain was unbearable. Lane knew he had to get away from these demons. They didn't call him Fast Laney for nothing. A burst of speed came to him as he shot ahead of the creatures, increasing his lead by several yards.

The lightning hit all around him, as the sky erupted in one last volcanic blast. The rain came down in torrents, pelting him with large missiles of hard water. Every drop felt as if someone had slapped him. The track immediately became a quagmire; the blackish ground of soft tar soon became a muddy mess, splashing up and on him as he ran. His legs kept pumping hard and fast, but he soon realized he was going nowhere. Every stride he made, his feet began to sink deeper into the black mess of goo and slime. The creature things raced past him to the finish line, as he continued to slowly sink. He was now up to his thighs, as he watched the wolf cross the finish line for the victory. He struggled and pulled, but it just made him sink deeper down into the hellish ground. He was up to his chest as he saw his two monstrous opponents walk back toward him, their mouths salivating, looking at him as if he was their next meal. They now stood over him as he was almost buried up to his neck.

"You lose!" came the booming words to his left. Lane turned his head and looked up into the burning eyes of the hooded specter. He stood over him, a long-handled scythe in his skeletal arms raised high up in the air.

"You lose," it repeated again, as the sharp gleaming blade swung down at his neck.

Lane sat straight up in a bolt of horror and dread. Cold sweat covered his body, his shirt soaked with sweaty fear. He realized he was still in his bed, in his room at the hotel the school had rented for him. He now knew it was nothing else but a bad dream. The clock on the nightstand read 5:00 a.m. He would try to sleep another hour till six, when they all had to get up. He trembled as he tried to go back to sleep, hoping his nerves would relax. He lay there contemplating the day ahead of him, praying what he had just dreamed wasn't a horrible omen of things to come.

*****

The crowd was enormous; the stadium was overflowing. The gigantic beehive was already at work. People shouting and screaming, waving to all the contestants on the field.

Lane had already done his warm-ups and routine. He was as ready as he ever would be. He surveyed the crowd, looking for his mom and dad. He couldn't find them, but he knew they were there somewhere.

Chet Cockburn walked over to him and leaned close to his ear. "Today I beat your ass, got it, Arnold?"

Lane looked intently into his face, praying it wouldn't dissolve into an image of a wolfman. When it didn't, he spoke quietly and calmly. "Do whatever you gotta do, Chet. Just don't take a chunk out of my shoulder."

Chet looked thrown by the comment. He stood dumbfounded. "What the hell…" was all he could get out. Lane smiled and walked away.

The runners were all at their starting blocks. Lane, again, was in the middle of the six and final runners. Of course, Chet was to his left, just like in the nightmare. He looked farther over to his left, at the man holding the starter pistol, expecting to see a hooded guardian of death. Instead, it was an older man in his fifties, heavyset, with a beard. He breathed a sigh of relief.

"Runners, on your mark!" the starter now cried out. Lane put his feet on the blocks and knelt to the ground. He lightly touched the earth, expecting it to give and his fingers to sink. It didn't happen. *Good*, he thought, *let's do this.*

"Get set." The man raised the black starter pistol, no enormous blunderbuss. Lane now felt this enormous surge of energy go through his body, gearing it up for what lay in front of him. In the distance, he quickly glanced and saw the finish line and tape. Beyond it, just a little bit out of his vision, stood a blurred form. A man, but he couldn't quite tell who it was; it was too far away. All that he could make out and knew was that this man was waving.

"Go!" the starter yelled as he fired the pistol. The loud clap of the gun brought Lane back to the now. He had let his focus slip for just that half second. The blurry figure had taken away that needed concentration. He sprung forward from the blocks, way too hard, overcompensating for his lapse. Two strides out, he was stumbling, his balance gone. He felt the upper half of his body going forward, lurching too much. He had fallen before, while training; he knew he had left the blocks with too much energy, surging too hard. It was all wrong. What lay ahead was complete disaster. In another second, he would be sprawled out on the track, watching the rears of the runners, as they ran to victory, while he lay there in defeat.

Lane thrust his right hand out as he stuttered with his legs. It caught the earth just right. He pushed off with it and somehow righted his body. He was up at least, but out of stride, he had to regain it fast. He heard his dad in his head, telling him to focus, just focus.

His legs were pumping the way they should. He was moving right again, moving like lightning. The group of runners was at least ten yards in front of him. His dad kept yelling in his brain, "Pick a point! Focus!"

Lane looked toward the finish line as he furiously sprinted. The blurred figure who had been waving was standing closer to the finish tape, in focus now. It was his dad. He was gesturing with his arms for Lane to come on forward, like he always did when he trained him as a young lad. He now stood just on the other side of the finish line, yelling Lane's name and beckoning him to victory. Lane felt that big wave of energy explode in him as he ran, propelling him ahead.

All the other runners disappeared around him. It was just him and his dad, yelling to him, to run to him. As he got closer, he could make out every detail on his father's face. He could see he was smiling, a big wide smile, his head shaking up and down, as if saying, "You've got this." His dad now put both arms out in front of him, motioning for him to grab them.

Lane flew down the track. He felt his chest hit and pull the finish tape. He ran the next ten yards with his face raised to the heavens, arms pumping, fists thrusting. He had won.

He turned to look for his dad, as spectators and teammates flocked around him. He hoped he hadn't gotten knocked down and run over by some of the runners. He searched frantically as people shouted in his face and hugged him. He couldn't find him.

His mother was in front of him now, tears running down her cheeks. She threw herself into his chest and hugged him hard, not wanting to let go. When she finally did, Lane yelled to her through the loud din, "Where's Dad? He was right here!"

The tears flowed from her as she spoke with a shaky, stuttering voice. "Your father…is gone… He…died this morning. Heart attack."

Lane thought, *How could this be? He was right here, right now, waving me to victory.* "That can't be. What? How?"

"It happened at the hotel...about five o'clock." She sobbed as she talked. "We were waiting for the ambulance... As he...lie there, he...he told me...don't tell you before the race. He knew it would... upset you. He wanted you to win so bad."

Now Lane was crying, head down, tears falling to the clay of the track. All the energy had left him; he felt like collapsing. He bent over, hands on his knees. The victory didn't matter. It was a hollow accomplishment without his dad. He needed his father there to hug and kiss him. His dad had worked just as hard, to be able to earn this too. Now everything was mute.

His mother put an arm around him and leaned into his ear. She spoke so only he would hear. "Just before he died...he said to tell you...and only you." She paused, as if unsure of what she should say. "He...he...said, 'Don't worry, I took care of the man with the hood.'"

15

Dentiel Reed heard both the top and bottom turrets open up. The sound of the four .50s combined were loud, booming.

"What the fuck is going on?" shouted Bernie Mossberg, as he looked out his side gunner opening. He stretched his head around in all directions. "I don't see shit. Don't know what the hell they're all yelling about."

Dentiel hadn't heard all the chatter on the ship's radio. He had taken off his headset after he got hit. "What they sayin'?"

Bernie looked down at him with disdain. "I don't know. Just something about some goddamn things attackin' us. It shouldn't matter to your black ass. You can't shoot that gun and help defend us now, can you? Can't even help defend my ass one little bit. Nope, not at all. Just lie there and die, you worthless piece of shit."

Dentiel looked up at Bernie with disgust and hatred, but it quickly turned to anguish as a stab of pain rocked his body. The blood was oozing out of him at a more considerable pace. The bandaged area around his midsection was soaked dark red, blood trickling from it, dropping to the cabin floor. A pool of it had formed alongside and under him as he lay against the bomber's side hull. Bolts of sharp and brilliant pain were racking his body, which felt hot and numbing cold, all at the same time. It was as if he were a blazing fire and someone kept stoking it, making it hotter. But yet there was ice and snow forming all around this raging inferno.

He knew he was in big trouble. Lane had helped him, but his type of doctoring couldn't fix this. Lane didn't have the know-how or the necessary equipment. No one on the bomber did, and it was still a long way to the base and hospital. He had pulled the short straw on this one.

But that didn't bother him. He knew he had been dodging the grim reaper for a while. Plenty of times the old man of death had come looking for him, reaching out, grabbing for him. But he had always managed to dodge him, elude him. He really wanted to go on this mission so bad; he knew the odds. Plenty of men had died already doing their part. Well hell, he just wanted to do his. If he had to meet his maker today, he would just do it as a happy, contented man.

"You ain't lookin' too good, boy. Ha-ha. Nigger, your time has come." Bernie's lips curled up in a smiling sneer. He stood over Dentiel, in the somewhat confined space, examining him with his eyes, hands on his hips.

The plane jumped sharply from turbulence, throwing Bernie up against the hull wall on his side of the cabin. He bumped his head, hard, on one of the support beams that ran throughout the compartment. A scowl of pain came to his face, then disappeared as the sadistic grin returned. "I think I'll just stand right here and watch you die. Yep, I just think that I'll just do that." He brought his knee up and rested his foot against the frame for support. He pulled a packet of cigarettes out of his jacket pocket, grabbing one out, then rummaging in a pant pocket, brought out a stick match, which he ignited against the heel of his boot. He lit the cigarette and took a long drag from it. He blew a column of smoke toward the wounded man and in the same motion tossed the extinguished match his way. His grin got bigger as he watched Dentiel.

"You do that, man. I hope one day you'll be in the same kinda fix, and no one will be there to help you."

No sooner had Dentiel uttered the last word than Bernie's face grimaced and his back arched forward. The cigarette fell from his fingers as they opened in a sudden reflex motion. Up through his midsection and flight jacket, three sharp, curled talons popped through into view. As they emerged out from his body, droplets of blood arced out, flying toward Dentiel. Pieces of flesh and intestines hung from the points on the claws. Bernie started to shake, in a spasm-like dance, bubbles of blood now forming on his open mouth and lips.

Dentiel watched in shock and disbelief as a hellish head appeared in the gunner's opening, not more than a foot from Bernie.

Dentiel thought it all a nightmare brought on by his wound and condition. He closed his eyes, hoping it would go away. When he reopened them, he saw the reddish-black devil's head looking at him, its orange-black eyes burning intensely. The creature then turned its head to gaze upon Bernie, its intended victim. The talons tore back out of Bernie's body as the creature extracted them from him, pulling his body, hard, against the cabin wall. Blood ran in torrents, as the torn particles of his body fell to the floor. The devil creature used its hands to grab hold of the .50-caliber gun, strapped in the harness setup, and with a single gesture tore it free, flinging it out into the open night sky, as if it were a piece of hard plastic and not an eighty-pound instrument of destruction.

The harpy monster quickly grabbed hold of the frame opening, digging its claws into it for support, and started pulling itself into the compartment. It was halfway into the cabin when its mouth opened, revealing rows of sharp, nasty teeth, dripping with gooey foam. All in the same motion, it plunged its mouth into Bernie's neck and shoulder and bit down hard. As it pulled its head away, pieces of tendon and meat came with it in long bloody strings. Blood pumped out of the severed arteries in a high spray, hitting the roof of the compartment. Bernie's head plopped back against the wall, staring up at the blood, but not seeing it. The eyes were wide open but glazed over in its death knell.

The harpy chomped and chewed hard on its savory treasure. Slivers and bits of its feast fell from its mouth. When it had completed this, it proceeded to pull itself the rest of the way inside the compartment. The creature seemed to pay no attention to Dentiel. In the creature's mind, his lying there wounded presented no immediate threat to itself.

Dentiel was enthralled at how big the harpy's wings were but yet fit so compactly close to the body, like a bird's wings did when it landed on a branch of a tree. The thing moved with fluid motion and ease as it stood over Bernie's body. It bit again, pulling away more meat in its mouth, chewing quickly and ravenously.

Dentiel's horror and astonishment were pushed to the back of his mind, as the sense of urgency returned. He knew this creature would start on him next when it considered itself done with Bernie. As a man who had always been steady under pressure, he knew there wasn't much time left for him to react.

He reached slowly down, undoing the cover for his gun holster on his belt. Moving as fast as the pain in his body would allow, he proceeded to pull out his weapon. He winced in sharp pain as the Colt .45 cleared the holster. He trained it up at the creature.

The harpy must have seen the movement; it suddenly spun around to gaze at Dentiel, remnants of Bernie still in its mouth and lips, blood running down its chin. It took only a millisecond for the thing to realize Dentiel was a threat. Its eyes pulsed brightly, mouth opening wide, emitting a gurgled hiss, as the arms and hands reached out to grab him.

The shot echoed in the tight compartment, like a sharp boom of thunder. The bullet caught the harpy under the left armpit, slamming it back into the bomber's side hull. With nothing holding Bernie's dead body up, it fell off to the left of the ghoulish intruder, hitting the floor in a clump.

The harpy recovered quickly, pushing itself away from the hull and at Dentiel. At point-blank range he fired twice more, straight into the thing's chest. The reddish-black skin was torn open with the impact of the .45-caliber slugs, throwing it back into the gunport opening. It would have fallen out the opening if not for its wings slightly opening back up. They lodged the creature half in, half out of the rectangular port. The harpy tore frantically at the framework, trying to dig its talons in for support. Dentiel would have none of that. He fired three more times into the creature, each bullet finding a spot on the thing, ripping more chunks away, and opening more wounds.

These last shots proved fatal. The top half of the harpy fell backward, out the window, to hang there, flopping in the wind currents. The bottom half of the creature's torso still hung on the inside frame of the gunport. Its sharp toe talons dug into the fabric, legs spasmodically jerking in a death throe. Smoke drifted lazily out of his .45 as his hand trembled from the ordeal. His eyes were wide, now adrenaline filled, as he stared at the thing in front of him.

16

The doors opened to the elevator on the first floor. The lobby to the hotel was very ornate, but elegant and grand. The floor was a polished grain-brown marble, walnut beams overhead, with walnut brushed wood trimmings all around. Leading out to the main doors was a magenta base-colored Persian rug. The doorman, in a splendid blue uniform, with latticed gold trim, held open the door for the couple and their entourage coming through.

Dentiel Reed had worked the Conrad Hotel for going on five years, first as a janitor, now as the elevator operator. He also had on the articulate blue-and-gold uniform. It was required for all male employees working the main doors or elevator. He didn't mind wearing it. It made him feel elevated, as if he really was someone important to the hotel, when in truth he knew he was just a hired hand, someone they could dispense with and get some other black man to quickly fill the spot. But the pay was good, especially during these hard times. He figured he'd hang on to it until something better came along.

It was a cold windy day in Chicago. He could feel the chill as the door to the hotel lobby remained open, letting the newly arrived group into its warm confines. The quartet was composed of a female and three males.

The woman walked as if she were floating on air. Her long stiletto high heels didn't hinder her gait one bit. Dentiel knew she had long slender legs, even though they were hidden under the long dress she wore. The dress was so tightly fit, one could clearly make out the shapely legs. It started out with her somewhat muscular calves, moving up to her alluring thighs, which were attached to the very curvy hips. The rest of the sexy body was hidden by the fur coat she wore.

The only areas she kept open were around her neck and breasts. Both, on the fur and the dress, the top buttons were kept open, especially on the dress. The buttons were unfastened down to the cleavage of her ample bosom. Her hair was dyed to a reddish-brown color, long, but semicurled in the fashion of the day. Her face was that of a young cherub. A creamy white complexion, full, pouty lips, now in a slightly off red lipstick. A nose that was of perfection, small, slender slope, with a slight upturn at the tip. The eyes were the killer, an almost emerald green, with just a hint of eye shadow, just enough to make them sparkle. She was perfection, and she knew it. This was Rea Hannity, and Dentiel had a pang in his heart for her.

Dentiel had first spied her four months ago, when she had become the arm candy for Thad Torrin. He was a businessman who owned the penthouse on the fifteenth floor of the hotel. She was a permanent fixture to Thad, lived with him, and went everywhere he wanted her to go. He adorned her with anything she wanted: jewelry, dresses, furs, you name it.

Thad Torrin could do that, with no monetary discomfort. He had money and wealth to spare. Times were great for him and his kind. His life was such that dealt with the unsavory of this world. The uncivilized dregs of the crime syndicates, the kill-or-be-killed vermin of the gutter, to the high and mighty czars of the underworld. He also partnered with the cream of the crop of society. Both could be as unscrupulous as one could imagine. He did the proverbial tightrope walk between the two, sometimes leaning and almost falling off to one side or the other. In the long run, he always had and made money.

Thad was a heavier man. His appearance was that of a man in his forties, overweight, medium height, starting to lose his hair. But he was still always a dapper man in what he wore. The best suits, hats, shoes, and jewelry always adorned his person. He never went anywhere in something you would say he just threw on. His face had the look of a falcon, small sharp eyes, always surveying the terrain, looking for prey. The weathered cracks on his face belied the tumultuous dealings he was evolved in. His nose hooked, in a Greco-Roman style. A pencil-thin mustache adorned his upper lip.

The two other men were his thugs, hired hands. Beefy gents who would clear the way for Thad wherever he went. They did all the dirty work for him, while Thad stood in the limelight and soaked it all in with smiling pleasure. Their names were Blinco and Dandy. That's all they went by that Dentiel knew; he never found out their real names.

Blinco was the taller one, Dandy the shorter man. Both were thick, sturdy cavemen. Take their brains and put them together, and you might, just might, have an acceptable one. Both men were dressed in simple but stylish suits, with fedoras to match.

"Good day, Mr. Torrin. Nice to see you and Ms. Hannity." Dentiel tipped his hat as he greeted them into the elevator.

Torrin let Rea enter first. As always, she positioned herself next to Dentiel, looked over at him, and gave him a beautiful come-hither smile. She always made sure she did that for him, every time she got in the elevator. His heart did a pitter-patter as he tried to calm himself.

The rest of the group jostled their way in. "How we doing today, Dentiel?" Torrin said, not paying any attention and seeing the way Rea looked at Dentiel.

"Just fine, sir. We headed all the way up today?" Dentiel had a nervous smile on his face as he looked past Rea to Torrin.

"Where else would we be headed, boy? Sometimes I wonder." Torrin shook his head in a dismissive way.

"What do you mean by that, honey?" Rea asked him, looking from Dentiel, then back to Torrin.

"Well, you know. Sometimes, with their kind, they just don't have all the working parts. It's just that, sometimes, I wonder what they even think about, or know. I mean, to really get through life." Torrin stated all this so matter-of-factly, as if Dentiel wasn't even there in the elevator at all to hear this exchange.

"That's just plain crude. You shouldn't say things like that when a person you're talking about is right here." Rea motioned with a nod of her head toward Dentiel.

Anger flashed across Torrin's face. A vile, mean expression pursed on his lips, eyes growing cold. Within a second, he caught hold of his emotions, checked them, and calmly reached a hand over to Rea's and gently caressed it with his.

"Now, now, honey. Calm down. We don't need to talk about this now, especially in front of the boy here. He knows what he is and accepts that. He can't help how his race is, especially with their brain capacities and limitations." Torrin said this all with a smile on his face, as he looked at Rea. Underneath something else was brewing. Dentiel could see it. Even though he wanted to reach over, at this moment, and smack the living shit out of Thad Torrin's face, he knew this would and could never happen. Retribution would be swift and deadly, coming from the two goons, standing directly behind him. He let it all flow by him.

"Yep. I didn't get brains, one, from either my mom or dad. I always gotta remember that before I talk."

"See, honey, he knows and even understands. That's surprising, but he realizes his limitations."

"Thad, just don't say things like that. It really isn't nice. I don't care what it is about a person. True or not, you just don't belittle them in public," Rea returned, looking compassionately at Dentiel.

"Rea, dear. Like I said before, we'll talk about this later. Okay?"

Dentiel looked down, not wanting to make eye contact with anyone. He had been told by everyone else who worked the hotel that you never cross Thad Torrin or get him mad. If you did, there would be hell to pay. They all told him the stories of broken bones, punched-out faces, even a story of a black janitor, before Dentiel, who had stood up to Torrin over something and had never been seen or heard from again to this day.

Dentiel kept his stare directly down at the elevator floor. But part of his peripheral vision saw Torrin's hand, the one holding Rea's. He was now squeezing it, hard. Her knuckles seemed to pop as he tightened his grip. Her hand became a disfigured form, as it was crushed inward, turning red and a light purple. Dentiel saw the pained look on her face, the tears forming in her eyes. She never uttered out a cry of hurt. She put her head down, slumped her shoulders, and accepted the rebuke for her verbal triad with Torrin. Thad never looked at her once while doing this, just looked straight ahead with a calm, pleasant disposition on his face.

The doors to the elevator opened. "Here you go, sir. You're home." Dentiel spoke, breaking the silence. Torrin let go of Rea's hand, the color quickly coming back to it. But in a lot of spots there was the red discolored, hurt look to it.

"Thank you, Dentiel. Have a good day." Torrin threw out as he walked out of the elevator into the small lobby and hallway, leading to the penthouse doors.

Rea followed, rubbing her abused hand with the other hand. She kept both hands low as she did this, trying not to attract any attention. Dandy, the small thug, pushed into Dentiel as he walked past him, raised his arm up, and gave him a push, sending Dentiel slamming into the side wall of the elevator compartment. Dentiel hit it with a muffled thud. Rea quickly turned at the sound and gave a look that seemed to say, "I'm so sorry."

No one else turned. They all kept walking, as if the incident had never happened. Dentiel watched as they got to the big double doors of the penthouse and opened them. He pushed the button to the elevator doors. The last thing he saw as the doors closed was Rea's tightly rounded ass swishing into the penthouse, as Torrin gave it a hard smack.

*****

It was days later when Dentiel got the call signal for the penthouse. His heart skipped a beat. Maybe today he'd get to see Rea. He hadn't seen her since the last episode with her hand. He counted the floors as the elevator zoomed past them, on its way up.

The doors opened, revealing Rea and Dandy. He couldn't help but not miss her face. The left cheek was bruised and puffy; the corner of that eye sported a partial black-and-blue mark. Someone had hit her, and he didn't have to guess twice about who did the smacking.

The couple stepped into the elevator, Rea taking her position next to Dentiel, Dandy on the other side of her. The smell of her perfume was exotic and sensual, all at the same time. Dentiel felt himself

THE DEVIL AT TWO

get hard. "You smell nice today, Ms. Hannity," he said timidly to her in a soft tone.

"Thank you, Dentiel," Rea replied demurely back. Her hand shot to her cheek with the bruise. She rubbed it, as if in embarrassment and humiliation.

"What the fuck did you say, nigger?" Dandy yelled as he pushed past Rea, slamming her into the back wall. He grabbed Dentiel by the lapels of his uniform, pushing him into the wall with a loud boom. The two men were nose to nose. Anger and rage in the white man's eyes, subdued hatred and venom in the black man's.

"You heard what I said," Dentiel spat out, still trying to hold all his emotions in check.

"I should bust your black ass right now!" Dandy spat out, spittle now painting Dentiel's face.

Rea squirmed herself between the two men, squeezing the front of her lithe body toward Dentiel. Her firm breasts pushed on Dentiel's chest and stomach, bringing his quickly receded hard-on back with a passion. She mouthed the word "don't" to him, shaking her head slightly. She quickly turned to Dandy. "You won't do a damn thing to him, got it? Or do you want me to tell Thad that you hurt me, that you slammed me into the wall and really hurt me? Do you? You know he won't like that, not one bit. What do you think he'll do to you then? Think about it. Just think about it." Venom shot out of her lips as she got in Dandy's face.

This caught Dandy totally off guard. Add to that his lack of brainpower and comprehension, he was completely stymied. Dentiel saw the fire on his face go out, as if smothered with a blanket. He backed away from the other two and muttered, "Okay, okay. I just thought... Aw, fuck it."

The doors opened for the first-floor lobby. Rea adjusted her dress, putting a hand to her hair, ensuring it was still fixed right, and went to step out into the empty open space. Dentiel shot his hand out and with his index finger rubbed the palm of Rea's hand. He did this in a manner as to not attract any attention. The finger did a slow stroke down her palm and fingers with a slight caress.

Dandy had already stepped ahead of Rea, moving toward the bell cap, to look for their awaiting vehicle. He never saw the incident transpire. She turned for a brief moment this time, mouthing to Dentiel, "Thank you." She quickly turned and walked away.

*****

Dentiel was working the afternoon shift. Rea and his path had not crossed since the last foray. He was bringing the Anderson couple down from the twelfth floor. He listened to them go on about their big plans for the evening. A lavish affair at someone's big mansion north of the gold coast. He half listened but acted like he was intent on taking everything in.

The doors opened to the lobby, and there stood Rea, this time accompanied by Blinco. He towered over her small frame, his arms loaded with several packages and boxes, a casualty of being with Rea on one of her shopping jaunts. "Good afternoon, Ms. Hannity. So good to see you again."

"Yes, I'm so glad to see you as well, Mr. Reed," she said with a sheepish smile, as she quickly lowered her head and slipped into the elevator.

"Please, don't be formal with me. Just call me Dentiel."

"Okay, Dentiel. That I shall." She quietly giggled as she spoke, casting him a glance.

"Hey, boy. You think you could help and hold one of these packages?" Blinco looked down at Dentiel with a mixed expression of disgust and anxiousness.

"Now, now, Blinco. Don't make him do that. He's got to handle the elevator and doors. That's his job. Don't make him do yours. Give me that package." Rea reached and grabbed a bag out of the tall thug's arms.

As she extended her hand, the fur coat she was wearing traveled up her forearm, exposing bare skin. The underside of her arm, the soft white skin, now had several purplish-yellow bruises on it. Dentiel figured they had to be several days old, but at this time of the healing process, they looked ghastly. He knew this was all Torrin's doing, the prick that he was, taking his frustrations out on her. His blood boiled a few bubbles thinking about it. He didn't realize he was talking till it was out. "He can't be doing that to you. He just shouldn't. He needs to be taught a lesson."

Rea saw Dentiel looking at her arm as he said it. She quickly pulled the arm down, covering it with the fur. A nervous look came over her face, as if caught doing something she shouldn't be doing.

"What'd you just say, son? Did I hear that right?" Dentiel could see Blinco's ire rise as he looked around Rea, toward Dentiel.

Rea shook her head no to Dentiel. Her eyes pleaded with him to stop. But there was a fire starting to blaze in his belly, and it wasn't going away just yet. He was mad. One, about Torrin hurting Rea, and two, he was just tired of the way he was being treated. He had turned the proverbial cheek too many times already; he was just fed up.

"Listen, Blinco. I'm tired of the way your boss treats this nice lady. A man just doesn't go around doing the things he does to her. It's just not right, got that?"

Rea turned quickly to Blinco, putting a hand on his chest, trying to calm the situation, before it got out of hand.

Blinco paid no attention to the lady. His stare was all on Dentiel. His furnace had just been stoked, and there was flame in his eyes. "You know, if I put these packages down right now, I could have you broke in half in ten seconds. You know that, black boy. Your life would be over in a blink."

Rea now had both hands on Blinco's chest, her fingers rubbing his dress shirt, trying to soothe the savage beast.

"Easy, Blinco, please, let it go. For me, please." She talked soothingly, looking up into his eyes.

Blinco seemed to come out of the clouded rage he was in the instant he looked down at her lovely face. Dentiel could see he had a soft spot for the girl. His heart also ached for her. He was relieved. He knew Blinco would have made good his threat. He would have been either a really broken man or a really dead one.

"All right...you win, little Rea." He touched her chin tenderly with his finger. The love shone on his face. Dentiel didn't know if it was a physical love or one of a fatherly bond. His age belied the fact that he could have been her father in another life. "I just can't have him going around saying things like that about the boss." He looked back at Dentiel and pointed a finger. "You can think those things, boy, but you can't say um out loud. Got me?"

Dentiel shook his head in agreement. He would let it lie for now, he thought. He just knew he couldn't let Rea take this kind of abuse for long. He was too much in love with her to let it go on. The bell dinged; they were at the penthouse. The door opened to an empty hall.

"Blinco, give me the packages, and you go open the door," Rea said and grabbed all the parcels in her arms.

"Here, I got it, kind lady." Dentiel smiled, as he reached for the packages. Rea gladly gave them to him.

"Why thank you. But I do have to carry some of my load around here." Rea giggled, as she kept one of the parcels to carry for herself.

"Okay, sharing is a good thing. That's what my momma always said."

"That's a good observation for your mother. It's always good to give and receive." Rea gave him a wry smile as Blinco opened the doors. "You working the rest of the afternoon?"

"Yep. I'm filling in for Jerome. He needed tonight off." Dentiel walked with Rea. As they got to the open double doors, he reached in and laid the packages on the oaken table inside the doorway of the lavish penthouse. He could hear Torrin on the phone in one of the other rooms, yelling at and about something. As he went to close the door, Rea caught his attention. Her back was turned toward Blinco, so only Dentiel could see her face. She smiled, with an expression of sexy sweetness, and blew him a kiss.

*****

It was about 9:00 p.m. when Torrin left the building, with his two guard thugs in tow. He wasn't in a very gentle mood, as he got in the elevator. No words were exchanged between him and Dentiel. It made him somewhat nervous. He thought maybe Blinco had said or told him about what had transpired earlier in the elevator with Rea. Dread filled him, as he half expected Dandy to push the stop button for the elevator and him and Blinco to proceed to beat the living shit out of him, all the time Torrin watching on, smiling in agreement and satisfaction. Then as he lay there, all broken and bleeding, to kneel down and tell Dentiel, "This is what happens to niggers when they forget their place."

He was pulled quickly, back to reality, when the bell dinged for the main lobby. A breath of relief left his mouth, as the trio exited the elevator and journeyed out into the night.

A half hour after the departure of Torrin, he got a ring on his floor button board. It was from the penthouse. It caught him by surprise. At this hour, he didn't think Rea would be on her way out, especially when it would just be her traveling out.

He thought about her as the elevator made its climb. The earthy, sweet smell of her perfume and her. He pictured her being in one of her sexy outfits, standing there, posing for him, as she spun around. The wisps of her negligee fluttering in the air. The more she twirled, the more of the garment fell away, exposing her luscious body. He envisioned her breasts like ripe young melons, dripping with sweaty dew that he would run to and lick dry with his tongue. The thought of it made him feel hard and ready.

The doors opened to reveal Rea. She wore no sexy outfit, just a pair of silky pajamas. But it was more than enough for Dentiel. The way they hugged and formed to her body made him get more aroused. He saw her pert nipples sticking through the pajama top, at perfect attention for him. She wore just the right amount of makeup and eye shadow. It made her face light up and pop with sexual beauty. Her lips had a red lipstick on them that glistened in the light. "Hello, Dentiel. Fancy meeting you here." A warm smile radiated from her face.

"Evening, Rea. Oh sorry, Ms. Hannity." He felt his face start to warm up. He was lucky he was black; it made it harder for Rea to see that he was blushing. "How can I be of service for you?"

She looked him up and down for a bit. "I'm so glad I have someone like you watching out for me. I adore that when a man wants to protect me. Keep me safe from harm and other things." She stepped into the elevator.

Dentiel could smell the alcohol on her breath as she got closer. She had been drinking; he just didn't know how much. "Is there something I can do for you?"

"Oh, I think there is." She took another step closer to him, putting a finger to her lips and slowly sliding it down both of them. He could feel her warm breath on him when she spoke. "It's just you and me, sugar. The assholes gone for a while. I hope a long while."

Dentiel could smell her body. It was a mixture of vanilla and citrus. An intoxicating blend that made him come straight to attention. "Oh, what would that be?" he returned with a smile, knowing she hadn't called him up here to just say thank you.

Rea reached up on her toes and gave him a long, slow kiss. He reciprocated with a more passionate one as he pulled her into his arms. She suddenly stepped back, keeping her eyes on him, as she slowly unbuttoned her top. Her well-rounded breasts fell out as she finished unbuttoning the rest of the buttons and took the top off.

She reached her arms out, grabbing the sides of his face, pulling it into her pear-shaped melons. The smell of perfume and body was even more sensual between her cleavage. Dentiel kissed and sucked her nipples. They soon were large and hard.

After a minute, she slowly moved him back away from her. "This is how I want to say thanks." Her eyes twinkled in green brilliance as she kept his gaze. Her hands slid in gently and quickly, undoing his coat buttons, and started on his belt. She accomplished the task, deftly, in seconds.

"My oh my" was all Dentiel could get out at this point. He reached over and hit the stop button for the elevator. He wanted no interruptions.

Rea unzipped him and let his pants fall to his shoes. She reached down and felt him, hard as ever. "Well, you're much bigger than Thad." She giggled slightly as she slid down to her knees and pulled the boxers down the rest of the way.

*****

She rolled from her position of being on top of him and collapsed on the bed. Beads of sweat were covering both of their bodies. The temperature of the room was very hot, compared to the cold weather outside. They lay quiet for several moments, trying to collect themselves.

"That was just truly amazing, sugar." Rea, finally able to talk, patted Dentiel's muscular stomach.

"It always is, when I'm with you." He leaned over and kissed her cheek, his hand moving and gently caressing her breast, nearest him.

The two had been seeing each other for about a month, sneaking around, the best they could, behind Thad Torrin's back. "I better get going. Thad will be back from his meeting in Pittsburgh later this afternoon. I've got to be home all cleaned up and ready for him."

"Damn, I wish it was just you and me. That we could leave this city, start our lives somewhere else," Dentiel exclaimed as he leaned over and kissed the nipple on the breast he was fondling.

"Dreams. That's all we can have right now. I'm Thad's girl, and that's that. Until he decides I'm not his anymore and kicks me to the curb, we have to live with that fact." Rea swung her legs off the bed, to the side, and got up.

"I know. But you've really got me under your spell. You've made me fall really hard for you, and you're all I think about." Dentiel sat up and kissed the back of her neck.

"I seem to always have that effect on men. Don't know what that's all about?" She giggled as she turned and kissed him hard.

There was a knock on Dentiel's apartment door. "Shit, I bet it's my brother Jonah. I told him to come by at noon. It's only eleven. Probably didn't have anything else going on. Just decided he'd come by early, I guess."

"I don't need him or anyone else knowing about us. Not just yet anyway." Rea looked at Dentiel nervously, as she jumped up and started dressing.

"I know. You get dressed and fixed. I'll close the bedroom door and get him to leave with me. Then you can leave after we're gone. Okay?" Dentiel was dressed in seconds as another knock banged on the door.

"I'm coming, Jonah, hang on!" Dentiel yelled from his bedroom doorway. He looked back at Rea, blew her a kiss, and quickly closed the door.

He crossed the living room and opened the front door, talking at the same moment. "Man, you sure are early."

"We sure are, aren't we now?" said Blinco as his punch connected with Dentiel's nose. There was pain and bright flashes as he went falling to the floor. He instantly tried to pull himself up and off the floor in his now confused and dazed state. This time Dandy was on him, straddling him and grabbing his shirt at the neck, pulling him to him.

"What stupid shit you been up to, nigger!" He wound his right arm up and brought it down into Dentiel's face with extreme force. There was a crunch of bone-on-bone impact, as all vision of the world faded from Dentiel's sight.

*****

Dentiel woke back to the world with a slap to his face. He felt the sting of it, but it was nothing compared to the other pain he felt. There was a throbbing, hot ache on the left side of his face to his nose. His eyesight was slowly returning, but the left eye was having trouble focusing. The world seemed blurred, watery in that one.

He could see quite well out of the other one. In front of him sat Thad Torrin, at a desk. Dandy stood to the right of the desk. Behind both of them, through a picture window, was Lake Michigan, looking rather splendid in the afternoon sun.

"Well, well, Sunshine is awake. Welcome back." Thad Torrin spoke, an evil grin forming on his face. It quickly dissolved into a look of anger as he continued talking. "We've been a real shit now, haven't we? You really think you could get away with this, behind my back? Boy, you really are one dumb black ape." Torrin stood up and walked around the desk to stand in front of Dentiel. "Welcome to my home away from home. It's my warehouse, down by the lake. In your neighborhood, on the south side." He swung his arms out, encompassing the building. "It's kinda funny, here you are fucking

114

my girl, and you're only a couple blocks away from where I do most of my business. Funny, right?" He moved closer to Dentiel, standing over him.

Dentiel knew he was in a chair. He tried moving his arms slightly, found resistance, and knew the scenario he dreaded. His arms were tied together behind the back of the chair. Not together per se. The rope tied around both wrists had a slack length of several inches between them, but still enough not to allow him to move them. He could stand, but he knew without control of his arms, he would just be fodder for Dandy.

"I don't think it's fucking funny at all!" Torrin's left fist came around, hitting Dentiel's right cheek. His head recoiled from the punch and came back to rest, with a new throbbing pain. He could taste blood in his mouth. "Well, what do you think I should do? Huh?" Dentiel didn't respond. He knew there was nothing he would say that would help the situation.

"Got no answer, boy? Well, what do you think, Dandy? What should we do with him?" Torrin never looked over at Dandy. His gaze stayed on Dentiel.

Dandy reached inside his suit coat and pulled out a .38 revolver, laying it on the desk. He then fumbled into his pants pocket and pulled out a switchblade, popping it open, slamming the blade into the top of the wooden surface. It stood at attention, vibrating from the slam. "I say we kill him. But fuck him up a little before we do."

"Oh, I agree with you, Dandy. We're going to do just that. You'll wish we had killed you straight off. But I want you to beg for me to kill you. Yes, that's what I want." Torrin sneered a smile at Dentiel, one of pure evil.

Dentiel now heard little whimpering tones coming from behind him. They were very low, but they were there. Torrin motioned to Dandy with his head, toward the sounds over Dentiel's back. Dandy walked out of view, but Dentiel heard him as he spoke. "Okay, bitch, up and at 'em."

Dentiel now heard movement, as Dandy gathered whom he was talking to, bringing them up, around into his field of vision. It was Rea. He had her by the back of her blouse collar. It was what she had worn when he was with her earlier, in the morning. Only now the nice peach-colored top was stained with splotches of blood, from her open collar down to her skirt waist.

He looked at her face. The once-beautiful face was now in ruins. Both eyes were almost swollen shut. One cheek had a ghastly gash in it, blood running down to her slender neck. Her mouth, on the same side as the cheek, was in shambles. The lips were split, swollen, and drooping, as if from a stroke. The once-cute button nose was puffed up and pushed to the right cheek, cartilage all but destroyed.

Rea whimpered harder as she looked down at Dentiel. Torrin grabbed her hair hard, yanking her from Dandy. "Look at her now. You still want this disgusting piece of pussy? I know, I sure don't. Not now. Not after she's had your black dick in her." He twisted her hair around his wrist. The sexy hair that it once was, was now all disheveled, matted with sweat, grit, and blood.

Torrin pulled the hair hard, making Rea yelp in pain, in the same motion he pushed her at Dentiel. She hit him, almost toppling them and the chair over backward. It teetered, righted itself, and fell back on all four legs. She slid down his body, collapsing to the floor, her head in his lap.

"I'm so sorry, Rea," Dentiel softly whispered from his lips, not knowing if she heard him or not.

She struggled back to her knees and looked at him through her slitted eyes. "I know...I...love you," she mumbled to him through broken teeth and mingling blood.

"Well, isn't that so fucking tender, isn't it, Dandy?" Thad laughed at the couple, arms extended, palm up.

"It sure is, boss. They deserve each other. The whore and the nigger."

"Go ahead, Rea. Kiss him goodbye. It's the last kiss either one of you are going to ever have." Thad Torrin seemed elated when he said it.

Rea reached up into Dentiel's face, trying to give him a kiss the best she could do, with her now pain-ridden lips. He could taste her blood as their lips formed together for the last time. She wrapped her arms around his waist and chair, hugging him. She leaned her head around by his ear and whispered, "I really...do love you."

Dentiel felt a little stab of pain in his left palm, as Rea pushed a metallic instrument into his grasp. He felt the shape and realized it was some sort of knife but, feeling the rough shaft, then came to the conclusion it was a very sharp long nail file. "Sorry...just...get him," she softly cried into his ear.

"All right, enough of that crap." Torrin grabbed her hair again, pulling her back away from Dentiel. Tears ran down from Rea's swollen, bloated eyes.

"You know what, Dentiel? You can't have this bitch no more. In fact, no one's gonna have her anymore." Torrin reached and grabbed the switchblade stuck in the desk. With Rea still on her knees, he yanked on her hair once more, pulling her head back and up, exposing her neck. With one swipe of his left hand, he brought the knife across her throat, slicing through skin and cutting her jugular. The blood ran from the thin slice, like a little forest spring, covering the front of her in a dark-red paint. He let go of Rea, her head falling back into Dentiel's lap.

Dentiel's emotions raged. His mind screamed in anger, but he knew he would be next. As his temper percolated, he adjusted the blade of the file and started cutting into the rope hanging between his hands.

"Now. Now you can have her. She's yours, you black piece of shit. You can watch her die. When she's dead, you're next." Torrin spat a wad of phlegm on Rea as she jerked and spasmed in her death dance.

Dentiel felt the rope give way as he sliced through the last of the fibers. He knew he had to move fast if he wanted to live. Rea's dying body fell off him, to the floor, as he jumped up. The sharpened nail file glistened in his left hand, the light from the sunny day reflecting off it, as he brought it up and slammed it into Dandy's neck.

The brute thug, standing to Dentiel's right, had been caught completely off guard. His hands came up, grabbing awkwardly for the file, stuck in the side of his throat. It must have caught the carotid artery; the blood spat out in large pumping spurts. Dandy staggered backward, hitting the wall by the picture window. Blood began decorating the glass, taking away the majestic view of the lake.

Dentiel moved as fast as his beaten body would allow. It took a lot of energy moving on Dandy; he was now moving in a slower motion as he grabbed for the gun on the desk. Torrin realized what Dentiel intended to do. He brought the eight-inch switchblade down into Dentiel's extended left hand. It dug and tore through flesh and cartilage, popping out of the palm, and mounting his hand to the desktop.

Dentiel screamed in pain as he grabbed the .38 with his other hand. His fingers caressing the barrel, he brought it up and around, swinging hard. The body and handle of the pistol connected with Torrin's left eye and nose, making a heavy, cracking impact. It sent him sprawling away from the desk to the floor.

With a hurried and excruciating jerk, Dentiel pulled his hand free from its position on the desk. The switchblade stayed impaled in his hand, as a testament to the gruesome ordeal. Another scream escaped his mouth as he fumbled with both hands, getting the gun into a firing position.

The door on the far wall of the office swung open in a quick flourish. Blinco stood in the doorway. "Hey, keep him quiet. The whole neighborhood can hear…" That's as far as he got. His face became a question mark as he surveyed the room. He let go of the door handle, as the door continued swinging, hitting the wall. The shock of what was playing out in front of him took a few seconds to register in his thick brain. He saw Thad Torrin, sitting up against the left wall, blood running from his nose. Rea Hannity, lying close to him, spasming in her death throes, a pool of blood forming around her body. His eyes shot to the right. Dandy was half leaning in the corner, gasping his last breaths, hands up to his throat, seeming to grasp some sort of knife thing. Blood splattered across the window and wall, his suit coat and white shirt drenched in the red fluid. Blinco's eyes and mind then registered Dentiel; he was standing close to the desk, sporting a gun, aiming it at him.

Everything clicked home for Blinco. The whole plan had totally gone awry. This wasn't how it was supposed to go down. He never thought his beloved Rea would be the dead one. It was supposed to be Dentiel, the cocky black boy, dying, with his neck cut. Now Dandy was dying, and the boy had a gun in his hands, pointed at him.

Blinco reached into his suit coat for the holster with the .45 in it. He quickly pulled it out, as the room erupted in a thunderous roar.

Dentiel fired three shots, using both hands to aim the gun. The pain of his hand and deafening explosions were lost in his world of survival and revenge. He watched through blurry, teared eyes, as the bullets raced toward Blinco. One flew over his head, hitting the doorframe, splintering it in fragments of pine wood. The second grazed his neck, putting a bloody crease across its right side. The third found his body, digging into the base, just below the neck and above the chest.

The impact sent Blinco flying backward, out of the room. He hit the floor, sliding several feet, before coming to a rest. He lay motionless, gun still in his hand. A second later, the hand relaxed, and the .45 slid to the floor. He was dead.

Dentiel turned the gun to Torrin, still sitting against the wall, in a state of shock over what had just transpired. A big gash adorned his face, under his left eye, blood running down his cheek. His hand was up, covering his destroyed nose, his life juice pouring from it, covering his expensive tie and tailored dress shirt.

"Don't…don't…please don't…shoot me," he stammered, as he looked pleadingly at Dentiel. "I…I've…got money in the drawer." He pointed at the desk. "It's yours. All yours. Take…take it."

"You think that will make up for this? You…you fucking bastard!" Dentiel screamed. Walking toward Torrin, he stopped at Rea's body, now motionless, swimming in an ocean of her precious life nectar. "I LOVED HER!" he blurted out, spitting saliva and blood at Torrin.

"I…I had to do it. You…and her made me look bad. Can't… can't have that."

Dentiel stood over him, gun pointed at his head. He swung the barrel at Thad's head. It clipped the forehead, opening another jagged gash. Torrin grimaced, as his hand shot out, trying to protect himself from more blows.

"You killed her just because it made you look bad? It hurt your feelings, hurt your appearance in the community, maybe?" With his gun hand, Dentiel reached over to the blade still sticking through his left hand. With a quick pull, he tore it out. Goblets of blood and tissue were flung through the air, as he yelped in pain.

"See how you feel about this." He put the knife back in his damaged left hand and in one quick motion slammed the blade into Torrin's right shoulder. He did it with all the pent-up anger and hatred he had left in him. The blade went deep, ripping and tearing, impaling Torrin to the wall with a meaty thud.

Both men screamed in agony and pain, from their damaged and traumatized bodies. Dentiel straightened up and spat a wad of blood and goo into Torrin's ravaged face.

"Feel any better, Thad?"

"Please, please. Oh god, just…just let me go. Take all the money in the drawer. Take…this too." He reached into his pants pocket, pulled out a thick money clip, and tossed it at Dentiel's feet.

"I don't want that. I wanted her. Wanted her bad. Now…I don't get her." A great wave of renewed anger and rage swept through him. He knew this would keep him going for a short time more. After that, he didn't know or care how he would be. "But you, big man. The big boss man over everybody and everything. This is what you deserve. You can have this." Dentiel stuck the black barrel of the .38 into Thad Torrin's mouth. He thrust it hard, hearing the crunch of teeth breaking and splintering.

Thad Torrin's eyes grew wide in terror, as his lips formed around the cold hard gun shaft. The next instant the gun exploded, tearing away his brains and life forever.

17

Dentiel's victory was premature. Out of the corner of his right eye, in the darkened gloom, he saw movement. The head of another harpy popped through his gun opening, a foot or two from him. Its blazing eyes peered at its fallen comrade, then at Dentiel. A type of screech howl pierced his ears as the creature opened its mouth and cried out.

In a blur of speed, the creature grabbed hold of the .50-caliber gun and ripped it from its support harness, the metal rivets holding it to the framing either sheared away or broke apart. With herculean strength, it flung the weapon out, away from the bomber.

Dentiel knew the creature was enraged and was coming for him. He swung his arm around to level the .45 at the harpy, as it attempted to crawl through the opening. In his dwindling and weakened state, it just wasn't fast enough. The harpy thrust a hand out, grabbing his wrist. He heard and felt bone and tendon snap and pop as the thing twisted hard. His hand involuntarily opened, dropping the gun to the floor.

The creature's jaws clamped down, hard, on his forearm, just below the elbow. As it pulled its head back, that section of arm went with it, in a ghastly ripping and tearing effect. Blood shot out in a stream as Dentiel screamed in pain. The harpy spat the forearm and hand out of its mouth as it proceeded to pull the rest of its body inside the bomber.

Dentiel looked down at his destroyed arm, in a dazed and numbed state, watching his lifeblood pumping out, like an old water hand pump he used to use when he was a child. Every time his heart beat, another surge of blood spat out of the torn opening. He watched in shock as the beats dwindled and his world grew dark around him.

18

Lane moved like he did when he ran, fast. He navigated around the empty bomb racks with oiled precision. He looked down at Dan Lanier, sitting at the main radio, as he raced past him. "What's going on?" Dan yelled over the drone of the remaining engines.

Lane held his arms out to either side of him, hands held palms up. He shook his head as if saying, "Don't know."

He bolted through the interlocking doorway into the next compartment. He could pick out Bernie and Dentiel in the dimly lit darkness, having a heated discussion. Bernie was doing most of the animated talking and pointing fingers at Dentiel, as the wounded man lay against the side of the cramped compartment. He stopped at the seat harness for his gun emplacement, when he heard the twin .50s of the top turret open up again. He looked up through the glass canopy, into the night sky. This angle gave him a good view of the large vertical tail fin of the plane. His brain exploded when he saw a creature hanging from it.

The thing sat high, perched on the tip of the tail. Its hands and feet dug into the material, hanging on for dear life, he thought. He quickly swung himself up into his seat harness and trained his lone .50 at the creature. He then realized it wasn't hanging there to save itself. It was there viewing, inspecting, watching the plane. Its head moved like a bird, quick jerking motions, in all directions. Its interest suddenly trained at Jessie and the top turret.

Lane's heart quickened as he saw its wings unfurl to the wind. They were large, massive appendixes. A word was thrust into his thoughts in that split second. It was the one Jessie had cried out over the radio: harpy.

The world moved fast. The harpy sprang from its perch as Lane's hand pulled the trigger to his machine gun. Most of the shells shot past the creature, but one found its target. The harpy fell out of the sky, hitting the roof of the B-17, just a few feet from Lane's canopy.

The next instant, gunshots filled the cabin. Lane stuck his head down and looked toward the report of the gunfire. He knew it had come from the waist gunner's section. He leaned down even farther to look. He saw craziness. Another harpy was half in, half out of the port gun opening. Bernie's body lay in a heap on the floor. Dentiel had his Colt .45 raised firing again, point blank, into the harpy. The top half of the creature fell out of the opening, but its feet claws kept it from falling the rest of the way out. Lane heard the animal-like shriek, making his blood chill inside him.

He jumped out of his seat, landing on the floor. A sharp staccato explosion pierced the cabin. It came from below the hatch cover, where Lanzo Torrida sat in the belly turret. His mind raced. The world was speeding up very fast, too many things happening all at once. The next instant he saw Dentiel swing his arm, with the gun in it, toward his gun opening. Lane saw another harpy was coming through it.

He moved toward Dentiel and the harpy, fumbling with his holster cover. His fingers were shaking; they felt like hot rubber, not complying with what he wanted them to do. The flap finally snapped open. As he pulled out his handgun, he witnessed the grizzly scene of Dentiel's arm being bitten off. This all seemed so surreal to him, like a nightmare. Just like another one he had had so many years before. Only that one was just a nightmare, nothing else. This was a nightmare in real time, in the real world.

The harpy was pulling its body into the craft, it blotted out Dentiel's stricken form. All Lane could see was the creature's well-defined, muscular back. He saw it was a dark ebony red in color, its mane-like hair dotting the head. He stepped to one side to get a better view of the ordeal.

The look on Dentiel's face was one of death, as blood jettisoned from his decapitated arm. The harpy was almost all the way into the cabin of the bomber as Lane trained the gun up to fire. At point-blank range, he fired four bullets into the back of the harpy. Two tore into the creature's upper torso; the other two caught the back of the head. Chunks of what he considered the thing's brains spewed out, all over the wall of the cabin and the now-dead Dentiel.

He stood for a brief second, appraising the situation. Dentiel and Bernie were both dead, plus two of those harpy things. Zack Prettner, in the tail gun, if he was still alive, he didn't know. He wasn't going to crawl through the tube to get back there and see, not with God knows how many of these creatures lurking about. The tube tunnel, as they all called it, was only a little over two feet in diameter and ran six feet to the tail gun compartment. He didn't want to be in it if he confronted another harpy. Realizing he needed to let the skipper know all he knew, he turned and headed for the cockpit.

He stopped when he saw Dan yelling at him, standing by the bomb racks. Another sound of gunfire erupted from somewhere, maybe .50s firing or something else, he didn't know. Whatever it was, combined with the droning engines, it blotted out whatever the man was barking at him. Lane's mind was heating up, bubbling to overload, and the damn thermostat wasn't working for it. He shouted a single-word response back at Dan, hoping he heard it. "Harpies!"

Glass shattered and fell on him. The next moment, intense pain rippled through his right shoulder, as talons tore through his flight jacket and entered his skin. He was jerked off the floor and pulled up and into the small window canopy for his gun. His shoulders and neck bones snapped and cracked as he became wedged in the cramped opening.

Lane paid no mind to this event. He was dead. The harpy that had tried to pull him through the small opening gave up. Frustrated, it bit his head off.

19

The glass exploded in the top gun turret, sending shards falling to the cabin floor of the B-17. Dan Lanier jumped in his seat by the radio transmitter. He didn't know what the hell was going on. Captain Davis was yelling over the plane's com, getting no response. He heard Jessie yell something about harpies, then firing his .50s. In fact, he thought he heard Lanzo's guns report too; something was attacking them.

Jessie's arms suddenly dropped limp by his legs. His body was still in its suspension seat, not moving at all. Dan thought, was Jessie injured or dead?

Jessie's body now fell to the left and came to a rest. Streams of blood began dripping profusely down from the sides of the turret opening, splattering on the floor, as if someone was pouring it from buckets overhead.

Dan jumped from his seat and stepped by Jessie's dangling legs and arms, looking up into the turret. The stars twinkled in the night sky, giving him some light, but still not what he needed. He could see the jagged remains of the turret and hear the wind whistling through its mutilated remains but couldn't see Jessie's face or head because of the way his body was positioned. Dan shook Jessie's legs and yelled, "Jessie, you okay?" All the time he knew he wasn't; he just knew it was bad. Getting no response, he grabbed his flashlight off his belt and turned it on.

Dan's heart leaped into his throat. He opened his mouth to scream, but nothing came out. The beam of his light gave him a full view of the turret assembly. Jessie Hildago's body, from the shoulders down, was completely intact and normal. It was from the shoulders up that made Dan wish he had never turned on his light at all. Jessie's head was completely gone. Where the neck should have been was in abject ruins. Pieces of ripped, torn skin and tissue sat above his flight jacket, as blood pumped out into the shattered turret.

Dan had gone to the movie theaters when he was younger and had seen the movies about the old wildcatters and their oil fields. Clark Gable and Spencer Tracy came to mind. They were the men drilling for oil. They would drill down into the ground. When the drill bit struck the oil cavity, it would let loose the black fluid from the earth into the air. It would shoot up into the sky so hard because of the gaseous pressure built up around that oil pocket. That's what this reminded him of, except this wasn't black gold pumping out of the earth; it was Jessie's lifeblood being pushed out of his body by his still-beating heart.

Dan stumbled away from the nightmare he had just witnessed, toward the cockpit. He didn't have to travel far, maybe four feet. He stuck his head into the cockpit. "Skipper, something got Jessie! Ripped his head clean off!" he yelled, making sure both men heard him.

"I heard it. Knew something happened, just don't know what the hell it was. No one's answering back on the coms. Dan, go see what Lane found out. Then get a message off to the base. Got it?" Cullum Davis shot back at Dan with a worried, agitated tone.

Dan raced from the cockpit, navigating around the carnage of the top turret and the bomb racks. That's when he picked out Lane Arnold in the gloom. He could see him through the doorway from his compartment to the next one. Lane was standing below his gun turret, the moon and starlight placing him in a tiny shaft of night light.

"What the hell is going on?" he yelled, figuring that was the only way to communicate with Lane. He knew that if he was running around the bomber and Lane was, neither one of them had their mic sets with them.

The single-word "harpy" filtered back to Dan through the heavy drone of the rough-sounding engines. He wished it was anything else besides that word. A flock of ME-109s attacking would be better right now. The vision that word conjured up in his mind was horrific. Everyone had always heard the tales circulating about the harpies and gremlins. The devilish creatures of the night that would come out and do their evil deeds. He had heard the stories of these winged creatures, flying on the winds of the sky, tampering with planes, messing with their engines, causing them to malfunction, leading to them crashing, and the destruction of their crews. The tales of planes falling from the sky inexplicitly, engines just stopping or blowing up, and them and their crew plummeting to their deaths.

In the next instant, any chance of communicating more with Lane was gone. Glass and debris rained down around Lane from his gunport. Dan's mouth dropped open as he watched Lane get pulled up into the canopy by an ebony-red muscled arm, with curved, sharp talons. These talons dug and tore into his body so quickly, there was no chance for Lane to react. Lane's legs pumped spasmodically about, dangling in the air, feet above the cabin floor. Within seconds, all his struggling stopped; his body went limp. It dropped like a stone, hitting the cabin floor in a clump. What light there was shone the same thing he had witnessed with Jessie. A pumping of blood was coming from an opening on Lane's person, somewhere, spraying it all over the side wall of the compartment.

Dan was now on the edge of shock and disbelief, almost insanity. He scampered back to his table with the main radio unit on it. With hands shaking, he started sending out a message to their main base of operations, back in England.

The position of his table was on the starboard side of the bomb racks, almost in the corner of the compartment, closer to the middle of the bomber. There was a walled partition and doorway between this room and the area where Lane had his navigation table and equipment. This compartment also included the waist gunners and belly gunner turret; it was the biggest room on the bomber.

Dan heard more glass breaking, followed by a heavy thump, something big and massive hitting the plane's floor, somewhere close to Lane's gun emplacement. He immediately thought of the .50, falling, hitting the floor. It had a metallic tone, this sound he had heard before when an old .50-caliber gun was being replaced for a newer one. Maintenance had dropped it that time. It was usually a two-man operation, but only one grease monkey had tried to handle the exchange, with those results happening.

A long screeching howl pierced his ears. It reminded him of a bird screaming in agony, or immense anger. The next instant the large .50-caliber gun hit the walled partition on the other side of the doorway, splintering and shredding it into chunks of debris. The massive weapon ricocheted off the port wall, tearing a large hole in the bomber's skin, and bounced its way to a stop by the bomb racks.

Dan leaped up out of his seat, pulling his Colt out of its holster. He never made it to the doorway. He stopped dead in his tracks, as a harpy-thing filled the opening. The creature looked at him with blazing orange orbs, opening its mouth wide and emitting another of those ear-piercing howls. He now knew this wasn't a scream of pain or grief, but one of intense anger and vexation. He speculated that this was all due to the reports made by all their guns, whether .50s or handguns, that he had seen and heard. This thing had probably lost some of its comrades to the firepower of the bomber and now was really pissed off.

Dan slowly stepped backward, away from the harpy, raised his .45, and pointed it at the ebony-red form. The harpy pulled it way through the destroyed wall and doorway, its taloned hands grabbing and breaking the remaining partition, wherever its clawed hands dug in. Dan saw the anger, pent up, in this creature building now to a climax. Its sharp, razorlike teeth glistened as heavy blackish saliva ran over its lip and down its chin.

The harpy made it two steps toward Dan, as he unloaded the .45 into it. Seven booming shots hit the thing at point-blank range, tearing huge gaping holes into its body. The impact of the shells sent the harpy falling backward, from where it had traveled. The gun clicked empty as the creature came to rest, dead, on the cabin floor.

Dan looked to the left of the fallen monster and spied another harpy rise from Lane's dead form. It held part of the forearm and hand that once belonged to his former airman. It took a large bite out of the meaty section of arm, tearing away flesh and tendon, chewing vigorously, as it made sense of what was happening before its gaze.

Now realizing another of its monstrous comrades had fallen, the harpy threw the section of Lane away in a fit of rage and bellowed the all-too-familiar anger, screech. It made its way toward Dan, as he stepped back a couple more steps, until his back hit the empty bomb racks. He thought of reloading his empty gun but knew the thing would be on him before he accomplished the task.

He looked at the creature as it wiped away the remaining bits of Lane it still had in its mouth, then down at the dead carcass that used to be his buddy and comrade. Lane sure didn't deserve to die like this, nor should he or anyone on this bomber. An anger started to form in Dan's head and body, as if a switch had been turned on, and now an engine was rumbling to life. Gone now was the fear and panic he had felt. All he saw was this harpy-thing in front of him, the creature that had hurt someone he cared for. All there was now was hatred and revenge in his head. To hell with the outcome.

20

"I'm gonna throw in the towel. You're done. Don't want to see you get hurt anymore."

"I'm good. I'm good," Dan replied, but he knew he wasn't. It was the fifth round of the fight, and he was running on fumes. He had been beat on by Harlon for the past three rounds, and he sure felt it. His ribs hurt bad, as if he had been kicked repeatedly by a mule. Both eyes and lips were swollen from punches thrown by this caveman boxer. He could taste the blood in the back of his throat from his now-broken nose.

"Like hell you are. I'm looking at you, and I know what I see. You can't make it another three rounds," Dan's trainer, Lenny Bush, said to him as they sat facing each other on their stools, Lenny wiping blood and sweat off Dan's face with a towel.

"If I get in close, I can work the body. He won't be able to throw the big shots with his arms." Dan spat a wad of phlegm and blood into the waste bucket, sitting next to his stool. He looked back over his shoulder at the crowd. They were all revved up, yelling and jeering, wanting blood. They were the predator sharks. The smell and taste of blood in the water had put them all in a manic mood. He could spot several people doing the thumbs-down gesture, like the spectators did, in days of old, at the Roman Colosseum, during the gladiator times.

Stacy sat in the front row, close to him and the ring. Her head was down, the long straight hair covering her face. She brought the back of her hand up, wiping her eyes; slowly lifting her head, she looked at Dan. He could see more tears in her eyes, as she wiped the snoot away from her nose. A faint smile adorned her face, trying to put a game facade to the situation.

She had been on him for a while now, to quit the fighting game. She wanted him to save himself, mind and body, from this brutal sport. She wanted for him and her to get married, have a family, and find a way better career for his life.

He looked back to her, trying to bring a smile to his bruised and battered face. He knew it was a hopeless try; instead, he gave her a thumbs-up. Dan turned back toward the ring, trying to prepare himself for the new round of warfare.

"Hey, gents, this gets any more out of hand, I'm stopping the fight." The referee had walked over to Dan's corner, looking sternly down at him and his trainer.

"Okay, Stu! We got it!" Lenny shouted back over the din of the crowd.

The bell rang for round 5. Dan pulled himself up and walked to the middle of the ring. Twain Harlon waited enthusiastically for him, bouncing on his toes, gloved hands swinging in the empty air, ready to pummel.

Dan walked right into a left jab, catching him square on the forehead. The right came around to land, but Dan blocked it. He threw a left back only to catch Twain's hard right shoulder.

Both men were of the same height, build, and weight. The only glaring difference was Twain Harlon was meaner and wanted this fight more. The arguing with Stacy and the love he had for her had softened Dan, had taken his edge away. His inner flame was low, down to just a flicker.

Harlon walked Dan back toward the ropes with steady jabs. Dan felt the top rope dig into his sweaty back and knew he had to get away from it. In this position, he was a sitting duck for Twain's barrage. He moved to get in close, but no luck, Twain had started the attack. It was quick and lethal. A right hook followed by two hard body shots to the ribs brought a labored grimace to Dan's face. He tried to cover up, as the blows rained on him.

The next instant, Stu, the referee, was pushing between them. "That's all, boys, break it up. The fight's over. I'm calling it."

Dan was relieved and upset all at the same time. Relieved to the fact that Harlon was ready to destroy him, upset that not going the full seven rounds lost him some money. Now, just going five, he'd just get the minimum purse.

He walked, staggered, back to his corner, where Lenny quickly started taking off his gloves, throwing a towel over his head. "Thank god Stu stopped it. You were a dead man."

Dan had no energy to respond. He reached down and grabbed a ladle of water out of the drink bucket and spat blood into the waste one. The second the gloves were off, he ambled back to center ring, to stand next to the ref and Harlon.

"The winner in the fifth round!" the fight promoter yelled into the microphone, dropped down from a line above the ring. "Twain Harlon!" The referee now raised Twain's hand in victory. The crowd roared in acceptance of the decision, disappointed there was no death or mutilation in the bout.

Dan reached over to shake the victor's hand. Both boxers moved in close. Dan could see Twain wanted to say something to him.

"You ain't nothin', just a piece-of-shit fighter. Why don't you do everybody a favor and just quit already," Twain said into Dan's ear. A sadistic glee formed on his face. Dan couldn't or didn't want to respond. He just knew he needed to get out and away from the goddamn ring.

*****

Dan had showered. Lenny fixed him up the best he could. Stacy was waiting for him outside the rear door of the arena. They walked in silence, Stacy keeping both arms around his waist in a desperate hug. It hurt his now-damaged ribs, but he wouldn't let her know this. She leaned her head against his shoulder.

"Thank god it's over. Is this it? Please, my love, please, I pray let it be over." She finally broke the trance of their silent walk down the deserted street.

Dan took a second to reply. "Yeah. That's it. This was the last fight of my career. Time to move on." He looked into her face, that sweet, beautiful face, saw the glistening tears, reached down, and kissed her.

*****

Twibel's bar was only a block away from the arena. It was a good place to stop, have a drink, and relax after a fight. The bar was still fairly empty. The main fight of the night was just starting at the venue. Dan thought that was good, sit down, have a drink, talk, and leave before the big crowd came in. At this moment in his life, he just needed his love, Stacy, to talk and be with, not a bunch of people telling him what he should and shouldn't do with his career.

They ordered their drinks and sat in a booth, away from the bar. "I'm glad it's over. I was dying inside watching him beat on you like that. It just scares me. I love you so much, don't want to see you hurt anymore."

"Harlon got me pretty good tonight. Don't worry though, I'll heal up, be okay." Dan brought the whiskey to his lips, taking a short swallow. It burned as he drank, the alcohol digging into the cuts; but it warmed his insides up, making him feel a little better. Stacy snuggled up to him, grabbing his arm in a loving embrace, as they sat together in the booth. He hurt every place she touched him, but he wasn't going to let her know this, not now.

"Well, well, what do we have here?" Dan's and Stacy's backs were to the door of the bar, not seeing Twain Harlon walk in. He had a full entourage of people with him, his manager, and several friends. "Trying to drink your pain and sorrow away, Lanier?"

"Just trying to relax, Twain. Just me and her." Dan tipped his head toward Stacy as he talked. "Don't feel like talkin' with anyone else, okay?"

"Touchy, aren't we? Don't see how you can be that way, especially after I just kicked your ass around the ring. Kicked it good and proper."

"Let it go, Twain. You won. Beat me good. Take that and me tippin' my hat to you and move on. I am." Dan gave Twain a tip of a finger to his forehead in salute.

Twain surveyed and scrutinized the couple. He was a good six or seven years younger than Dan, in the prime of his career, and he knew it. He was, as one would say, feeling his oats. "I just can't, for the life of me, see a pretty lassie like this sitting with a loser like you. I think you could do a lot better than him, girl." Twain looked intently at Stacy. A disgusting leer came over his face. "In fact, why don't you just come over and have a drink with me?"

"No thanks, mister. I'm fine right here with my man," Stacy replied, looking back at Twain with disgust. When they had first sat down, she wanted the outside seat of the booth, so she was closest to Twain.

"He ain't no man. I proved that in the ring. Now, if you'll just go with me, I'll prove just what a man really is." Twain put a hand on Stacy's shoulder, squeezing it generously.

Stacy pushed his hand away and crowded closer to Dan. "Leave me alone. Please go to the bar and find another woman. There's plenty that would go, be with you."

"Yeah, but you're a lot prettier. And now seeing you've got a little spunk in you, I really want you." Twain again put a hand back on her shoulder.

"She told you no. Just leave us be. Go do what you gotta do, and let us move on with our life." A cloud, a red haze, started to form in front of Dan's eyes, the ire prickling on the back of his neck.

"Nope, that ain't gonna work. I want this lassie. She's coming with me. I'm gonna let her feel my man thing. Let it split her open, the way my fists did to your face." One of Harlon's entourage came over and grabbed his shoulder, trying to pull him away, back to the bar. Twain briskly shoved the hand and the man back several paces.

The anger was bubbling in Dan. "She said no. Now leave."

"Sorry, mate. I've decided she's with me. Come on, baby. Come taste a real man." Twain grabbed Stacy's arm, yanking and pulling it hard, dragging her out of the booth.

Dan followed her and in an instant was between Stacy and Twain. "What you gonna do, Big Dan? Hit me? You couldn't hurt me in the ring, and you sure as hell ain't gonna hurt me here."

Dan pulled Twain's hand free from Stacy's arm, giving it a vigorous shove. The same arm of Twain's came back up in a roundhouse swing, straight for Dan's face. He ducked as the blow missed him but connected with a heavy splat. Stacy was the casualty of the hit. Her body lifted off the ground and flew into the heavy wooden side post of the booth. Her head hit it hard with a crackling thud; her body quickly crumpled to the floor.

Everything in front of Dan was engulfed in a red storm; his eyes saw nothing but fiery rage. The anger in him was at a zenith. The only image in front of his sight was Harlon. Everyone and everything were blotted out by the red swirling winds of hatred and vengeance. He knew Stacy was hurt, but he had to exact revenge right now, make Twain pay for what he had just done.

He strode into Twain with a swinging right, which Twain blocked, but with lightning speed drove his left into the man's gut. The air left Twain's body in a large expel of breath. He sagged slightly, leaving himself exposed. Dan recoiled his right arm and brought it around in an uppercut, connecting with the man's chin with savage force. This lifted Twain off his feet, and he went sprawling toward the bar, hitting it hard. In a burst of speed, Dan followed Twain to where he fell. Harlon was sitting against the wooden base of the bar, trying to get his wits back into perspective, but at the same time leaving himself open for an onslaught. Dan slid to his knees, pulling his right hand back to gain power. He brought it forward into Twain's face with a devastating effect, catching the bottom and tip of Twain's nose, breaking bone and cartilage, sending the fragments up into his brain, killing him instantly. Twain's eyes glazed over in an open look of shock, as he dropped over on his side to the floor.

Dan jumped up and ran to Stacy. She lay motionless on the floor by the booth. Several people had rolled her over to check her condition, to help her if they could.

Dan jerked them out of the way and knelt beside her. Her head had an awkward twist to it, as she stared up at him. He saw she was going to have a whopper of a black eye, but he would take care of her. Her eyes were open, but he was dumbfounded. Why wasn't she saying anything? At least acknowledge him, tell him she was all right.

"She's gone, mate," one of the women who had been kneeling by her said to Dan. "She broke her neck when she hit the post. Don't think she felt a damn thing."

The red storm was just about faded from Dan's eyes and brain, as he looked around at the crowd gathered around. "Get her some help. Please!" he screamed.

"We called for a doctor. They're on the way," the bartender stated, as he put a hand on Dan's shoulder. "I'm sorry, Dan, but I've seen this before. She's gone."

Dan looked at all the people, then back at his love, Stacy. Poor, fragile Stacy, who only wanted him to survive, stay alive, be healthy. And look where it got her. It sure didn't get her a good and pleasant life with him. One that they would have had together till they grew old. One where they would have shared their love for each, till the light grew faint in the sky, and they watched the sun set, together, arm in arm. Nope, that wasn't going to happen now. All it got her was dead. The red storm around his eyes was gone; in its place was a shower of tears.

21

Dan positioned himself against the empty bomb racks, pumping a fist at the harpy. "Com'on, you fucker. Why don't you try me out? See how I taste, you bastard!"

The harpy slowly approached him, apprehensively stepping from side to side, like a panther warily questioning its prey. Talons opened and closed on its hands, making a metallic clicking sound as the sharpened claws touched each other. "What're waiting for? Com'on, let's do this!"

The creature was only a couple of feet from him, as it stealthily crept toward him. The left hand of the harpy swung in a long, wide sweep. Dan ducked under it and delivered a coiled right fist to its face. It sounded and felt like he had hit a brick wall; the skin of the harpy was hard and cold. Pain swept through his hand like a thousand electric needles, but he had no time to pay it attention. He brought his left arm up in an uppercut, striking the thing squarely on its chin. The same pain coursed through that arm, but double-fold, because of the amount of force he generated in the punch.

These two blows staggered the flying devil; he wobbled back several steps. Dan's hands and arms burned, in fiery torment. He knew one hand was definitely broke. The harpy seemed to regain its senses, opening its mouth, screeching disapproval at him.

An explosion reverberated from the nose of the bomber. The whole plane lurched and leaned to starboard. The harpy, losing its balance, fell in that direction. Dan used the shift of the plane as momentum, throwing himself at the creature. Hitting it with his full weight, he sent it crashing into the radio and desk. The desk splintered, radio shattering into dozens of pieces of debris.

Dan fell on top of the harpy, his fists swinging in a flurry of punches, exploding with stinging pain every time he connected with the beast. The harpy's left arm reached up and dug its talons into Dan's shoulder. Shards of pain exploded in his brain and body as his right arm went limp.

With his left hand, he dug his thumb into the glowing orange globe of the creature's eye. Digging in deep and hard, he jerked his hand away, popping the eyeball (orb) out of its socket. Blackish goo ran from the now-open hole, down the harpy's cheek. The thing screeched again; this time, Dan knew the bellow was more pain than anger. The harpy dug its claws deeper into Dan's shoulder. If he thought the pain was intense before, it now was magnified beyond his pain threshold. It was his turn to scream. A shattered piece of chair leg lay by the harpy's head. Dan grabbed it, as the creature used its remaining arm to push itself up. With what strength he had left, Dan brought the jagged, splintered piece of wood up over his head and down into the harpy's chest.

The skin of this monster was coarse and tough from living on the winds of the world. It had to be tough over the course of untold years, this thing had endured the onslaught of rain, snow, hail, and many other of nature's forces. The wood pierced the skin and went in. But not as deep as Dan expected, maybe only an inch. It was enough to enlist another shriek of pain from the monster.

The harpy swung its right arm, hard, across Dan's face, the talons ripping into his eyes and forehead. The world in front of him that had been a red storm now turned into one of red liquid. His sight was destroyed beyond repair by the creature's claws. The harpy delivered another hard blow, knocking Dan off it. He bounced and landed against the port side of the bomber.

Looking up through whatever bloodied vision he had left, he saw another harpy come through the destroyed doorway. It looked over at its wounded comrade, then at Dan. In one quick blurred leap, it landed on him. Its talons dug in, and its mouth bit down hard. There was no time to scream in pain, no time for anything but death.

22

The night was electric around them. The darkness alive with life brought more zeal to the pair. He could feel the energy coursing through him. The tingling of sensation was astounding. His heart was pumping strong, blood flowing, letting him know he was alive and one with the earth. The ground and air moved with him in unison, reminding him of the symmetry of the world.

The bodies of the man and woman were in perfect rhythmic union to each other. The male on top, the female below him. Their sexual ballet, leading to an orgasmic climax, was very close.

The world was waking now from its quick sleep. Birds were starting to talk, squirrels running, searching for the bounty of the day. The sun was still an hour away, but the telltale hint of it was on the eastern skyline. The stars twinkled their last rays of brilliance before departing.

The moment was fast and spasmatic. The man completed his task and collapsed next to the woman, on the blanket they had slept on. "That was fantastic, my strong bull," the woman stated between gasps of air.

She was a slender, lithe woman. Short-cropped black hair hung just to the kerchief hanging on her neck. The hair matched her sensual dark eyes. Her bodily proportions matched her appropriate physique, but one could tell quickly she was a dynamo. The muscles in her arms and legs rippled as she made any type of movement. There was no doubt she was a Spaniard, a gypsy woman from the mountains of Spain.

"It was for me as well, my love," the man replied, wiping sweat from his brow.

The somewhat coolness of the night was leaving, bringing the warmth and heat of July to the quickly arriving day. "You're sweating already. I think maybe it's more the nerves starting to grow in you than us making love. Don't you think?" stated the woman, now sitting up, undoing her kerchief, and starting to wipe off her body.

"I know it is. But a lot of it is still you. You know you're astounding, Benet." He leaned over and kissed her passionately.

"Yes, it very well could be. But now, no more talk of this. Let's get going. The sun is coming quickly. It is time. We need to move with the rest of the group." She rapidly started putting clothes on.

"It's gonna be a hell of a day," the man, Slade Driscal, replied as he stood to put on his pants.

The day in question was July 24, 1938. The place was Spain, on the bend of the Ebro River, just north of the town of Fayon. The Spanish civil war was in full swing. A big conflict was in the brewing, starting at about six o'clock this morning. The hour was a little after four.

Slade and Benet were part of the Republican Army. Their adversaries were the Nationalists, a fascist regime tied in with Italy and Germany. This conflict was the precursor for the Second World War. The struggle between the two groups had been going on for two years. The reward ahead for this impending battle was control and possession of Spain proper.

"Make sure we have everything we brought with us. We can't leave anything behind. We'll need it all." Benet finished dressing by tying the kerchief back around her neck. She grabbed her backpack, slinging it over her shoulder, and picked up her heavy Lewis MK1 machine gun.

"My, my, you're a strong one," Slade said, watching her do this. He tied up his pack and snatched up his Erma submachine gun.

"I have to be, especially to handle a bull like you." She smiled a devilish grin as she looked at him, shaking her head. "Don't forget the bow and arrows. We'll need them for sure."

Slade had his pack on and walked over to a large rock, where the bow and quiver of arrows leaned up against. He quickly inspected them, slung the quiver over the other shoulder, and proceeded to follow Benet to the ridge, which she was headed for.

At the top of the ridge lay six men, all Republican loyalists. They looked down the ridge, at the Ebro River. A small secondary road ran along the river, from the west up to a single-lane bridge. It ran across the river to the north side, which was Republican territory. On the south side, the side the group was on, was Nationalist land. On the left side of the bridge, a small guard shack sat, on the right side, a gun emplacement. Sitting behind the sandbags of the emplacement was a lone soldier, smoking a cigarette. A heavy gun lay on the bags, facing the north shoreline. Across the road, on the slope of the small ridge, sat another gun emplacement. Two men sat, enjoying what was left of the night. By their faces, lights flickered bright then diminished, indicating cigarettes also. Sitting between them was a Maxim 08 machine gun, a relic of the First World War, but still a deadly weapon. Its barrel pointed straight down the length of the bridge, guarding for anyone or anything coming across its span.

"Anything new going on?" Slade asked quietly as he and Benet settled down with the rest of the group.

"No. Just the three soldiers. The rest are in the shack, sleeping." The man who said this was Torrida Leone'. A grizzled old man, but nevertheless, a rough and sturdy one. He was a veteran of this war, a man of killing.

"Let's kill them now," Guano, another of the group, whispered out. He had long hair, tied in a tail, a young man.

"Don't be so impatient, my young friend. We go in a few minutes," Torrida replied to him.

"I'll go down the ridge on the left with Benet and Delaneo. Torrida, you and the others go down on the right. I'll take out the one on the left of the gun. That should distract the other, then you take him, okay?"

"Fine by me, Americana." Torrida and the rest of the group always referred to Slade as that. Since he was from America, the shoe fit.

Benet now asserted herself. Besides Torrida, she was the other leader of this band of men, and his daughter. Her hair stirred in the soft morning breeze. "When we take care of those two, be quick. We then take care of the one sitting at the bridge and the ones in the building."

The group split and crept swiftly down the slope of the ridge. There was a soft glow in the east sky as the sun approached. Slade looked down at his watch; it was just about five, the main operation starting in an hour.

As Slade's group of three slunk down the ridge, they kept a keen eye on the duo sitting with the machine gun. He knew they had to take them out quickly so they wouldn't alert the other Nationalist soldiers. At this moment, these two soldiers were oblivious to anything around them. This hour of the late night made them tired and lax. They were talking and smoking, just trying to stay awake.

Slade and his group slid into position, about forty yards from the gun emplacement. Benet nodded to Slade, letting him know now was the time to take out the soldier. Sweat had started to dot his shirt. The heat of the day was coming, but this was all nerve sweat right now. He had left his backpack on the ridge. His quiver of arrows adorned the center of his back, the shafts and feathers facing right. His Erma (gun) was slung to his left shoulder.

Slade had learned how to shoot a bow when he was young, living in Oklahoma. Indian reservations were quite close to where he lived. He had had many a personal relation with the boys and girls living on them. They had all taught him quite well the art of this weaponry growing up, he became very proficient at it.

He slowly pulled an arrow out of the quiver and placed it in his bow, slowly drawing back and taking aim. He pulled the bow as taut as he could, needing as much velocity on the travel of the arrow as he could get. He needed to make sure one shot would take out the soldier for good, not just a wound.

The bow string made a sharp snap as he let it loose. The arrow sailed rapidly, striking the sitting man in the throat. The cigarette in his mouth fell to the ground, as his lips opened in shock and death. He fell over to the earth as his comrade looked on in disbelief. The disbelief only lasted a moment, as the soldier hopped to his feet, grabbing his rifle. Slade grabbed another arrow and quickly fired, not knowing if Torrida and the others could get to the man and stop him before he yelled or fired his rifle.

The soldier arched his back in pain and shock, long before the arrow reached him. He was falling backward, as the arrow struck his chest, but dead from the knife that had been thrown that pierced his back and heart.

Both groups converged on the gun emplacement. The light was brighter now; day was almost upon them. The soldier sitting behind the sandbags by the bridge, seeing them clearly, barked out a word in warning, to any comrades who could hear him.

Benet slammed her Lewis gun on the sandbags as she jumped behind the emplacement. It barked loudly, as its shells tore apart the yelling soldier. The rest of the group were either behind the sandbags or lying on the ground by it, as they trained their weapons on the guard shack.

Guano had the other Lewis machine gun that the band possessed. He extended the tripod, to hold the gun firmly in place, as he took aim, lying flat on the Spanish soil.

Two Nationalist soldiers came bolting out of the door of the little house, guns in hand, as Guano let loose with the Lewis. Dirt kicked up as he found his aim. The next second, splinters of wood filled the air as parts of the shack's door and walls were torn into by the bullets. The soldier's bodies did a dance of death as they fell to the ground.

Rifle barrels appeared in the two window openings facing the attackers, shots firing in retaliation. Torrida motioned Delaneo to go left and then Raspera, another comrade, to go right. The two men moved quickly as the guns of their friends barked out to give them cover.

Delaneo made his way to the roadway. Coming to sit behind a large rock, he pulled a stick grenade from his coat pocket. Gunfire erupted in the side window of the shack, closest to him. The bullets pinged off the boulder as Delaneo pulled the pin out of the grenade and began rocking his arm to gain momentum. The throw was a good twenty yards as he heaved it hard. It flew end over end through the air, arcing its way toward the building. It hit the wall with a thud, falling to the ground. The next instant the earth exploded in a deafening blast, opening a large hole in the guardhouse wall.

Raspera had made his way almost to the roadway, off to the right of the building. Bullets zinged and popped all around him as he crouched behind a larger rock he found for cover. His would be a more straight-on throw, directly into the heavy hail of fire. He squatted and ran all at the same time, raising his arm and throwing the grenade, the same instant falling to the ground. His comrades roared a heavy volley of gunfire at the same moment toward the shack, hoping to deter the return fire of the enemy. The grenade, with luck, landed a foot inside the open doorway of the building. It exploded, sending wood and dirt high into the early morning sky.

Torrida yelled for everyone to stop shooting. Silence came over the landscape of the skirmish. He was sure they had prevailed. After thirty seconds, he motioned Delaneo toward the guardhouse. Everyone else kept their guns trained on it. Delaneo scurried across the road to his side of the shack and looked in through the window. He motioned for the rest of the group to come forward. They had accomplished their task. The bridge was theirs.

Raspera slowly got to his feet, holding an arm that had been damaged. A bullet had caught his throwing arm, just below the shoulder. Blood was staining his shirt.

"Donal, take care of him!" Torrida yelled to a tall lean man with a bearded face. The man ran to Raspera with a bag carrying medical supplies. He had Raspera sit on the ground as he attended to him.

Two shots rang out from the guardhouse, as everyone turned toward the building, guns raised. Delaneo walked out of the shattered building with a smile. "They are all done for sure now."

A rumble of thunder could be heard far off in the east. "The offensive has started, right on time," Benet said as she looked in that direction.

"Yes. Let's get things together. We want to be ready for when our troops get here. Let's hope the enemy doesn't come first," Torrida exclaimed, looking around, surveying the situation.

*****

Two hours later, things and people had been patched up and repaired, giving everything a normal-enough look. The guard shack, with its gaping wounded walls, had things put over or piled against it to try to hide its damage. Three of the band had donned Nationalist uniforms. Guano, Roberto, and Causill had rummaged through the dead bodies, picked, and sorted out enough pieces of garb to make them look presentable, alive, and well, not shot and blown to death.

Slade Driscal was talking with Guano at the gun emplacement at the bridge. "Okay, you understand how this works, right?"

"Yes, Americana. It is like any rifle. The big bullet goes in, you slide the bolt back in, aim, and it kills," said Guano in an ambivalent manner.

"You're right, but it's much more than that. Why don't you take a practice shot and find out?" Slade motioned toward the rifle lying against the sandbags.

It was a German Mauser rifle, a Panzerbuchse 39 model, but much larger than a normal one, and accepted a way larger bullet. It was considered an antitank gun, able to pierce through several inches of metal plating.

"This shell is able to get inside a tank. But it's got a big kick to it. So hold on tight."

Guano laid the gun on the top of the sandbags, got behind them, and knelt. He set the rifle into his shoulder and sighted it back west, down along the river. He picked out a medium-sized rock, about sixty yards away, and pulled the trigger. The Mauser fired, sending a sharp, heavy recoil into Guano's shoulder, throwing him back.

"Madre de Dios!" he shouted in pain. "It's like a small mule just kicked me."

"I told you. My advice, hold on tight when you fire, put some extra padding on either your shoulder or the rifle. And you might want to use the bipod it has, to help support it. Set up something off the bags to place the legs on. That's just my belief. You can do what you want."

"No, no, Americana. I see what you mean. I will do that." Guano smiled at him, happy with his new prize of a weapon. He looked up and down it, admiring it. "Let me ask you something, Americana. How do you know so much about all these guns? Have you killed a lot of men?"

Slade looked at Guano, not smiling now. "I've killed some, had to. It's not a fun game like you think."

Guano's smile faded. "I don't mean it like that. It's not fun to just kill, but it makes me happy to kill Nationalists. Them and their German and Italian scum that are with them. If you had seen what they did to my village, you would be happy to kill them. They came and killed what men they could, even some children. Then they raped our women. Ah yes, Americana, it makes me happy to see them die."

Slade nodded in agreement and walked away up the slope toward the gun emplacement that had the big 57 mm machine gun, the Maxim 08. To the east, he could still hear the rumbling from cannon and tank fire. Large columns of smoke rose high in the sky, indicating the damage and destruction of the assault.

"It's two hours now, and still our troops haven't come yet. I wish they would hurry." Benet stood up to greet Slade. Raspera sat, still cleaning up the machine gun, getting it ready for the fight that was sure to come. His wounded arm was bandaged, in a sling. It didn't hinder him. He worked with zest, wiping and loading a belt of ammunition into the great gun.

"Hopefully they get here soon. I'm surprised the Nationalists aren't here also with their reinforcements."

Benet wiped her forehead with her kerchief and smiled at him. "Well, we can hold for a while." She pointed at the Maxim and then swept around to everyone else. "We've got good firepower now."

"We do. But if they send tanks, we don't," he said grimly.

As he finished his last word, Raspera shouted out, "Here comes Torrida! He's running hard! That's not good!"

Benet whistled loudly to everyone, beckoning with her arm to assemble by her. Torrida bounced down the ridge and arrived out of breath, hands now on his legs, bent over, trying to pull in new air. He waited till the whole group was together, then began talking. "The Nationalists are about two miles up the road. Moving slow, one tank leads them. Followed by four trucks, I think. All are filled with troops." He looked intently at everyone. "We get set now, with haste. Delaneo, take the other Lewis gun. Set up on the east side of the road where it curves to the bridge. Stay hidden behind the rocks. You only get up and fire when you hear everyone else fire. Roberto, Causill, you stand by the guardhouse. Wave at them like brothers. When they are thirty steps from you, open fire and throw grenades. Then find cover fast. I don't want you two dead that soon. Guano, you have the big gun. Take out the wheel treads on the tank so it can't move. Then kill it with your bullets." Guano nodded in agreement. "Does he have a lot of bullets?" Torrida looked at Slade.

"Yes, he's got a box of fifty."

"Good. The rest of us will be up on the slope. Benet and Raspera at the big machine gun, you and I"—he pointed at Slade—"in the rocks. All of us hiding, out of sight." Torrida looked around at everyone with a stoic glare. Everyone nodded or grunted back grimly.

"Then go, be ready. Pray our help comes quickly. Glory to the republic." The group broke and ran to their different destinations.

Benet grabbed Slade, pulling him into her body. "Stay alive, my love. I want to be able to feel your body again." She reached up and kissed him hard. As he pulled away, she slapped his face with the palm of her hand affectionately. She grinned. He blew her a kiss and ran off carrying the other heavy Lewis gun.

It came to him that Benet was such a hard-skinned and tough woman, but he knew he loved her just the same. He also knew she loved him too. She was a warm and loyal person who would fight with the last ounce of breath for a person or thing that was close to her. Her last drop of blood and passion would be spilled for that thing or one she truly loved and believed in.

*****

The rumble of the tank echoed louder as it approached. Slade found it hard to think about what needed to be done. The vibration of the tank treads as they rolled across the loose rocks and pebbles on the ill-maintained road, obliterating them to dust, permeated his thoughts and mind.

Slade recognized the tank. It was a Panzer Mark 1 model, a German design. The Germans had really incorporated themselves into this civil war, maybe not as much with troops, but definitely with their equipment and firepower. This tank was the first of its design. It had no cannon but instead housed two heavy MG 13 machine guns in its turret. A lightly armored vehicle, but still very deadly. He hoped the Panzerbuchse rifle would help stop it.

Roberto was waving and smiling as the column approached the bridge. The tank ground to a halt, twenty yards from the guardhouse. Causill came forward, standing next to Roberto, waving also, one hand behind his back, holding a stick grenade, the other hand holding the rifle slung across his shoulder.

The top hatch of the tank opened. A soldier (an officer, by the markings on his uniform) pulled himself halfway out and yelled to the pair, over the rumbling engine, "Has anything tried crossing the bridge yet? Have you been attacked?"

"No, nothing has come. The only things we have seen is your scummy asses!" Roberto shouted back. The man sitting atop the tank had a puzzled look on his face.

The startled delay between the two speakers was short. Roberto swung his submachine gun that had been hanging by his side, from a strap around his neck and shoulder, into a firing position. He had acquired this Spanish-made Star Si35 gun from one of the dead Nationalists. He was happy to have made it his own, knowing the damage it could inflict. Holding it in front of him at waist level, he fired a long stochastic burst. The pattern of the bullets started at midturret as he raised his arm up toward the hatch. The shells tore into the openmouthed soldier, pushing him back into the hatch cover standing up behind him. As Roberto stopped firing, the man fell forward, to lie dead across the turret top.

Causill stepped forward, pulled the pin out of his grenade, and heaved it at the tank. Its trajectory sent it flying into the side of the turret. It hit the armor plating, falling to the ground and exploding harmlessly. The only thing it did was send dirt and debris sailing in all directions.

Things moved fast now. Guano, who had been standing, quickly knelt down behind the sandbags of the gun emplacement, on the river side of it. He brought the massive Panzerbuchse rifle up to his shoulder, resting its bipod on boxes stacked in front of him. He aimed and fired. The shell found the left tank tread, blowing chunks of it apart, sending cotter pins, bearings, and shrapnel into the air. The bottom half of the tread fell to the ground.

Delaneo was up with his Lewis as the first burst of Roberto's gun spat out. Laying his gun on the large rocks in front of him (he had picked two that let him have full control and vision of the road), he fired on the first truck behind the tank. It was his good fortune that the truck was not directly behind the tank, but slightly off to its left, closer to the river. His bullets slammed into the cab, straight on, decimating it and whoever sat in it.

All the firepower on the slope opened up now, sending a multitude of shells into the remaining troop trucks. The canvas covers on the beds of the vehicles quickly became perforated with holes from the projectiles. Benet was feverishly firing the Maxim, spent shell casings spitting out from its side. Slade and Torrida, lying behind rocks, on their bellies, barked out bullets from their respective weapons. The holes in the tent covers of the trucks soon turned into large rents or lacerations, as the bullets tore into them. Screams of death and pain could be heard over the sound of the battle.

What soldiers who were not already dead, or severely wounded, came pouring out of the vehicles, looking for cover to hide behind. Torrida had hoped for this element of surprise, and it had come to fruition.

Guano slipped another bullet into his rifle and slammed the bolt home. He fired at the still-viable tread on the right side of the tank. It struck at an angle, ripping great chunks of material from it, but it still held in place.

The same instant, the Panzer roared forward with a growl from its engine. With only one working tread, that made any attempt to propel forward not viable. The tank spun on its axis, slightly to the left. This strain on the remaining damaged tread was too much. It snapped apart at the point of Guano's wounding shot, the tread rolling off its wheels, to the ground. The tank and its crew wasted no time with its dilemma. The turret quickly rotated to its left, guns lowering to fire.

Roberto was still standing in position, firing his submachine gun at the trucks and soldiers. Causill took another grenade and hurled it high and long. This time it landed under the first truck in the column. It exploded, raising the truck off the ground in a short lurch. A moment later, the gas tank erupted in a second explosion, sending flames and burning metal into the atmosphere. Out of the corner of his eye, Roberto saw the turret swing toward him. He turned and ran, grabbing Causill by his uniform jacket, trying in vain to drag him with him, away from the impending death.

MG13 shells travel much faster than a human's feet. The heavy guns let loose with a loud growl. Causill's body was ripped into chunks and pieces. Roberto, a step ahead, threw himself toward the sandbags of the gun emplacement. Shells tore into his left shoulder, ripping the arm away from his body in a bloody spray. He landed on the ground and began crawling the last few feet to the safety of the bags, his good arm digging and pulling him along.

The tank's turret rotated to follow his progress. The guns spoke again, tearing the rest of his body apart. A bloody mist quickly formed in the air.

Guano took all this in, as he slammed another bullet into the rifle and fired, this time, directly at the guns of the turret. He saw it punch a hole in the tank, just to the left of the machine guns. This did not stop the progress of the guns, as they rotated to him. The sandbags exploded in a storm of grit and dust, blinding his eyes. He could feel and hear the heavy shells screaming past him, as the safety of the gun emplacement slowly dissolved around him. He fumbled for and grabbed another shell, bringing it up to the rifle, feverishly putting it in the chamber, grabbing the bolt, locking it home. That was the last thing he did, the last recollection he knew, as an MG13 shell obliterated his head.

Torrida saw what was transpiring. He knew their bullets or grenades would not be able to stop the tank's guns and its deadly onslaught. He looked into his backpack, dug down, and pulled out the only satchel charge the group had. The satchel charge was the equivalent of about ten grenades in one. It was a smaller version of a canvas backpack. It had a small pin or lever on it for use. The one drawback was it had to be put in position and the pin pulled manually for it to work. It came with a ten-second timer or could be detonated by a heavy blow to it, such as a bullet.

Torrida looked back toward Slade and waved to get his attention. When he did, he held up the charge and motioned toward the tank. Slade knew exactly what he wanted to do and shook his head no. The Nationalist soldiers were returning fire, hitting the rocks and dirt all around them. Torrida's run to the tank would lead him right into the hail of fire. But he knew this wouldn't stop Torrida, not now, not ever. He motioned for him to go; he would return cover fire for him the best he could.

Torrida pulled a grenade out of his pack and hurled it toward the burning trucks. When it exploded, he was up and running, staying as low as he could. Firing the Erma, wildly he ran for the tank, a good twenty yards away. Bullets flew past and around him. He jumped and landed behind a rock at the edge of the roadway. Bullets tore into and sheared pieces of the rock away, as he lay there, somewhat safe. He could feel the heat coming off the truck that was blazing, close to him. A yard away, part of a hand, probably from one of the soldiers of said truck, lay in the dirt, smoking, the skin bubbling from the intense fire. He took off the backpack he had slung over his shoulder, pulling out the satchel charge and his last grenade. He pushed the activator lever, setting the charge, but not the timer. He wanted to place it on the tank and have a bullet ignite it. He pulled the pin on the grenade, looking back at Slade, their eyes meeting. A melancholy grin came to Torrida's face, as he threw the grenade, over his head, toward the trucks. As it exploded, he ran.

His ten-yard jaunt was interrupted at five, as a bullet hit his left side. He fell to the ground and rolled, still holding on to the charge. He rolled the next several yards in pain as Slade and Benet's guns barked in response. His body smacked the side of the tank, as a wave of stars and painful explosions clouded his vision. With one hand on the tank, the other holding the satchel, he pulled himself up.

The tank now swung its turret back around to the east, looking for Delaneo and his Lewis gun. Delaneo paid no attention to it as he kept spitting death at the soldiers trying to cross the road from the destroyed trucks. They were trying to get to the river's edge, where some bigger rocks lay. Rocks that would give them protection and life. The only problem was they had to traverse the road, and Delaneo wasn't letting this happen. Many bodies lay dead in the roadway from his gun. He thought to himself, just a few more blasts of the gun, and then he would crawl away to safety, behind the bigger rocks. He just needed to kill a few more of these Nationalist bastards before he did.

The tank, again, was faster than his thoughts. It sprayed the rocks where he lay with wanton destruction, chewing and churning Delaneo into pieces of blood and bone. His Lewis gun fell to the earth from dead hands.

Torrida jammed the charge pack in between the turret and body of the Panzer. Another bullet shattered his thigh bone, spinning him around and down to his knees. He tried to rise up, but there was no more energy or strength left. The next two shells hit him in the chest, ending his life, as he slumped to the earth, leaning against the tank.

Rage came to Benet as she witnessed this event. She screamed in grief and anger as she fired the Maxim at the last truck in the convoy, the only one still viable. The fuel leaking from its ruptured gas tank erupted in a large fireball of flame and destruction. Soldiers close to it were either hurled to their death or ran away like blazing fireflies, their lives ending shortly after.

The tank's turret, now content with the dispatching of Delaneo, kept turning to the west, toward the group on the slope. Slade knew their end would be quick in coming if that satchel charge wasn't exploded. He brought his Lewis around, trying to hold it in his arms and fire at the same time. The Lewis, being a heavy and massive weapon, was hard to shoot, precisely, in this way. Without any other support but just his elbow resting on the ground, Slade's aim was off. His bullets pinged off the tank's armor as the turret made its slow turn.

"Goddammit!" he screamed in despair. The next burst his gun emitted caught the satchel charge. The pack erupted in a cacophony of flame and debris. The turret lifted a foot off the body of the Panzer and slid off to the left, resting half on, half off. Slade covered his face and head, as hot chunks of metal shrapnel buffeted him. Some came to rest on his clothes, and immediately small fires sprang to life. He felt his skin and hair singe with the burning waste. He hurriedly brushed off the hot metal.

A gnarled, serpent-like flame sprang up from the bowels of the tank. He perceived no movement from inside. The occupants were all dead.

The pause in the fighting was brief, just enough to reflect on the quick death of the metal beast. Rifle shots began ringing out, striking the ground and sandbags around the remaining band of Republicans.

Slade, Benet, and Raspera returned fire, this time aiming and rationing their shots, not just firing wildly into the fray. Slade counted his grenades; only three left. He yelled to Benet, "How many grenades do you have?"

She returned the answer by holding up two fingers. Raspera also obliged, holding up one finger. An explosion shook the ground, yards from Slade. Nationalist soldiers were advancing on them, throwing grenades. Whatever was left of them, which wasn't many, were trying to climb the ridge to get a better advantage. Their only problem was that there was too much of an open killing field to cross to accomplish this. As soon as a soldier made a run, the machine guns spoke, and their life was ended.

A soft rumbling whine from a distance came to Slade's ears. With each passing second, it became louder. He looked west, up the river, and saw it, a plane. He knew at once, coming from that direction, it wasn't one of theirs.

It came in, streaking fast, above the waters of the river, at a
height of only a hundred feet. Its engine sounded angry as it zoomed
past the bridge, headed west. Slade recognized it as a Fiat G.50 fighter
plane. An Italian craft, a single-seater, a newer-model plane. He had
read about them before he came to Spain and the civil war. They
were Italy's new pride and joy, fresh off the assembly line, and here to
destroy the enemies of the Nationalists.

Slade knew they were in trouble the second it passed the bridge
and then banked to the left. It was circling back, coming back around
to investigate the trouble below it. Somebody, somewhere, had a
radio and probably informed it of what was transpiring at this bridge.
The plane stayed at its height and came over them, tipping its right
wing down, to get a better look of the situation. As it passed, it made
the same banking turn to the left; it was coming around again. Slade
knew the pilot had deduced the situation and was coming back to
circumvent it. Slade heard the tone and whine of the plane's engine
change as it came back around, now dropping down lower, seeming
to hug the water. It came in low, thirty feet off the water, heading
straight for the guard shack and them.

Slade saw the flashes from its guns before he heard them. The
tracer patterns of the lethal machine guns started halfway out on
the river, making two identical columns of water geysers. They ran
straight at the guard shack, where chunks of wood and debris were
torn apart from the structure with a crackling, ripping sound. The
line of bullets continued past the building, straight at Benet's gun
emplacement.

Slade watched from twenty feet away, as the bullets buffeted
the sandbags. They popped, exploded, and broke open, sending sand
spraying all about. In a brief second, the plane flashed past, over their
heads, and started another wide circling arc. It was coming back for
another strafing pass. The fighter rose high in the sky, to make a
sufficient altitude bank, so it could come back with a longer, more
lethal spray of bullets.

The same instant, Slade heard and saw movement along the
north side of the river. It was a column of trucks headed to the bridge,
their reinforcements. If the plane spotted them after this next strafing

pass, the column would be in for a world of hurt, as exposed as they would be; they were sitting ducks.

Benet popped her head up. Slade could see blood trickling down one side. A bullet had grazed her scalp. She looked at him and grimaced in pain. Her dark-brown eyes emoted a look of despair and resolute determination, all at the same time. He knew she was hurt more than just a grazing shot. He pointed toward the far riverbank. She looked, shaking her head in acknowledgment. She then pointed up at the circling plane. Using her forefinger, she made a cutting gesture across her throat.

Slade understood; they had to take this fighter out, right now. He gave her a thumbs-up. She smiled back, grimly, then blew him a kiss. He watched as she locked the gun belt for the massive Maxim gun in place, raising its angle up, to meet the returning plane. Raspera now appeared, shakily, laying a rifle across the destroyed sandbags. His hands were covered in blood. The sling holding the wounded arm was partially torn away. It wafted in the late morning breeze. Slade knew he had been wounded even more from the strafing run. Hell of a man to still be willing to fight, even in that kind of wounded state. But the whole group had been like that. They believed in their cause, this cause. They would all, and did, give their lives for it.

Slade inspected Benet's face closer now. The blood was running down the side of her face to her neck in a steady stream. The head wound was worse than he had first thought. Anger swept through him. No one hurt his girl, his woman. He snatched the ammo drum from his Lewis and slammed a fresh, new one in its place. He would make the plane pay for this. He flipped up his sight finder on the machine gun as he positioned it on the rocks.

The fighter swung into the center of his sights, as it came into position for its low-level strafing run. It was just coming over the water on the far side of the river as Slade started firing. The Lewis chattered like a swarm of angry bees. He heard the Maxim start to scream in unison. His vision was clear as he fired. He saw in detail the enemy plane. It hadn't started firing yet, probably didn't want to waste ammunition, wanted to be a hair closer. He saw their bullets start to hit home. Pieces of the fighter broke apart, turning into a somewhat powder state, and fall away from it. It was all too late for the fighter when flashes appeared from its guns. Larger sections of the plane were falling away from it now. Smoke and sparks drifted out from the engine.

Slade didn't let up; he kept firing till his gun went silent, out of ammunition. Benet's gun kept hammering the doomed plane. Slade peered through his sights, watching as a spectator. The gun flashes stopped on the fighter as big plumes of smoke shot out of it. An explosion erupted in the engine, sending large pieces of fiery debris, dropping away. The wings began to wobble. It was out of control, in its death knell. The nose dipped down, not far from the shore bank, its propellers clipping the water, tipping the plane down, where the nose smacked the river, sending it tumbling end over end, toward the shore and the guard building. The sound was deafening as the shack and plane met. An explosion obliterated them both, sending large sections of metal and wood high into the sky.

For a split second, Slade's and Benet's eyes met. There was a mixture of relief and happiness in them. They had achieved their victory, Slade thought. They had stopped the plane; it wouldn't be able to inflict damage on the reinforcements or on them. A split second later, that thought and realization was gone, evaporated on the hot, smoky, burning air of this hellish day.

A large chunk of the fighter's engine crashed down on the gun emplacement in a thunderous boom, sending smoke and debris careening in all directions. Pieces of hot metal hit and pierced Slade's body. He pushed his head into the dirt, screaming, not in pain, but in grief. He knew she was gone, incinerated in that brief moment of time and space. There was no surviving that. Even if she did, she would not survive long, out here in the field of battle. No doctors or hospitals were nearby to help with the situation. Even then the chances would have been slim. No, she was gone, dead. But someone would pay; someone would compensate him for his grief and pain.

As Slade sat up, bullets started to hit the ground around him. The remaining Nationalists had recovered from the tumultuous ordeal and were pushing the fight back at him. He grabbed a grenade, pulled the pin, and hurled it. Not waiting for the explosion, he threw another, and then his last. The three concussive blasts almost erupted simultaneously. He heard someone screaming. It seemed far away. Maybe it was the hurt Nationalists? Then he realized it wasn't them; it was him. He was venting his anger and hatred any way he could. His blood was boiling, seething for revenge. They would pay for Benet, his love, his life. They would all pay with their dear lives. He slapped in another drum of ammunition, staggered to his feet, and began firing.

23

Slade Driscal snapped out of his dreams, his nightmares of yesterday to another nightmare of the present. He heard Skipper Davis over his headset. "Anyone that can hear me, answer, dammit! We've got craziness going on! Everyone, stay alert, watch out!"

Without any warning, the port window, in his nose section of the plane, exploded, sending shards of glass flying in all directions. He was lucky he had his head turned. Otherwise, his face and eyes would have been pin cushioned by it.

A large taloned hand swung in, clearing any broken shards that were still in the frame out of the way. Once that was accomplished, the hand retreated; and a reddish-black face, the face of a demon, Slade thought, looked in. He gazed into blazing orange eyes. The creature opened its mouth, exposing rows of sharp, serrated teeth, dripping a blackish goo. Next came an ear-piercing screech, bringing a ringing pain at once to them.

The harpy began tearing apart the framing, making an opening for it to get into the small compartment. Pieces of fabric and wood were slung away from the lumbering bomber into the black sky. Slade's shock and awe lasted only a second; his battle training and past hardships kicked in. He unholstered his .45 and quickly crawled the short distance between the two, raising his gun up at point-blank range, pulling the trigger. To his surprise, nothing happened. There was no bark of sound or discharge from the firearm. To his dismay, he realized the gun had misfired.

By this point, the harpy had made a big enough of an opening and was pulling its body in. With a swing of its right arm, it hit Slade's hand, knocking the gun free and sending it bouncing away from him. The creature's backswing caught him across the side of his face, tearing through his leather flyer's cap, ripping a section of bloodied flesh away from it. The blow sent Slade falling back and hitting the small doorway to his compartment. He steadied himself, quickly grabbing for the starboard wall to gain support. His hand felt his flight jacket, hanging on a hook in the corner. He remembered what was in the jacket.

Whenever he flew a mission, he always carried two grenades, the small pineapple-shaped ones. Ever since Spain, he always did this when he went into action. It gave him a sense of security and safety, of being prepared for anything than might come his way.

The harpy was struggling to get its legs inside the cramped quarters but, at the same time, swinging its clawed hand at him, realizing he was still a living threat. Slade dug a hand in the jacket's pocket and felt one of the grenades. All in one motion, he pulled out the grenade, pulled its pin, and flung himself at the monster.

The harpy, unprepared for this movement, caught the whole weight of Slade's body full on, sending it and Slade falling toward the nose glass, and the Norden bombsight structure. The weight of Slade Driscal was a good 230 lbs. at this time of his life. The cold metallic hardness of the Norden sight was very firm and rigid. As the harpy made contact with it, Slade heard the snap and break of the creature's back. It screeched in pain, as its now-broken spine was semi-impaled on the bombsight. Its arms flailed wildly as it belched black phlegm from its mouth.

Slade stood and straddled the beast, holding the grenade above its head. The activation lever snapped, when he let go of it, making a metallic popping sound, as the countdown started. With a quick thrust, he jammed the bomb into the monster's yawling mouth. Slade screamed in pain as the sharp fangs tore into his skin. He pushed as far and as hard as he could, feeling the tendons and muscle of the creature's jaws give way to his to mighty shove. He jerked his hand back, leaving strips of his flesh, hanging on the serrated teeth.

Slade flung himself backward, hard and fast, hitting the exit wall to the nose section. Twisting, he tumbled through the small doorway and into the tight tunnel channel. The harpy clawed violently at its mouth, trying to extract the grenade. But with only a five-second fuse, all movements became mute.

The concussion of the explosion was somewhat contained inside the harpy's mouth. But skin and muscle are no match to the blast of a grenade and its aftermath. The whole nose section was blown apart, almost as if a giant hand had reached out and plucked it away, leaving just jagged, mangled edges of a framework. The wall and tunnel had helped to shield the blast from Slade, somewhat. The now-lost compartment gave view to a vast black night sky. The wind whistled and buffeted through gaping holes in the wounded wall at a tremendous pitch.

Burning pain stabbed at Slade's right leg. Looking down, he saw several pieces of metal shrapnel stuck in his calf and thigh, a last parting gift from the Norden. He reached down with his right hand to pull them out but quickly realized he couldn't grasp them. His hand and fingers were useless; they were numb. The pain farther up his hand was throbbing white-hot fire. His wounds there from the harpy's teeth were deep and ragged. Blood was running from them like an open faucet. He knew there had to be severe nerve damage, probably even that the nerves and tendon were severed.

It was difficult, but after some twisting and distress, Slade managed to reach over with his left hand and jerk the pieces out. Yelling in agony, he watched the blood flow out and soak his pant leg. He lay there for a few seconds, waiting, and hoping the pain would recede a bit. He tore off a section of sleeve from his uniform and made a tourniquet around his thigh, using a piece of broken wood framing to apply pressure. He now decided he had to start crawling through the tunnel to get help for himself, plus find out just what the hell was going on.

Several shots exploded from up above him, in the pilot's cockpit. He just knew it had to be Cullum. He was in trouble, one of his best friends, over the last year and a half. He needed to help. Screw anything else. He had learned over his life, you help your friends. Whether it costs you your life or not, you just do.

His mind raced. He looked around for a weapon. The gun he once had was definitely gone. It was in the nose section, and that was history. He surveyed his surroundings, nothing, till he saw his jacket fluttering. It had somehow survived the blast. It was now hanging on to a jagged rib frame of the bomber, tattered and torn. In fact, it had been impaled through by the metal shard. It now flapped briskly in the brisk wind currents. He reached up and snatched it with his still-functioning hand, pulling it to him. He grimaced as he felt in the pocket. The pain in his wounds was ramping up.

A sense of newfound energy and urgency burst up in him as his hand came across the grenade. He yanked it out and eyed it; it was still usable. A small smile of pain came to his face as he pulled himself up and started moving up through the small tunnel shaft that led to a hatch just behind the pilot's cabin. These fucking monsters weren't going to take the skipper and the rest of the ship from him. Not without a fight, his fight.

24

"No one's answering, Cull! But some shit's happening, though. Just listen to all the fireworks going on!" Terry Graynor blurted out as he looked worriedly at Cullum Davis.

"Yeah, I know. Shit! Watch the controls. I'm going back to check things out!"

Terry reached over and put a hand on Cullum's shoulder, trying to hold him in place. "No, you stay here and fly this bird. I don't think I can handle it, you know, the shape it's in. This poor girl's in trouble. You know how she handles better than I do."

Cullum hesitated, then shook his head in agreement.

Terry was half out of his seat when the nose erupted, with a rupturing blast, in front of them. It was a sharp, quick blast, blowing the glass out on all its sides, taking pieces of metal ribbing and turning them into gnarled, twisted caricatures. The debris hit the cockpit windows, causing severe cracks and creating dime-sized holes. The whole bomber rocked sharply to starboard, slamming Terry into the wall of the cabin. He fell, jamming himself between the wall and his seat.

Cullum held on tight to the steering wheel, trying to compensate for the unexpected explosion. He fought to help keep the bomber flying straight. Another death groan came from the remaining engines; they valiantly ran, trying to do their job.

"What the fuck!" was all Cullum got out, as he fought the wounded, dying plane.

Terry pulled himself back up and into his seat, looking out at the damaged nose section. "Was Slade in there? If he was, he's gone now."

"Quick, move your ass! Go see!"

Terry went to move and, in the next second, froze. The line between reality and insanity skewed intensely for him. He didn't know what he was looking at. Was he knocked out from the blast and just dreaming this, or had the real world been ripped apart and they all, including him, were in the crazy world right now?

Peering in at him from the overhead windows of the cockpit was a face. It was a face like none he had ever seen before. From what he could judge, in the normal world, the face was upside down. The body attached to this face was lying on top of the bomber. How could this be? Any person trying this stunt would have been blown off by the intense wind draft. His eyes then picked out what held this being in place. A foot or so past the window, he saw what appeared to be claw tips that had perforated the skin of the plane and had dug in to hold it there.

But it was the face that questioned his sanity. The face had a hardened look to it, a weathered reddish-black look. The eyes, oh my lord, the eyes, he thought, were two bright, blazing orange globes of fire. Their intensity, in the blackened sky, made him wince to their glow. The mouth on the thing opened, revealing sharp fangs. The sound the creature emitted was shrill. As it came through the broken holes in the windshield, it reverberated into a devilish cry of madness.

That's when Terry's blood turned ice cold and froze in his veins. His heart, which had been beating so hard and so fast, seemed to stop. His childhood nightmare came back and played out in his mind. All the trauma of it slammed back home. He lost control of his bladder and urinated on himself.

25

The cold whistled through the trees; frozen in place, they yelled in low murmurs of pain. It had snowed the week before, ten inches in fact; but the temperature had risen above freezing, melting some of it away. But in the previous day, artic blasts had reappeared, icing everything back into a state of frigid trauma.

Terry Graynor huddled with his two sisters around their fireplace. It roared, valiantly trying to keep the cold out of their house and keep the toasty warm in.

"You kids have to start getting ready for bed now!" Jeanie Graynor, their mom, called out from the kitchen sink, cleaning up the last pot. Drying it, putting it in the cupboard, she puffed with exhaustion, as she wiped her hands on her apron.

"I told you before, Jean, have the girls do that. Dammit, you've done enough! I don't want them thinking they can get lazy and not have to do a damn thing!" Ted Graynor yelled from his wooden rocking chair, sitting in the corner of the living area. He sat in this small meager room, behind the children, a bottle of Wild Turkey in his hands.

"They helped with everything but this. This pot is too big for them. They'd probably drop it, dent it, and then you'd be madder than hell!" she called back, never turning her shoulder to look at him.

"Well, it's to blame bad enough. The boy's lazy as hell. I don't want the girls being the same way." He took a quick swig and licked his lips, wiping them with his shirtsleeve.

"Dad's really getting liquored up," Terry's elder sister, Clarice, whispered in his ear.

Ted and Jeanie Graynor had born three children to their family: Clarice, nine; Terrance, eight; and Glennalen, six. Ted was a cattle farmer, out of Edgemont, South Dakota, just north of Rapid City. For the last couple of years, times had been lean for the upstart family. Troubles with drought and battles with wolves, bears, and other wild animals had taken a heavy toll on his herd. It had been tough at times to make ends meet. That's what drove Ted to the bottle, and he hit it hard. When he got, as Clarice had stated, all liquored up, he got mean and troublesome. Sometimes he took it out on his wife, most of the time, on his kids. Terry especially became a common target. No matter how hard he busted his butt, his father always rode him. He was never working hard or fast enough to suit him.

It was a cold early spring night in the Dakota territory in 1931. The winter was not about to let go her grip just yet; she wanted to hang on to the very last. The icy cold fingers of her soul were wrapped around the minds and bodies of the Graynor family. They had lost more cows to this new freezing weather. The wolves and bears had stayed away for a while now, probably hunkered down for this last part of the winter, waiting it out. But come the spring proper, they would be out in full force, with empty stomachs that needed feeding.

Terry also got the brunt of helping his dad. Even at eight, he was quickly enlisted as a cattleman first class. His father pushed him from dawn to dusk. Many a night he went to bed crying, listening to his mother and father fighting, her sticking up for him and Ted mad she was doing just that.

"All right, everyone out to the toilet to do their business." Jeanie had come into the living area to hustle the kids into the routine of going to sleep for the night. This meant them having to go outside to the outhouse. Most rural houses, or farms out, away from a town or big city, didn't have indoor plumbing. So this meant going to an outside toilet, usually twenty to thirty yards from the main house. It was always put a distance from the main living dwelling because of the smell. Lime was always used to eat up the feces and urine and quell the odor, but when it got hot in the late summer, there was no helping the rankness that came out of the defecation hole.

"You kids get your asses out there, doos your thing. Terrence, take the lantern so yours sistas can see and not step in anything." Terry could hear his father's words starting their usual slur. The Wild

Turkey was starting to take hold. He knew not to cross him when he got to this point.

"Yes, sir." He grabbed the lit oil lamp closest to the trio. All three helped each other don their coats and pull their boots on.

"Now remember, let your sisters go first and you last." His mom patted him on the head.

"Yes, Mother." He didn't like going last, not in the cold weather. His dinker, as his little sister called it, tended to shrivel up and his bladder shut down, making it hard to go. Sometimes all he got out was a little trickle of pee.

Terry opened the door off the kitchen and was greeted with a cold, frigid blast. "Oh, that's cold!" Glennalen cried, starting to shiver under her big coat.

"I don't give a damn. Gets your asses out theres. Ifs youse don't, I'll give youse somethin' to cry about." Their father had gotten up and come into the kitchen. He looked at the group with a half sneer on his face.

"Well, at least we got a full moon. We'll be able to see better," Clarice added, as the trio stepped out.

The outhouse was a small shack of a building about six feet high and a three-by-three square area to sit. The toilet was a round hole, elevated up a couple of feet off the ground sitting in a wooden platform. In this weather, the wood seat became very cold.

The group made their way quickly, wanting to get this done and over; the warmth of the house awaited. Glennalen went first. "It sure feels spooky out here tonight," Clarice whispered to Terry. Her head did a 360 turn, looking around at any and everything. The brightness of the moon casting monstrous shadows everywhere gave the landscape an eerie, nightmarish quality to it.

"I know. The trees sound like they're talking to us." Terry and Clarice listened as the wind made the trees do a low moan.

Glennalen did her duty quickly; the door to the outhouse swung open. "Next."

Clarice ran in, closing the door quickly. Terry saw movement out of the corner of his eye.

"What is that?" his little sister screamed in panic. Terry swung the lantern to his right, at the row of pines behind the little shack.

"It's nothing. Just the trees moving from the wind, that's all." He let out a sigh of relief. Terry could feel his nerves building up also. The snow freaked him out as he and his sister stepped around. It made a crunching, breaking sound that seemed to go right through him. The wind was picking up in speed, giving the air a soft talking sound, almost as if there was a lilting scream carrying over it.

"I'm scared."

"Don't worry. We'll be done quick," Terry said, trying to comfort Glennalen. All the time his nerves kept revving up. He had seen what wild wolves had done to the cattle, when they got a hold of one. The pack would gang up and rip it to shreds. It was not a pretty sight. He prayed the pack wasn't out tonight, hunting for prey.

The door to the outhouse slammed open with a bang. The pair jumped in unison. "It's all yours."

"Jeez, Clarice. Don't do that. You scared the hell out of us." Terry handed her the lantern and stepped into the proverbial shithouse.

As he closed the door to the outside world, the light that there was quickly faded. It was almost total darkness inside the squared area. A little shaft of moonlight shone through a small slatted opening between two planks of wood on the side of the building. He knew the inside of the outhouse by heart. All the times he had used it, every nook and cranny was etched in his mind. He lifted the wood seat. He didn't need to poop, just pee into the round opening. He dropped his pajama bottoms, grabbed his member, and waited. Nothing. It was too damn cold. Anything that needed to come out was frozen up in him now. Also, it didn't help that in his mind he had visions—visions of a demonic, gnarled hand, one made of hanging skin and old creaky bones, rising out of the toilet hole, rising up to grab his penis and twist it hard, ripping it away from his body, and pulling it down, into the black depths below.

"Hurry up, Terry! I'm scared!" yelled Glennalen.

"Hell, I'm just froze," added Clarice. "Just hurry."

Terry pushed from his gut, straining with every fiber of his body. All that came out was a small trickle of urine. He tried several times, only getting a few small droplets; otherwise, it was to no avail.

"Please hurry, Terry. Please." Glennalen was really pleading now. He could hear the fear and cold mixture in her tone. He pulled his bottoms up and opened the door. Both girls stood in front of him. The light from the lantern shone clearly on the pair; he could see they were both shivering.

"All right, let's go." He grabbed the lantern from Clarice and led the girls back to the house.

"Did we all do our duties out there?" their mom asked as they took their boots and coats off.

"Yes, ma'am," they all replied in unison. In the back of Terry's mind was the thought, *I hope I can make it through the night without getting the urge.*

*****

Terry only made it four hours. The urge was strong, it woke him out of a sound sleep. He didn't want to get up, but he had to. There was no way he was going to pee his bed. His mother had a jar she kept under the sink, a pee jar. She had made sure to tell Terry about it. It was just for him on occasions like this. She told him to use it and, when he was done, put the cork back in it. By god don't spill it, but make sure to put it back under the sink. She swore to him to tell her when he used it so she could empty it out before their father found it. She knew he wouldn't take a liking to something like that, no, sir. She told him it would turn into big trouble.

Everyone's sleeping quarters were upstairs in the house. His parents had one room, and he and his sisters shared another. His father had told him if he carried his weight, maybe next year he would split his and the girls' room in two, giving him his own room.

He slowly crept out of his room; his sisters were sound asleep. Quietly he made it down the stairs. The fireplace still crackled life, a soft glow and warmth coming off it. The last step of the staircase made a slight creaking sound as he stepped on it. It didn't matter. Everyone was upstairs asleep; they wouldn't hear it.

As he made his way to the kitchen archway, he heard the rocking chair come to life, the chair his father had been sitting in earlier that evening. He made it two more steps, praying it was just the house breathing and sighing from the cold winds. Praying it wasn't his father, still sitting there, asleep after drinking too much. Left in the chair by his wife because she didn't want to have to contend with him in the state he was in. It was better, she figured, to just let him be, let him sleep it off. The next sound he heard was the bottle of Wild Turkey hit the rug under the chair. It made a soft thud, rolled, and clanked against the leg of the chair. A hollow clank, stating that it was empty. He crept, another couple of steps, to the sink and bent down to open the cabinet door, praying his father was still asleep. He reached for the pee bottle, praying he slept the sleep of a drunken man. His prayers were quickly dashed on the rocks of despair.

"What the hell's youse doing, boy?" His father was standing in the archway to the kitchen, silhouetted in the glow coming from the fireplace.

"Nothing, sir. Just had to go pee." Terry closed the door to the cabinet. He turned and faced his father in the semidarkness of the house.

"What the hell you doin' under the sink? Gos on outside and dos your chore."

"Okay." Terry wasn't going to say anything about the pee bottle. He sure as hell didn't need his mother to be catching hell for it, let alone himself. He reached for the lantern.

"Youse don't need no damn lantern. Theys a full moons out there. Youse can see just fine."

He quietly put his boots on and grabbed his coat. "Don't needs the coat either, you lazy sissy. Youse won't be out theres that long. Just get your ass going." Ted walked over, half staggering, and opened the kitchen door, swinging his arm in the direction of the outhouse. "Com'on. Get going, boy."

"Can…can you at least watch out for me, sir?" Terry's stomach rolled over, panic rising in his voice.

His father wobbled a little as he swung his arm even more exaggerated at the outside. "Just get going. Ain't nothin' wants to eat your scrawny, skinny ass."

Terry walked to the door, fear starting to well up in his gut, his heart racing. He looked out into the dim moonlit night. The moon was at the end of its race across the sky, almost done for the night. Shadows hung at every turn. Right now he didn't feel like peeing.

His father shoved him out the door. He trembled and fell into a small pile of snow. The door slammed shut behind him. Terry was alone, adrift in the night world. He felt the dark dread from all around him close in. A claustrophobic state seemed to invade him all at once. The blowing pines wanted to grab him, snatch him up in their branches, rip his body apart, piece by piece, then place his detached head atop the highest point of the tree, for the birds to come and pick his eyeballs out, and fly away with them.

He staggered to his feet and slowly stepped toward the outhouse. His head jerked hurriedly from side to side, forward and backward, at any little noise or movement. Hulking and shrouded forms rose up all around him, wanting to grab and tear into his body. He knew this wasn't true, wasn't real; but to an eight-year-old boy, the night and all its sinisterness created these images in his young mind. In his fragile young mind.

His hand found the door to the outhouse. A sense of relief came to him. Inside he would be somewhat safe, for a while, till he finished his business and had to step back out into the night and begin his trek back to the house and safety. Terry turned to look around one last time, to really make sure things were all right. Only they weren't all right. His senses broke into a dozen fractured pieces.

A larger, hulking form appeared out of the pines on his left. He smelled and heard it before he really saw it. The smell was one of a wild oldness and dead. A mixture of rot and decayed blood, something that had been tucked away for a long time. The smell of stale sweat and damp fur permeated his nose. The massive form grunted several times. The grunts began low but in a quick procession rose in volume; the last one turned into a semigrowl. It rose up, high in the air before him. The shaggy furriness of it made his blood freeze in his veins. A large bellowing blast of a growl exploded from it.

Insanity stood before him now, in the shape of a grizzly bear. A bear that stood at least ten feet high on its hind legs. The bear was just out of hibernation and was hungry. This hunger and ravenousness led to anger and meanness, and a desire to eat anything it found that fit its criteria for nourishment. Terry was one of those things that topped its list for immediate replenishment.

Crazed fear set in on Terry. Running wouldn't save him, and the small shit shed would provide zero protection. All this filled his head in a flash of sheer terror. He did the only thing left that he could do, he peed his pants.

The grizzly's mouth opened wide, exposing sharp canine-type teeth. Large specks of saliva flew out as it bellowed its hungry crazed growl. Its meaty hooked claws rose above its body, ready to swat Terry and incapacitate him, making him easy prey for dinner.

The next sound was deafening, like a huge, booming thunderclap in a storm. Whatever beastly sounds the bear was making, they were suddenly evaporated away by this new roar.

The fur below one of the bear's raised paws seemed to blow apart, as if a mighty gust of wind blew across it. The section of skin underneath ripped apart in fragments, as the bear was thrown backward.

Through whatever moonlight was left, Terry followed the movement of the animal as it fell and rolled on the ground. Within a second it was back up, its animal instincts of defense kicking in. It set its back legs, positioning itself for a lethal jump. The maw roared back in a sense of rage and anger.

The next explosion caught the fur just under the bear's neck, tearing it apart, lifting the animal off its front paws. Twisting, the bear fell on its side to the frozen ground. Silence fell over the scene. Only the wind was left, talking to the pines.

"That son of a bitch almost got ya!" crackled Ted Graynor. In his two hands, he held a twelve-gauge Winchester pump shotgun. The barrel was still smoking as he held it close to his stomach and hip. He turned toward Terry, swinging the barrel at him. For a brief instant, Terry thought he was going to shoot him.

"Don't worry, boy. He's a dead un. And it only took two shells. Hot damn!" Ted walked over to the boy, slapping a hand on his shoulder. The other hand, in a quick jerking motion, grabbed the shotgun at the pump stock, raising it up and quickly down, locking another shell in the chamber.

"Well, you better go do your thing in the shed. But I bets you've already done it in your pajamas. Man, that thing would've scared the shit out of me, if I was your age. I bets it's at least four hundred pounds, a big un. Weez gonna eat bear for a while." Ted was really cackling as he spoke, adrenaline and whiskey all combining to his nature and attitude.

Within a split second came the huge bellowing growl, and a mighty hooked paw slammed against the head and neck area of Ted. His body and gun flew away into the darkness.

This time there was no urine left in Terry for him to spill out, but there was shit. He felt it leave his bowels, out through his sphincter, and down his legs. He stumbled back and landed on his ass in the cold snow. Shitting his pants was totally forgotten and the least of his worries. The bear, its fur, a bloody and tattered mess, screamed at Terry. Blood mixed with saliva tattooed itself on his face. The animal was fighting, trying to get itself back up on all fours, but having a hard time doing so.

The Winchester spoke again. It seemed as if the bear was kicked in its side, throwing it away from the boy, toward the pines. This time it landed hard and slid. It lay there breathing heavily, in labored gasps, not able or wanting to move at all.

"Terry, get behind me, by your sisters!" Jeanie Graynor now stood next to him, the shotgun in her hands. Holding it tight, she pumped the stock, placing another shell in the firing position. "Do it now, Terry, hurry!" she yelled.

Terry got up and staggered to Clarice and Glennalen, both standing close to the back stairs of the house, sobbing and shivering. Ted Graynor lay several yards from them. Terry looked down and saw the damage the animal had inflicted on him. He could only see the left side of his father's face; the right was in shambles. The bear's mighty swing had crushed in his skull, the talons tearing great rends into the flesh. He could not discern where the eye was; it was all just a bloody pulp. The other good eye stared blankly into space. The mouth, a contorted vision of shock and surprise.

Terry grabbed his sisters and huddled with them as they both extended their arms to accept him. They watched as their mother slowly and with great trepidation approached the bear. It lay on the frozen ground, steam rising from its massive form, mixing with the frigid air. The body lay silent, lifeless, as Jeanie stood over it, shotgun aimed down at it.

The blast made them all jump in shock; none of them expected it. But with this type of animal, its size and breath, one had to make sure of its death. Ted Graynor thought he had killed it, and look what happened to him. It cost him his life.

Jeanie Graynor joined the trio, putting a hand on Terry. "Okay, let's all get in the house. No more we can do out here. I'll make a few calls, get things taken care of. But right now, we all need to warm up." She looked at Terry and sniffed. "And you need to be cleaned up."

"What about Dad?" Clarice mumbled under a sigh of sorrow and tears.

"He'll be okay till morning. Nothing else is gonna bother or hurt him now. He's not really here anymore, is he?"

26

The shriek that came through the holes in the windshield was magnified twofold. A sharp pain shot through Cullum's ears, making him wince and tense up. The thing (or harpy that some of the crew had called it) was looking in from the overhead glass and screaming. He saw it had frozen Terry where he sat. He jabbed Terry hard. "That's what's attacking us! We need to kill it now! Shoot it, Terry, shoot it!"

Terry didn't respond. He sat looking up at this upside-down-positioned creature, as if in a trance. He didn't notice or respond as the harpy reared one arm back and slammed it into window glass in front of him. The glass exploded inward, shards biting into Terry's face, cutting serrated slits, some sticking home like thumbtacks. The harpy's arm extended in, reaching its extreme length, talons closing in on Terry's cheeks and chin, the sharp ends of its fingers grasping and digging in. His skin popped, blood spitting out of the punctures.

This brought Terry out of his daze. He screamed in pain, arms flailing at the creature's arm. He pounded his fists, with all his strength, down on the extended appendix. The harpy's reach was at its longest, not having as firm a hold on him. With one last blow, Terry broke free of its hold. The talons pulled free of his face with a sucking, popping sound. Terry slid out of his seat, crashing to the floor, next to Cullum. He pushed himself back against the wall of the cabin, curling up in the corner like a scared little child. He shakily wiped the blood off his face from the now-closed puncture wounds. All the time his terror-stricken eyes watched the movement of the harpy, as the tears ran down his cheeks.

Cullum wasted no time. Trying to keep a hand on the control wheel, he reached down into his holster, grabbing his firearm. He raised the .45 up at the harpy. Letting go of the wheel, bringing

174

the other hand over to give him a better firing grip on the gun, he took aim. The bomber's nose lurched downward, acting on its own, without anyone controlling its flight. Cullum fell forward into the control panel.

The harpy slid forward, its claws trying to dig in to get a firmer grip. The upper half of its torso now hung in front of the windshield. Its lone extended arm flailed at Cullum, fingers and talons opening and closing, as it reached for him. The sudden dive of the bomber gave Cullum the few precious seconds he needed. Holding the gun firmly with both hands, he fired. Four bullets dug into the harpy at point-blank range. The first two went into the monster's chest, the next two squarely in the face. The head of the creature seemed to explode, like a hollowed-out pumpkin did when a firecracker was lit off inside it.

Heavy black goo splattered and spewed down into the cabin, as all movement from the harpy stopped. Its frantically groping arm dropped limply to the broken window frame. Dead, it slowly slid off the roof of the cockpit and fell into the night sky, tumbling away from the plane.

Cullum quickly grabbed hold of the wheel, pulling with tremendous effort, trying to straighten out the dying bomber. Within several seconds, the plane started to level back out. He could hear and feel the concerned groaning of the remaining engines, as they fought valiantly to accomplish what he wanted them to do.

Cullum looked back at Terry. "Get up now! I need you to help me fly this thing right now! Move your ass!" he yelled, more to get Terry out of his state of traumatic shock than anything else. He knew he was on the edge of insanity, after all he had witnessed; and looking at Terry, he knew he was sliding over the edge, into the abyss.

Terry seemed to snap to a somewhat composed state. He was still shaking, and the tears were flowing like a river, but most of the terror had left his face. He shook his head as if to get clarity then rolled to his feet. He held on to the wall as he slowly grabbed hold of his seat and pulled himself into it. Trembling, he put his hands on the other steering wheel. Turbulence and the bucking of the engines made it jump in his grasp, but he held on to it for dear life.

"Good. That's good. Maybe with a little luck, we can get this baby home." Cullum's tone was more even, trying to calm Terry, settle him down. Both men looked at each one with a concerned look, but a little more assured. The other with what could only be called a shell-shocked persona on it and tears that were starting to dry.

27

Slade Driscal crawled through the small tunnel from the destroyed nose compartment of the cockpit. It was a journey of about four or five feet, but it felt more like forty yards to him. The hatch cover for it was now in reach. When he opened it, he would be just behind the two pilot seats. His right hand was numb, bloodied, useless. The right leg throbbed, blood still seeping from the wounds. He pushed the hatch up and over, with his remaining good hand, and stuck his head up.

"You guys okay? I heard firing."

"Are you okay? When the nose blew, I thought you were gone. What about it?" Cullum motioned toward what was left of the nose.

"Yeah, one of them bastards wanted to get in at me, I guess to eat me. Well, he ate a grenade instead. Those fucking things are gonna kill us and this bomber." He patted the floor compassionately, as if trying to calm and settle the dying plane.

"One of those things, or harpy, as Jessie called them, tried to get in here. Got Terry pretty good in the face." Cullum motioned his head toward his terrified copilot. Terry was white as a ghost. The puncture wounds sported the bottom of his chin and lower cheeks. Little droplets of blood oozed from them and trickled down onto his flight jacket. Small shards of window decorated the rest of his face, resembling a bad case of measles. Every couple of seconds, he would reach up, wipe the blood away, and feel, inspect, his wounded face. When he found a shard, he would delicately pull it out.

"Shot the fucker in the chest and head. He definitely bought the farm."

177

"Yep. They sure are killable. But they're strong and crazy. Just not of this earth." Slade rubbed his limp hand, hoping to massage life back into it, but knowing that it wasn't going to happen.

"They're from this earth, just from a time long past. A long-ago, forgotten time." Cullum looked Slade up and down as he watched him attempt to crawl out of the hatch opening, struggling to get to his feet. "You're lucky you're still alive. I can see you're banged up pretty bad. Losing blood down there?" He saw the blood pooling up on Slade's pant leg, spilling into his boot and onto the floor. His limp arm was also dripping like a faucet, one that needed to be shut off. "Don't know who or if anyone's alive back there. Can't raise anyone on the com. Better see if you can find Lane. Maybe he can help fix you up a little, patch you up."

"I think I will. Skip, can you lend me your pistol? Mine got lost in the skirmish over there." Slade pointed at the mangled nose of the *Fallen Angel*. "Don't know what I'll run into back there." He flicked his head back at the rest of the bomber.

"Yeah, let me fill her back up so you have a full mag, okay? Terry, hold the controls. I'm letting go." Terry looked at Cullum with semi-glazed eyes but nodded in acceptance. The plane jerked and bounced up and down, as he let go of the wheel. Terry quickly held on and straightened it out. "If you get to someone's com, call me. Let me know the situation," Cullum said as he pushed more bullets into the magazine, slamming it home into the pistol and handing it to Slade.

"Will do, Skip."

Cullum held the gun between him and Slade, looking at him for a moment. *This time*, he thought, *I'm bringing everyone home that I can. I'm not giving in. This isn't the Sahara. I've got a bomber under me that's still flying. God willing, I'm getting them and it back to the base.*

28

The wall of sand rose in front of them, like a never-ending sea of grit and debris. It came out of the northeast with a vengeance. One could see the wind swirl in different shapes and patterns inside the towering storm front. In some portions of it, the sand was of a lighter quality; in others, it was dark, foreboding, as if the sand was gathering more in one area than another. It brought no rhyme or reason to its nature.

"This is *Golden Goose* to the rest of the flight. This sandstorm is going to hit us in another minute. I'm taking my plane up to try and fly over it. The rest of you can follow or try to outdistance it on the left or right. Good luck. See you in Algiers, over."

That was the last communication Cullum Davis had with Flight Group 205. It was the fall of 1942. His bomber, *Alley Cat*, was one of a group of five Boston Mk III light bombers, headed for Algiers, in North Africa. They had arrived by ship in Casablanca, Morocco. Their bombers had then been semi-reassembled and refitted. The Allies thought it better to do it this way instead of flying and landing the planes on the shores of Algiers, while the invasion and fighting were still going on there. They deemed it too messy. It would be easier to have the group fly from the already-secure Casablanca airfield, across the vast Sahara Desert, and hopefully land at the airfield in Algiers, providing it had been captured by the Allied forces.

The invasion was already two days in. Word had gotten back to them the airfield was in their possession, so there would be no problem in landing. The one big problem staring them in the face was the mighty Sahara, a very intimidating and unforgiving desert. The air group would only be flying over the northern tip of it. The distance from Casablanca to Algiers was 757 miles. Their commander said that wasn't too bad of a distance, especially since it would be a day flight. Yes, not too bad at all, as long as everything went right, no monkey wrenches thrown into the works, as they say. Well, this sandstorm was one massive, major monkey wrench.

The flight was over halfway to their destination. It was a beautiful, clear sunny day. This was normal when it came to weather in the Sahara. Just about every day was sun drenched in the desert. There was very little precipitation to be had. The desert looked like one massive sea of sand. Its tall dunes resembled the crests of high waves in the ocean. Once in a great while, they could see some vegetation, but that was far and few.

The weather reports they had gotten before the flight hadn't mentioned any storms on the horizon. But it had been said that this type of event happened quite frequently without any warning. It had something to do with the heat and circulation of the winds in the atmosphere, sometimes coming out of nowhere on the drop of a dime. Cullum saw the sky darken miles away. The speed of its travel was impressive. Within five minutes it was on them.

Cullum saw his commander of the flight pull the nose of his bomber toward the sun and gain altitude, followed by another plane. Two other crafts went left, or west, to hopefully outrun it. Cullum's decision, right or wrong, was to go right, east, to get around it. He kicked himself afterward; he should have followed the commander and tried to go up and over. But he was a cocky young captain. This was his first assignment and flight. He thought he knew what he was doing. He thought so until five minutes later after he had banked to the east.

He realized the storm was too massive and wide, it ran almost to the horizon. He didn't want to get hit by it traveling parallel to it; so he turned into the wall of sand, trying to climb, gain altitude.

The storm front hit his bomber like a large wave breaking on the rocks on a shoreline. The plane groaned and shuddered in shock, the engines whining at a high pitch. He realized quickly that he had to level out, fearing that having the belly of the plane taking the brunt of the blast might send it tumbling end over end and to their deaths. The sand sounded like small rocks pinging against the windshield and propellers. This design of bomber was small, its type called light, only carrying two engines. He didn't have the luxury of four, like a heavy bomber would have.

"Goddamn. This is one hell of a storm, isn't it, sir?" his copilot, Lieutenant Harold Landers, shouted over the loud din of sand and wind pelting the plane.

"It sure is. Hold the wheel steady and tight, Harry." A look of concern came over Cullum's face. They had been flying at five hundred feet; they were now at a thousand.

"Joe, come in," Cullum called over his headset to his radioman, Joe Reyes.

"I'm here, Skip," he replied.

"Try to get *Golden Goose* on the radio. See if they made it over this mess."

"Okay, over."

Anxiety and fear began to creep into the back of Cullum's mind. He didn't know if the plane could stand up to this kind of thing for long. Plus the fuel capacity he had was only good for the trip there; there could be no deviations. Fighting the storm, the wind resistance, would eat up a lot of that fuel, leaving him short on getting to his destination.

"You think we'll use up more fuel fighting this?" Harry Landers asked.

"I was already thinking the same thing. I think it will, just like heading into a strong headwind."

"Skipper? I can't get anything on the radio. This stuff is just too much interference, over," Joe Reyes called back over the plane's radio.

"Okay, Joe. Just keep trying, over." Cullum called out to his navigator and bombardier, Jim Covanski, "We still on the right heading, Jim?"

"Yes, sir. Still headed north. Can't see nothing, but the compass tells me where we're headed."

"Well, crew, I guess we'll just keep flying and see what happens," Cullum replied to his small crew, and for the next twenty minutes, there was silence, just the heavy pelting of the sand and the roaring intensity buffeting on the bomber.

"Cullum, I'm looking at the gauges. Don't know if you were? But we're starting to lose more fuel, and the engines are heating up fast." Harry finally spoke, his index finger tapping the gauges in front of him.

"I know. I've been listening to the engines. Could tell they're starting to lose power. It's the goddamn sand. Probably tearing the insides of them apart. Filling them, through every little nook and cranny, with that stuff."

They both watched the altitude gauge as the bomber slowly started an unrequested descent. Their one thousand feet flying height was now down to eight hundred feet.

"Joe, send out an emergency broadcast. Tell whoever we're about two hundred miles or so from Algiers, due south," Cullum said over his mic, knowing it wasn't going to amount to anything; no one would receive it.

"Okay. Don't think anyone will hear."

"I know. Just do it, okay?" Cullum looked at Harry. "Looks like we're gonna have a sand landing."

"Hot damn. Can't wait," Harry replied, a sarcastic smirk came over his face.

"Jim, you better get out of the nose. When we land this crate, and we're going to, the nose will be the first to get the impact. Joe, you and Jim strap yourselves in. This could get very bumpy, over."

"Roger that, Skip," both men replied.

"We're at four hundred feet, falling fast!" Harry exclaimed. They could hear the engines dying, starting to choke, flailing with the last gasps of energy.

"Hopefully we don't land in a gully or straight into the side of a large dune. You can kiss our asses goodbye if we do." Cullum was peering intently out into the swirling sand. Harry was looking down, trying to see any ground.

"I've still got some more living to do, although I guess if the sand doesn't get me, the Nazi bullets will. Can't get a fucking break, can I?" Harry snorted a small chuckle.

A small gulp of an explosion shot out of the starboard engine. It was followed by some sparks, but no fire of any kind. If there was, the sand would have quickly extinguished it. The prop came to a startling stop. With that loss of power, the plane dipped dramatically to that side.

"Hold on tight, son! The hairiness has started!" Cullum yelled as he gripped the wheel, trying to compensate for the sudden power loss.

"I killed the fuel for the starboard engine. Altitude is two hundred feet, falling fast." Harry strained his neck looking out the side window, praying for any glimpse of something.

A loud pop bang came from the port engine, as the propeller came to a slow halt.

"That's it, we're going in. Get ready, guys. I'm looking for a good spot," Cullum said as he keyed his mic.

"One hundred feet."

"Start looking. Tell me what you see?" Both pilots looked down into the sandy soup. The bomber was leveled off and gliding now, through the buffeting storm. Wind gusts pushed it up and down.

"Fifty feet. Anything?"

"Nope. Nothing but blowing sand."

At twenty-five feet, Cullum started to make out the sandy floor below them. At ten, he could see a little of their trajectory in front of them.

"Dune on the right, watch it!" Harry yelled and pointed toward a sand dune of about twenty-five feet.

Cullum pulled the flaps and twisted the wheel to compensate. But it was too late; the starboard wing tip caught the dune, twisting the bomber at an angle. The port wing dropped, dragging into the packed sand floor. The frame of the plane screamed in pain as a tearing, ripping sound came from it. The next instant the whole port wing broke away from the main body, turning the bomber over upside down and sending it tumbling across the desert floor.

Cullum heard the other wing break free, as he closed his eyes to the impact and the resulting rolling of the bomber. His head and shoulder felt the effects of the 360-degree spin on the sandy sea of the Sahara. He felt sharp pain in his collarbone; a blow to his head brought stars and darkness for a moment. Then, as quickly as it started, the sound of ribbing and framework being demolished stopped. The crash was over. The plane creaked and groaned one last time as it came to a rest.

To Cullum's amazement, after all the rolling, the plane sat in a sort of upright position. The windshield in front of him was still in one piece. His side window did not fare so well; it was completely gone. The wind and sand whipped in sharply through it.

Cullum looked over at Harry; he seemed to be in one piece. He was trying to shake his head, trying to extract all the cobwebs. "You, okay?"

"Yeah. Just feel like somebody gave me a quick and thorough beating all over. How 'bout you?"

"Same here. Got punched a couple times, pretty good, feels like." Cullum unstrapped his seat harness and tried to get up. The main body of the bomber lay at a slight list to port, so he was careful as he stood. He gingerly put weight on his legs checking for any breaks or injuries, feeling and looking at the rest of his body for any damage.

Harry tried to stand and quickly collapsed back in the seat. "What's up? You okay?" Cullum asked.

"A little pain in the side. I'm gonna sit a minute, catch my breath. I'm fine," Harry said as he pulled off his flight helmet and eased back in the seat.

"Stay here. I'll check on the others." Cullum carefully walked out of the cockpit and toward the back of the plane. The cockpit seemed untouched compared to the rest of the bomber. The tail section lay at a ninety-degree angle to the body, almost ripped away. The ribbing and framework were severely twisted and bent. Large holes of missing and ripped fabric were gone or hung down in long rends like torn tissue. The wind and debris howled through the wounded holes. Jim Covanski and Joe Reyes lay motionless on the floor of the dead plane. They were still strapped into their seats, much smaller than the pilot seats, but harnesses still intact. The rolling of the plane had broken their seats away from the main frame, though. Cullum knew they had to have taken a wild and hard ride when they tumbled across the desert carpet.

He knelt down beside them, touching Jim. "Jim, you okay, fella?"

Jim groggily answered back, talking very faint and weak, "Not really, Skip. Something happened to my leg. I'm on fire from my shoulder down to it."

Cullum peered down at his legs through the gloom of light barely pouring into the cabin. Jim's right leg from the knee up was okay; from the knee down was the problem. His foot and shinbone sat at a forty-five-degree angle from his knee. The shoulder wasn't any better. A large gash of a wound ran from it down to his rib cage, bleeding profusely. It was as if someone had taken a jagged knife, jerked, and pulled it down his body. His eyes looked above Jim and spied a broken, ragged chunk of plane frame jutting out, with bits of uniform on it. He knew what the culprit of his wound was immediately.

"Let me check on Joe. Then I'll fix you up, okay?" Jim nodded weakly in agreement.

The whole time of talking with Jim, Joe had not moved or made a sound. As Cullum crawled over to him, he knew instantly there was no way of helping him. Joe's eyes stared blankly up at the ceiling of the cabin, his mouth agape. The neck told the story. It lay at a grotesque angle from the rest of the body. It had snapped violently, ending his life.

"Let me go get the first aid box. I'll be right back." He patted Jim softly as he walked past him, back toward the cockpit.

"The storm seems to be letting up," Harry stated, a little more energy in his voice.

Cullum saw a little more life in him now. "Yeah, looks like it might be ending, blowing past us." Cullum put a hand on his shoulder. "How do you feel? Think you could come back with me and help?"

Harry looked at Cullum with a shocked, worried look. "Why, what's happened?"

"It's Jim. His legs broke pretty bad, and he's got a bad wound. We need to try and stop the bleeding."

"Sure, let's go." Harry nodded and grabbed the first aid box on the wall by his seat.

Jim had unbuckled himself and was trying to roll out of his seat, as the pair approached. "Hold on there, soldier, don't move. We gotta fix you up first before you can move around." Cullum and Harry gently moved him to a semi-lying position up against the wall of the bomber.

"What about Joe? He okay?" Jim asked between grimaces.

Cullum shook his head negatively and spoke softly. "He bought the farm. Crash, broke his neck. He probably died instantly."

"I sure hope so," replied Harry, as he looked over at Joe's motionless body.

*****

The storm had finally left, leaving the sun to sparkle down on the destroyed bomber. It was late afternoon as the two pilots sat around Jim, talking.

"Well, we've got your wound patched up. It's not bleeding too bad now." Cullum looked over at Harry, knowing he was stating a lie. He knew Jim needed better medical attention than they could give.

"What we need to do now is set that leg." Cullum motioned down at Jim's grossly bent appendix.

Harry pulled a small flask from out of his flight jacket. "You need to take this all down. It'll help some when we do it."

Jim grabbed and shakily drank the contents, handing back the empty container. "Okay. When you do it, do it fast, right?"

"Sure thing. You might pass out, but that's good. When you wake up, you'll feel better."

"Yeah right." Jim shook his head pensively.

"Hey, just think about something else. Like all that pussy we're gonna get when we get to Algiers," Harry said with a hopeful grin on his bruised face.

"Hell, it'll be all gone. Those bastards in the infantry will have got it all before us," Jim said, a weak grin appearing on him.

Cullum had positioned himself down by Jim's leg as the other two talked. With a quick press and jerk, he snapped the bones back in a somewhat acceptable position. Jim yelled in a quick scream and then passed out. "Okay, let's get him splinted. Then we gotta bury Joe."

"Whatever you say, Cullum. You're in charge." Harry did a fast and comical salute, all the time knowing there was nothing funny about their situation.

*****

It was dark by the time Jim woke back up, shivering. He could feel the cold around him, figuring it was just the injuries that had brought that on. He did not realize that November in the Sahara, the nights got really cold.

A fire was blazing nearby, in the open section of the tail, where it had been so savagely torn apart. He still lay against the wall of the craft, a pillow of jackets behind his head. Harry and Cullum were feeding stripped parts of fabric and wood into the firepit in the sand. Smoke and sparks of flame drifted up into the starry night sky.

Harry turned his head to check on Jim. "Hey, you're awake." He got up and knelt beside him, opening a canteen of water, putting it to his mouth. "Take a little water. It'll help. If you still feel groggy, it's 'cause I gave you some morphine. Hope it's helping with the pain."

"I hurt, just not as bad as I thought I would." Jim took another gulp of water and then pushed it away.

"Well, when it wears off, you will." Harry closed the cap on the canteen and set it aside.

"You hungry yet?" Cullum had walked over and joined the conversation.

"Nope. Just tired."

Cullum grabbed a blanket and laid it over him. "Looks like you're starting to shiver. This and the fire, I hope, can help keep you warm." He covered Jim as well as he could with the skimpy army-issued blanket. "It'll probably get down in the forties tonight. It doesn't stay warm all the time in the desert, like everyone thinks."

"Here, I'll give you my blanket. I've got the fire. I can sit closer to it, to stay warm." Harry laid a second blanket on Jim, tucking it in around him.

"What's gonna happen to us, Skip?" Jim asked in a feeble whisper.

"Well, the radios done in. We've only got what rations and water we were able to salvage. It will last about a week, maybe stretching it thin, two weeks. So I think we need to start heading north to Algiers." Cullum pointed off into the distance. "But right now, get some sleep. We'll talk about it more in the morning."

Harry and Cullum walked back over to the fire, as Jim settled in back to sleep. "What we gonna do about him?" Harry nodded back over his shoulder at Jim, keeping his voice to a low murmur.

"We're going to take him with us. He needs help bad. The legs set and splinted, but I know infection's going to set in soon. His shoulder's the other problem. It's still bleeding, and at a good rate. We used up what antibiotics we had on him, but I don't think it will be enough."

"What we gonna do, carry him? That's gonna be hard, the way he's all busted up." Harry looked pensive as he talked.

"We'll tear off a section of the wall from the plane, use it as a sled. Lay him on it. We've got our chutes, tie them to it, and you and me drag him." Cullum put his hands over the fire, rubbing them together for warmth. "That sound good?"

"That sounds like a plan to me, Cull. We'll drag him as long as we can." Harry knelt, grabbing a tin of K rations, popping the lid, digging a finger in, pulling out a chuck of food (if you could call it that), and putting it in his mouth. "Right now, let's eat."

*****

The sun was almost straight up in the sky. The temperature had risen considerably since the night. Even though it got down right frigid at night, the days turned into a blistering affair.

"I bet you it's at least eighty-five degrees now," Harry said, wiping sweat from his brow.

"I know it is. Let's take a break." Cullum motioned to stop. Both men looked back at the direction they had come, the long, furrowed depression of their makeshift sled running back from the direction they had just traveled.

"Bet we covered at least five miles. Don't you think?"

Cullum looked up at the sun starting to blaze in the sky, heating up their whole surroundings. "Think we can cover more ground at night. We don't have the luxury of a fire to keep us warm. The fact of us moving will keep the blood warm and flowing. During the day we can hunker down and sleep." Both men looked dubiously down at Jim. The bandage for his wounded shoulder was soaked in blood, the overflow dripping down onto the fabric material of the plane's wall, now his own personalized stretcher.

"The poor guy ain't doing so good. We barely got any food or water in him this morning, before he conked out again," Harry conceded to Cullum.

"Probably better this way. We'll give him what morphine we have left, keep him as comfortable as possible. That's all we can do."

"You're right. I'm just saying his odds aren't very good."

Cullum looked around at the massive expanse of sand. "I really don't think none of our odds are good right now. Let's walk a couple more miles, then rest so we can start again when the sun goes down." Both men grabbed a handful of the parachutes, put it over their shoulders, and started dragging their sleeping cargo through the sand.

*****

As the group came to the rise of the sand dune, they rubbed their eyes in disbelief. Below them, about a hundred yards away, sat a small oasis. There were maybe ten or twelve palm trees, interspersed with some brush and bushes. In the middle was a small pool of water. A luscious, cool, lifesaving elixir of fluid.

"Do you see what I see?" Harry yelled, pushing Cullum's shoulder hard.

"Yep. Thank the Lord. Let's get Jim and us down there pronto." Cullum and Harry started down the slope in a swift walk-run, trying to keep the sled angled up so Jim wouldn't slide out.

They got to the edge of the oasis and smelled the freshness of the trees and bushes, the life essence they were emitting. The water beckoned them. They dropped the sled and ran to the small pond, knelt at its edge, and slammed their faces into the liquid gold. The semicoolness of the water brought them back to life. They drank for a while. When they had had their fill, they dragged Joe over to it, splashing water on his face and body. Jim woke in a feverish start, but in a second of the water soaking his face, he was grinning.

"That feels so fucking good" was all he could say.

Cullum and Harry sat against the trunks of two palms, while Joe remained on his stretcher, but under the shade of the trees. "We'll fill our canteens up, stay the rest of today and tomorrow, then leave for the north that night. Okay?"

"That's a good plan, Cull," Harry chirped, arms behind his head.

"Hey, Skipper. What is that on the far ridge of that dune?" Jim asked, his head turned to the north, looking at the dune.

"Looks like people. Maybe four. They're headed this way." Harry was up, cupping his eyes, looking. As they got closer, the group could see they were carrying large pitchers on their shoulders.

"I think they're coming here for water. They must have a camp or village close by. Hope we can get help from them." Cullum was standing and speculating.

The closer the group got, the more it became evident they were women. Their small size and the way their hips swayed back and forth assured the men that they were female. This band of women was covered head to toe by a silky fabric, a haik. This was normally worn by people in this region. The only piece of skin or flesh visible was around their eyes. As the women got to the edge of the oasis, they all waved in a friendly gesture. The men reciprocated in kind.

"Do you speak English?" Cullum asked.

To his surprise, they did. "Yes, we do. Are you English soldiers?" the lead woman asked, as she stepped forward.

"We're bona fide Americans. That's what we are," Harry said proudly, almost laughing with glee.

"Our plane crashed back south." Cullum pointed back from where they had traveled. "We've been traveling for weeks. Food and water gone, till we got here. The oasis saved us."

"The oasis saves us all. We come here when we are close, to get water. Our camp is about a half day's journey that way." The female pointed in the direction over the northern dune.

"We have a man, hurt bad. Can you help us with him and get us to Algiers?" Harry pointed over toward the stretcher with Joe.

"Yes, yes, we can. But first let us attend to your injured one and give you what food we brought with us." All four women put down their ceramic pitchers and gathered around Jim. They touched and examined him with great intent.

The women had pouches of food, containing dates and dried meat. They offered them to the starving trio. "We don't want to take all your food. What will you have to eat?" Cullum asked, his eyes and mouth watering at the sight of food.

"We can do without for now, till we get back to camp. You brave and beautiful men need this now. Eat, eat it all," the lead woman declared. The rest of the women giggled in response.

Harry didn't wait for a reply from Cullum. He grabbed some of the dates and ravenously devoured them. Cullum waited a second and then did the same. The fruit had a pungent perfumy odor but tasted sublime to their empty bellies.

With their bellies content, the two pilots sat against the trees and watched as the women now attended to Joe. They ceremoniously took his bloody dressing off, cleaned his wound, and dried it. To the two men's amazement, they proceeded to strip him of his clothes and wash his naked body. It seemed like they examined every inch of his body with fervor and glee.

The sun was now in its setting state, running down toward the western horizon and night. Cullum looked over at Harry. He was in a state of semisleep, his eyes opening and rapidly closing, trying to fight off the impending dream world. Cullum felt his eyes and body getting heavy, too heavy, he thought. Something was amiss. Even being tired from their long trek through this barren land, he knew tired; this was something totally different. He had never felt like this before. His body seemed to be completely shutting down.

His mind and eyes were still functioning as he watched the females begin to take their garments off. They disrobed with a sexual relish. They wore nothing underneath their main haik robe. Their soft supple skin was soon exposed for all to witness. One of the lithe women cuddled up next to Harry and rubbed her pear-shaped breast against his mouth, slowly pushing its erect nipple into his mouth. His eyes opened in shock and a sexual arousing.

Cullum's skin started to tingle and become numb. He felt as if he was staring down a long tunnel. The lead female of the group, Sliwo, he had learned in talking to her, now stood over him disrobing. Her hair was long; the color of a sultry brown, it fell to her shoulders. As she slid the garment to her hips, her large breasts bounced in sensual delight. Her garment dropped at her feet, revealing her crotch, hairless, and glistening in sweat. As she stepped away from her robe, Cullum's heart raced in terror more than sexual arousal. Her feet were more like a horse's hooves, sharpened claws at the tips.

"I want you badly, American soldier," she proclaimed as she knelt down in front of him. Her hands deftly undid his pants and slid them off. He was naked from the waist down as she purred over his aroused member.

Cullum looked over at Jim on his stretcher, scrubbed clean, naked to the world, but totally asleep, as if in a coma. The two naked females attending him rubbed and licked his body joyously. The female closest to his head thrust her hands and arms up to the now-twinkling stars, as if offering him up to some greater power, the other woman talking, incanting, in some unknown gibberish. The praying female brought her hands back down to his chest, then leaned her head down and into his throat. With a deep and hard bite, she pulled away a chunk of flesh and tendon, blood running out from her mouth, down onto her pert breasts. Cullum watched, aghast in horror, as the blood lingered on her nipple, then was quickly licked away by the other woman.

Cullum's gaze found Harry, whose body was now in bloody tatters. Loose pieces of skin were ripped and draped on his chest. Cheek flesh hung in long bloody strips from his face. The female's hands were now sharp claws rending his body apart. Harry's body jerked in its death throes, his eyes wide open in terror and shock.

Cullum looked back down at his female devil. Her eyes had the look of a cat's, sparkling a rich yellow-gold color. Her teeth had turned to fangs, sharp and deadly. He sat viewing all this, paralyzed to the core, unable to move a muscle. He now knew he shouldn't have eaten their food. It was tainted, made to cause this effect.

"My friends and I always find our food at this oasis. Sometimes it is far and few. Sometimes we wait forever. But when it comes, we enjoy it to its utmost. We were almost starved to death, before you three came along. Now we feast for a long time."

Cullum watched in unbelievable terror as she opened her mouth wide and bit down, hard, on his rigid member. He jumped up in a state of fading sleep and nightmare, grabbing at his crotch, finding everything still there, attached, safe. It was just a dream, a horrific one at that, but nothing more. He looked around. It was late afternoon. Night would arrive in about an hour. All three of them lay in the shade of several small ragged trees. It was all they could find to protect them from the sun's heat and glare. It was going on five days now. Their journey out of this hellhole was still proceeding at a slow pace. Their water and food supplies were getting very low. Water would be gone after tomorrow, food maybe a day later. He gave Harry a soft tap to wake him up.

Harry jumped with a start. "Wow. I'm having some wild dreams."

"It ain't just you, brother. Me too, and they're not all roses either. Night's coming. We gotta get going." He could feel the temperature and air already starting to change. A brisk coolness was starting to waft across the dunes.

"Cullum!"

"What?"

"He's dead. Jim's gone" was all Harry could get out, as his hand rested on Jim's chest.

Cullum looked over at Jim and knew immediately. His eyes and mouth were semiopened, his head tilted far to the side, leaning over, way too far. A new heavier pool of blood had formed underneath his bandaged wound, puddled up on the stretcher. He reached his hand over and felt for a pulse. "He's done."

"Shit. I knew it was getting close. He wasn't talking or making noises anymore, wouldn't eat or drink. He was really burning with a fever." Harry shook his head in despair.

"Yeah, I kept smelling his leg. It was getting worse with infection. Well, let's dig him a hole and put him in. That's the least we can do." Cullum got up.

Harry rubbed his side and winced in pain. "Then we gotta get moving. I don't want to end up like him."

*****

The sun was behind them as they hurried. Harry looked nervously over his shoulder. "They're still following us. I think they're gaining ground."

"Then keep moving, dammit!" Cullum yelled, trying to pick up the pace. But he knew they couldn't. They were tired, dead tired. Harry stumbled, trying to walk faster and still keep an eye on the pair following them. He had lost all his dexterity being out here in this godforsaken wasteland; it just wasn't there. As he fell, he reached out for support from Cullum. It was a domino effect. His weight was too much for Cullum to compensate for, trying to walk with what meager energy he had left. The pair went down, landing hard; but in the soft sand, nothing was injured. They both crawled to their feet, spitting granules out of their mouths.

Cullum stood and gazed at the figures trailing them. There were two, walking—maybe the right word would have been "staggering"—toward them. Still, their stagger was constant, never a break in the stride. He knew they would catch him and Harry before the next dune. "We stand and fight!" Cullum pulled his .45 out of his side holster.

"No, let's keep moving. Please, let's just keep going." Harry grabbed Cullum's arm, trying to weakly pull him back into a gait.

"We're too weak. No water or food for four days now. We won't make it to the next rise. No, we make our stand here and now." Cullum grabbed the front of Harry's tattered shirt, his eyes gleaming grim determination.

Harry lowered his head in defeat. "All right, all right. Let's just end this then."

Another hour, it would be dark. Cullum didn't want to fight in the dark, no way. He turned and started walking toward the advancing figures.

"What the hell are you doing?" Harry yelled, grabbing for Cullum.

"Finishing this right now!" Cullum brought the gun up as he advanced. It was shaking in his weakened hand.

Harry stumbled after him, bringing his gun out of its holster, preparing for the confrontation. Within a minute, the two groups were thirty yards apart. Cullum watched as the pair in front of him lurched from side to side, as if in a death walk. At twenty yards, he was certain it was a death march.

The two figures were Jim Covanski and Joe Reyes, both dead to the world for over a week, going on two. The clothes they had on hung on them in tatters. If they weighed a hundred pounds each, they were lucky. Their skeleton look was magnified by their skin. It had an old grayish tint to it, wrinkled and shriveled, in an almost mummified state. The eyes sat deep in their blackened sockets, never blinking, just keeping a dead gaze on their intended victims. The birdlike arms, swaying in unison at their sides, now lifted up in a grabbing, clawing motion at Harry and Cullum.

At ten yards, Cullum fired his gun, two bullets striking Joe in the chest. Large puffs of dirt and sand exploded from the body, as if that was all that existed in the body of the man. Cullum saw no trace of blood at all exit the frame. The thing that was Joe staggered back slightly from the impact, shook off the impacts, then righted itself and resumed its forward progress. Harry's gun answered in response to Cullum's, a bullet striking Jim dead center in the forehead. No blood or bone spewed from the hole that was created, just a large cloud of sandy dust. It too staggered backward, but seeming to have no effect, it continued its walk toward them. The two men watched, amazed, as the large hole in its head quickly closed back up to just an indentation of shriveled skin.

Feverishly both men fired continually at the dead things advancing on them, with no effect of stopping their forward momentum. The guns finally clicked empty with the things just feet from them. Harry screamed in fear and terror as Jim Covanski grabbed hold of him and leaned in to bite with ragged, ancient teeth.

Cullum threw his pistol at Joe Reyes, striking him in the head; it staggered the thing for just a moment. Then, with cold, dead eyes staring up at him, it opened its mouth, revealing teeth that were ready to bite, to tear him apart and eat him. He heard himself scream in terror.

This brought him to his senses. He was breathing hard and sweating as he bolted forward in a sitting position. Another goddamn nightmare, he told himself as he looked around.

It was midday, hot and sticky, way over eighty degrees, probably closer to ninety, he figured. They had collapsed here at daybreak, at the slope of a large dune. One they hoped would give them some shade from the sun, especially if they stayed on its northern side. The shadow it would cast might give them a little respite. A little was better than none at all.

The sun had been tearing them up for the last couple of days. The area they were in had no trees or bushes to hide under for shade. Mostly they just used their shirts for makeshift tents, propping them up and lying under them to shelter from the sun's rays. It provided whatever little shade it could, but by now the sun and heat had done their damage. Their skin had gone through the whole process, from reddening to blistering, and now back to deep browning and shriveling.

They had been without food or water for days now. Death was getting near; their luck had run out. Whatever luck that was sure hadn't amounted to much. They were both beyond weak and drained; it was to the point Cullum thought that maybe they should just lie here and wait for death. In the back of his mind, his wife, Jane, would appear. She would be holding their little son, Thomas, tightly in her arms, both of them waving madly to him as he left for the war. He wished he was with them now. That thought and picture was the only thing that kept him going. Kept him wanting to stay alive, fight for life.

Cullum thought he had maybe a day or two left, but Harry was fading faster than he was. Over the last couple of days of travel, he had caught him holding his side whenever they would stop, as if it pained him deeply. His skin had a different look to it besides the normal drying and shriveling-up look, more of a waxy paleness. He thought he knew the problem but needed to talk to Harry about it, not that it would matter for them in the long run. They were dead men if help didn't arrive in the form of water and food.

Harry came around from his sleep about a half hour later. Beads of sweat were flowing off his forehead, his face hollow and sunken. "You don't look so hot, Harry. I know I don't, but…"

Harry stopped him before he could finish what he wanted to say. "I can't go any further, Cull. I've tried, but I know I'm done. I wanted…to say something after Jim went but decided not to. I…I guess I was hoping for the best. That help would come over the dune and save us. Praying for that little possibility that maybe the odds would work out for us. I can…see now that they aren't or won't work out. I'm torn up inside. It was from the crash. I know I got hit hard in the stomach and side when we rolled the plane in the sand. It hurt, but I figured it was just bruising or contusions. But it just kept getting worse. I…kept checking it and knew after a while what had really happened." He raised his shirt up, revealing a large purplish-black area around his stomach and left side ribs. Fluids were building up, storing themselves under the skin, next to organs and other vital body parts. It had a sheen to it that screamed internal damage. Severe damage with blood filling up inside him from a tear or rip of something or organ inside his body.

"You've got internal bleeding for sure, Harry." Cullum shook his head in agreement with what Harry had said and just showed him.

"And it's really hurting like hell now. I was lucky I made it this far. I just kept hoping our luck would change, that we'd get that help."

"I'm sorry, man" was all Cullum could respond. He knew Harry was a goner.

"I know you are. That's why you're still gonna go on and save yourself. You're going to beat this predicament. That's why any of us go forward in life, we strive to find and embrace the future. To find that reward, that happiness, eternal bliss ahead of us. None of us want to stay in the past. That's over, done with. We need to go forward, to find and see the ones we love and hold dear. We need and have to see them again. That's our connection with this screwed-up world. The connection between the planet and our families is a strong one. It goes back all the way to the beginning of man. That connection to love, to live, and strive for life. You have that link on this planet with your family. Your wife and child are out there waiting for you to return." Harry swept his shaky hand toward the north. "They want to feel that love, that connection you have with them. So you're gonna get through this and go home. That's what you're gonna do, and I'm gonna help you do it."

Cullum looked somewhat perplexed by this. Was Harry burning up with fever, delirious, out of his head, saying crazy things? he thought. "I don't understand, Harry."

"I'm going to be dead soon, less than a day. It's just gonna happen. We both know that. But I've got my blood and my flesh that will save you, keep you alive a little longer."

The premise hit Cullum's tired and blistered mind like a sledgehammer. "You can't mean that. I could never do it."

"You can, and you will. You have to, for me. It will be my way of…keeping you moving forward…keeping you alive…so you have a chance of getting back to your life, family, real life." Tears formed in Harry's eyes as he spoke. "In a little bit, I'm going to take my gun, put it in my mouth, and…end my already-dead life. You're going to cut my wrists and collect my blood in our canteens. My blood will be your water… You need that. Cut some of my flesh away, dry it out in the hot sun. It should last for a little bit…nourish you."

"I...I...can't," Cullum stammered, his own tears forming.

"You can. Like I said, you've got to keep moving forward. As long as you've got an ounce of breath left in you, you go forward. I'm just...helping you...giving you a little push." Harry struggled in pain to pull his pistol out of its holster. "Now go. Stand away from me. Turn your back. Once I do it, move your ass and get what you need from me, like I said." Harry waved Cullum away with the gun.

There was nothing else Cullum could say. He knew Harry's mind was made, and how the dice were rolled for him. They definitely had been rolled snake eyes against Harry. He put a hand on Harry's leg and gave it a pat. He got up and started walking away, tears running down his face. He knew this whole thing was a brutal, terrible act; but it was the only act that could save him, get him back home to his family.

"Good luck, Cull. You were a good skipper to have." It was the last thing he heard before the gun went off.

*****

He had been walking for three days now. Walking was the word he used, but it was really more like a mild stagger. The sun was starting to peek its head up on the eastern horizon. In the distance, off to the right, he spied some bushes. Bushes he hoped were big enough to supply him a little shade from the sun. He needed to sleep, rest up. Harry's gifts had gotten him here, but as far as going much farther, he didn't know. He had one canteen of fluid (he couldn't think of it as blood), maybe half full. He had eaten the dried meat. He had cut and dried very little, just enough to replenish him (he had almost vomited the meat up several times as he ate; it revolted him to do it), to get him to this point. But now it was gone.

He stumbled a couple more steps, then heard the noise. A soft rumble of machinery, slightly to his left, north of him. He strained his weary vision, spotting a rising dust cloud, approaching him. Some kind of vehicle was coming his way. Cullum didn't know or couldn't tell if it was a truck or tank. At this point, it didn't matter. At this point, it just mattered that it was another human being who could save him. It didn't matter if it was a Brit or American. Hell, it could be a crummy Jerry, who would take him as a prisoner. At this point, it just frankly didn't matter. Christ, the Nazi might even kill him on the spot. At least the ordeal would be over.

Cullum held his hands high over his head and waved feebly. The vehicle kept coming toward him. It had seen him. His mind raced. He reached and grabbed his last remaining canteen from his belt. Opening the cap, he turned it over; the remaining blood trickled to the sand. The sand eagerly soaked it up. He tossed the canteen away from him. No one needed to know about any of this, what had transpired out here in this sandy, hot hell.

The vehicle came to a stop, twenty yards from him. Cullum's heart beat with joy and sick triumph. No dying today. It was an American armored car, an M8. It sat idling, looking at him. The top hatch opened, and a man's upper torso came up. He wore leather headgear with googles. He quickly grabbed hold of the machine gun mounted by the hatch and trained it at Cullum. Cullum raised his hands in a gesture of surrender.

"No funny stuff, buddy. Who might you be?" the soldier barked over the rumble of the engine.

"Captain...Cullum Davis...United States Air Force," he spat out.

"Well, were you a part of that bomber group from Casablanca that was headed to Algiers?"

"Yes...yes, I am. Our plane...went down back there." He pointed back south with a waving gesture.

"Well, thank god you made it. One of your planes had radioed through about a huge dust storm. Everyone figured you guys wouldn't make it. They sent us out to look. Found a bomber, a couple miles back that way." The soldier pointed west as he pulled himself out of the vehicle, making his way down the side and landing on the ground. "That one we found, sad thing, was burnt to a crisp, including everyone in it." He talked as he approached Cullum, holding out a canteen, offering it to him.

Cullum grabbed it and greedily drank the precious water. Droplets ran from his mouth down his chin and neck.

"Easy, chum. Take your time. We got plenty more of that." The soldier looked Cullum up and down, examining him. "How the hell did you survive out here, in this wasteland?"

"I...just did. Just kept...moving forward." Cullum felt his stomach turn as he took another swig from the canteen.

29

Slade Driscal turned and stepped out of the cockpit, straight into the face of primordial terror. The thing in front of him was something from the dawn of time itself. Something that had survived and thrived for eons, feeding on other lesser life-forms to sustain itself, eventually finding man and using him for their food supply. It had been around to watch man crawl out of the slime, stand on his hind legs, and progress. All the while it stayed in the shadows, being the quiet predator. It only would come out of its lair every so often to feed and destroy. To wait for the right chance and opportunity to pounce and strike its prey, kill it, and drag it back to the brood, to feed on it.

The screech from the harpy stunned Slade's ears. He hesitated just for that instant, that split second of bringing the .45 to bear on this creature. The gun came up and fired point blank. The harpy was quicker. Its taloned hand swatted the pistol out of his hand and sent it flying.

The shot was meant for the creature's face. Barely missing, the concussion of the discharge caused the harpy to stagger back in shock and pain. Slade tensed himself and sprang with what strength he had at the vile thing. As their bodies collided, he delivered a blow to its head, with his still-usable left hand. Needles of pain laced through his fist, as he reared back to deliver another blow.

Over the ages, the harpy's stamina and tolerance for pain had become twofold. It recovered swiftly and grabbed Slade, running him across and into the wall of the bomber. His head slammed hard against a metal frame post. Stars and darkness flashed before his eyes. The harpy's talons dug into his chest; blood ran from the punctures.

It bit down hard on the top of his left shoulder, digging in with its teeth. Slade screamed out in agony.

The earsplitting blast of the gun and coinciding scream brought Terry Graynor out of his dazed and frightened state, as if a switch had been flipped. He was no longer cowering like the scared little boy of eight. Comrades and friends were getting hurt (and he assumed killed) all around him. He realized he had to do his part, carry his load, to help with this screwed-up situation. The devil had come knocking on this bomber, and he sure as hell wasn't going to let him walk right in. He bolted from his seat, pulling out his .45. He saw the monster slam Slade into the wall and clamp down on his neck. Anger flooded his brain as he brought the gun up and fired. Two bullets dug into the harpy's side, breaking free its grasp of Slade; it twisted and fell to the floor.

The minor victory was short lived. The dead body of Jessie, still hanging in the turret seat, was ripped away, like a piece of wrapping paper, and tossed behind the enraged harpy standing there. Jessie's thick, coagulating blood splattered on Terry's face as he turned to face the demon. "Fuck you," he spat out as he pulled the trigger of his .45. The explosions came in rapid succession as the shells struck the creature straight on. There was a brief look of disbelief on the harpy's face as it was slammed backward. Terry emptied his gun into the tumbling body. He saw the energy in the blazing red eyes twitch and go dark, as quickly as snuffing out a candle's flame.

He turned back to Slade, to find the second harpy picking itself back up. Terry pointed and pulled the trigger of his pistol. A dry click was all he heard. He realized the gun was empty. In a half-crouched position, the harpy began crawling toward him, favoring its wounded side, its mouth dripping a bloody, gooey venom, the eyes burning bright, death and hatred in them. His vision turned to Slade. Bells and whistles went off, as he saw what was going to happen. He spun around and dove for the cockpit doorway, at the same moment screaming at the top of his lungs to Cullum, "Cover, grenade!"

30

Slade folded to the floor of the bomber like a bloody, wet blanket. The pain coursing through his body was now turning to a great numbness. Time slowed around him but rushed like a cyclone through his head. He could see a bright light in the distance, shrouded on all sides by utter blackness. Forms, bodies he could make out, were passing from one end of the dazzling tunnel of light, across it, and into the darkness on the other side. The bodies or shapes were people he knew. Some of them were from long ago, back in his childhood, through his life, to the now present. Some waved as they walked but never stopped. He called to them to stop, help him, get him out of this terrible ordeal; but none ever did. He screamed now, or thought he did, at the top of his lungs. A new form walking stopped, looking intently his way. It seemed to peer and then recognize him. It waved in a frantic gesture and stepped closer. It was a woman, a beautiful woman. She had short black hair, slender, having the look of a lithe cat, dressed in a small diaphanous-type white outfit, one worn by the ancients, back in the days of the Spartans.

The realization came to him now; he knew this woman, this female. But what was her name? He couldn't remember. He had known her from the past, had strong feelings for her, but still the name wasn't there. He had loved her dearly, with all his heart, and had connected with her spiritually as well as physically. Her name and identity were there at the edge of his thought recollection; he just couldn't pull it to the forefront.

His ears picked up the harpy. It was off to his right, growling, a moan of pain mixed in with its anger. It was still alive. The shots that had knocked it down had hurt it but not completed their task. It was starting to move again, getting its bearings back, its adrenaline flowing. In a moment it would be up, ready to attack again, to cause death and mayhem. Not just of him, but to others on this bomber. Others whom he had strong feelings and attachments for, just like the young woman gazing at him. He couldn't let this happen, not like it had happened to the woman. That thought came forward and hit him bluntly, the realization all too clear. The woman had been hurt, hurt to the point that she had lost her life. This wasn't going to happen to his other friends, not if he could help it.

His left arm was still somewhat functioning. The pain and numbness were still there, just being held off; he strained to hold them at a distance. He felt his hand fumble by his belt, feeling for the grenade. Was it still there? Or had it been knocked away when he and the monster grappled? His fingers felt the cold, corrugated metal of the explosive; it was there.

The shadow of the harpy came across the bright corridor of light he was looking into. The woman was blotted out for an instant, as the creature's form went past; but just as quickly she came back into view, still waving enthusiastically, yelling to him, as if from a great distance, not the several yards it seemed she was standing from him. Her voice became stronger, closer, each time she spoke. What was just a mute response soon became a booming chorus. Now, the word hit his brain like a hammer. She was yelling his name over and over. The ringing of it was strong and bold, in a cacophonous chime. "Slade, Slade!"

Her name was Benet. He knew it now. She had loved him, as much as he had loved her. He had lost her years ago, many memories past. He wanted to be with her again, to feel her, love her, envelop her. The rest of this damn world didn't matter to him now. That's how strong the feeling was flowing through him, coursing like a raging river. He needed to cross the bridge, to stand with her in the brilliant light.

Slade felt the pin on the grenade. His lone finger fumbled but finally slid into the ringlet. He pulled it with what energy he had left. The small metallic pin made a popping noise as it left the tiny hole in the grenade. The timer lever set.

He would be with her now. They would be together forever. The harpy in front of him would be gone, sent to its own hell or purgatory. His friends and comrades would be safe.

A resounding blast of noise and light sent Slade Driscal from this plane of existence to the next.

31

Cullum Davis thrust himself off the seat he was on, to his left, jamming himself between it and the side wall under the blown-out window. The eruption of the grenade was a blast of incredible force and fury in the cramped quarters of the bomber. He threw his arms up trying to cover and protect his face, as shards and pieces of fractured debris pelted him and everything around him. The sound of it left a deafening buzz in his ears, blotting out any other sound or noise. He remained balled up for another second waiting for any secondary repercussions from the blast. He lifted himself up after he thought it was all clear. Pain stung his arm, the one he had used to protect his face, closest to the explosion. A piece of shrapnel had pierced his flight jacket and impaled itself in his flesh. The heat of the metal burned his fingers as he yanked it out, throwing it to the floor.

Wind buffeted wildly through the cockpit across his face. His ears were deaf to its sound; all he heard was a buzzing roar in them. He saw the wall separating the compartment from the rest of the plane was completely gone. What was left of it was lying atop the instrument panel and pilot's seats. The port wall of the bomber proper, just behind the cockpit, now had a gaping hole in it. It gave him an unobstructed view of the port wing. The one of two last viable running engines, closest to the body of the bomber, was ablaze and smoking badly. He watched as several small explosions erupted from it, sending more flame and sparks shooting out into the night sky. The prop came to a quick and dead stop.

Cullum's hearing slowly started returning to a somewhat acceptable level. It was still muffled but now able to pick noises out. The wind was whistling and howling through all the open wounds in the bomber. Sparks and pops of electricity fell from the damaged wiring, now ripped apart, hanging from the ruptured overhead electrical troughs.

The bomber was vibrating and shaking with an alarming motion, as if it were having some form or type of seizure. Cullum felt the energy and momentum of the plane start to decrease rapidly. He looked out the starboard cockpit window at his last running engine. It was still alive, maintaining a somewhat respectable whirling prop, but at the same time struggling, doing a jerky dance of its own. He saw hints of smoke and sparks gesturing to him from its body. He knew it was not long for this earth. Even if it was running normally, with three of the four engines now gone, the bomber wouldn't be able to stay up in the air much longer. In another minute or two, it would start to lose levelness and start to drop from the sky. A stall would happen. After that, it would fall into its death spiral, one from which there would be no recovery out of.

Cullum cleared debris off the control panel. Finding the flaps, he extended them, lowering its stall speed, then raised them to get more lift from the plane. He pulled back on the wheel. The bomber responded lethargically, as it fought to his request of rising, telling him it didn't want to stay up in the air much longer. Spying a piece of metal bracing from the destroyed wall panel, Cullum jerked it out of the rubble and wedged it through the steering wheel and into the floor against the control panel. He hoped it would hold the plane in its current pattern for a bit, giving him enough time to do what he had to do.

He heard Terry before he saw him. The pain in his moan said he was still alive, but not doing so well. He spotted his boots under the rest of the debris from the walls and framework. Frantically clearing the pieces away, he had a good look at his injuries. Blood ran from a jagged gash in the side of his head. A large splinter of wood had pierced his side and sat there like a figure on a trophy stand. Without any thought, Cullum yanked the wooden spear out of him. Terry yelled out in a grimace of pain, as he rolled over. "Help me, Cull. Help me."

For a second, Cullum thought he was looking at his old buddy Harold Landers, the copilot he couldn't save from years ago. The expression in their eyes and mouths seemed the same. This time he hoped the outcome would be different for this copilot. He held his hands for a second and spoke to him. "Hang in there, buddy, this time I'm getting you outta this mess."

Cullum looked under his seat, or what was left of it. His parachute pack was in shambles, ripped and torn to shreds from the blast. He looked under Terrys' seat; the blast had spared his to a better degree. The chute pack was torn but still appeared to be usable. It might still function.

Cullum donned the pack on his back, strapping the harness around his legs and arms. He knelt down beside Terry and grabbed hold of him. "Help me get you up the best you can so we can get the hell out of here."

Groans and moans of pain laced Terry's mouth as he pushed himself up with Cullum's support. Terry's bloodied hand slipped on the back of his seat, almost sending the duo back to the floor. Cullum held him tight and jerked him to an upright position. The pain was too intense for Terry; he slumped in Cullum's arms.

"Stay with me, Terry. I know you can do this. Just a little bit more." Cullum spoke into his ear, shaking him a little to get his attention and clarity back. The duo stood side by side as Cullum positioned Terry, putting an arm around Terry's waist and slowly guiding him through the debris. "You can do this. Just put one foot in front of the other." They traversed the destroyed bomber's floor, moving toward the gaping hole in its side. "Slade made a doorway for us with the grenade."

"Poor guy didn't realize that. Just wanted…wanted…to kill the damn beast," Terry said in a feeble croak.

He was leaning on Cullum with all his weight, and Cullum could feel him fading. The hand and arm he had around Terry were damp, soaked with blood. The wood that had impaled him had left a nasty wound.

The bomber started to dip to port. The lone engine, not strong enough to hold the bomber level, was spitting and coughing itself to death. Cullum knew in another minute it would dip even farther to port. Once it did, the plane would go into its spiral, the death spiral. He knew it would be near impossible to jump out of it then.

"We've got to go now, Terry. The plane's gonna tilt a little more and give us momentum to run and jump through that hole." Cullum pointed at Slade's handiwork, as bits of debris and loose items were being sucked out of it by the increasing wind draft. "Just keep your head tucked close to me and hang on tight. You've got to run with me. Your life depends on it. Got it!" Cullum yelled in Terry's ear, making sure he heard and understood him fully. He looked down and saw the left leg of Terry's was perforated with bits of wood and shrapnel darts, as if he had just encountered a porcupine and it had given him a present of its quills. "I know you're hurting, but you gotta hang on. Once we're outta the plane, wrap your legs around me, like you're in love with me!" Terry looked up and smiled a weak grin at Cullum, nodding in agreement.

The bomber was now at a forty-five-degree tilt to port. Larger pieces of debris and equipment started sliding toward the wall and falling out of the wound in its side. Cullum put both arms around Terry in a bear hug. Terry leaned his head down onto Cullum's chest, as if they were going to dance and did his attempt at a hug.

They moved rapidly toward the hole in a walk-run-type gait. Cullum lowered and tucked his head at the same moment they got to the opening. The wind buffeted the pair as they dropped out of the bomber into the black sky.

They did one end-over-end tumble, close to the bomber. Cullum felt the wing of the plane, perilously close, as they slid over and past it. The heavy wind current spat them up slightly and away from the stricken bomber. He counted to five and pulled the rip cord for the chute.

The opening of the parachute sent the duo shooting back up, high in the sky, giving them a good view of the bomber, once called the *Fallen Angel*. She looked like a mighty albatross, dying a slow death. Flames and smoke were pouring from the engine that had taken the brunt of the explosion from the grenade. The last good engine was sparking little firework-like sparks and flames from it. Its finish had arrived. The plane dipped awkwardly to port at ninety degrees, the wing sections standing perpendicular to the earth. That's when it started an end-over-end spiral to the ground and certain destruction. It gave one the impression of something being sucked down a bathtub drain when the plug had been pulled and all the water was going down the hole.

Cullum felt a sad pain stabbing at his heart, a grieving pain. He didn't know who was alive or dead on the bomber. In all the turmoil and speed of the attack, he hadn't gotten responses to the calls he had sent out to the crew. Some could very well still be alive right now, spiraling to their deaths. Or they could all be dead, killed by these demonic creatures.

All he knew for sure right now, at this moment, was that he had saved at least one person. It was a small victory, but a victory none-theless. Terry held on to him grimly and determinedly, legs locked tightly around Cullum's waist, as they floated, slowly, down to earth. His face still remained buried tightly into Cullum's chest. Cullum looked below them. In the distance, he saw the bright glow of flames, indicating where the bomber was in its fall to Mother Earth.

In minutes, they would be on the ground, and the new ordeal of finding help and safety for himself and Terry would begin. This was still enemy territory that they would land in. Maybe patriot help would be below. The French resistance groups fighting the Nazis were all around. Maybe luck could still shine on them. They might still get out of this and back home to their loved ones. The thought of his wife, Jane, and son, Thomas, floated in his mind. Oh how he wanted, needed, to see and be with them once again. Just to be able to touch them, hold them, tell them how much he loved them. To feel their life energy flowing through them to him. Him giving it all back twofold.

All these thoughts were dashed from his consciousness in an instant. Eviscerated from his mind just like his bomber and crew had been. From above and to his right he heard the sound. Cullum had never heard anything like this before in his life. But as clarity and reason rolled over in his mind, he knew what it was. It was the loud, thunderous, flapping of great wings. Not of a large bird, no, but of some winged demon, more deadly than any other winged raptor. It was descending, down, toward Terry and him. He turned his head toward the approaching thing. He had no time to warn Terry or even scream. In an instant it was on them.

32

The bomber was burning, as if it were a Roman candle, the kind a person fired off on the Fourth of July. The flames were intense. They grew brighter every second. Soon the whole plane proper was engulfed in the flaming cauldron.

That's when she saw Cullum. He was trying in vain to climb out of the cockpit glass. His face and hands were bloodied from the shards of the broken windows. Pieces of the shattered glass had stuck into his skin, making it look like a pin cushion. Streams of blood ran from his forehead into his wide, terrified eyes. Soon his clothes became scorched by the licking flames. They smoldered for a brief second then ignited in a fiery blaze. She watched as he tried patting then pounding his body, trying to put out the fires. It was all just a futile attempt. The fires spread, leaving his face the last thing not ablaze. His mouth opened wide, as horrified howling, screams belched out of it. Everything moved quickly. Cullum's head ignited in a splash of fire as if it were a matchstick being struck against a hard surface.

The burning mass of the bomber began its plummet toward the earth. Cullum's blazing body now stood outside the cockpit, on the nose of the craft, whirling around like a maddened dervish. He then threw himself off the burning pyre into the sky, flapping his flaming arms, trying to fly. Whether he was trying to ascend to the heavens or just to get away from the hellish flames, it didn't matter; it was all in vain. He plummeted to the earth, screaming out in pain and terror, as he raced to his death.

That's when Jane Davis screamed and bolted upright in her bed. Beads of sweat dotted her forehead. Her skin felt clammy. It was all a dream, a bad dream, she thought.

"What's wrong, Mommy? I heard you yell," Thomas Cullum said from the doorway of the bedroom, rubbing his eyes with his hands. The four-year-old boy stood in his pajamas peering at her through the darkness.

"Nothing, honey. Just had a bad dream, that's all."

"Was it about Daddy?" he asked as he closed the distance and crawled into her bed.

Jane's blood turned cold in surprise at what he had said. "No, no. Just other bad things. Don't worry, baby, it was nothing." She quickly dismissed the whole incident, trying to steer Thomas away from any of his questions.

"I have dreams about Daddy. Sometimes good, sometimes bad," he said as he snuggled close to her. The summer night was hot and humid, but she knew the boy needed to be by her, to be in her love and safety right now. If he asked about her excessive sweating, she could always blame it on the weather. She dared not let him know it was due to her having one of her own bad dreams about Cullum.

After what he had just said, though, she knew she couldn't let it lie. She needed to know more. "What are your dreams about, the good ones?"

"Those I really like. He is always running and playing with me in the park. The sun is always shining, and everything is nice. I am happy that we are having fun," Thomas half whispered, half talked in her ear.

Jane had always shown Thomas pictures of his father, but the boy had never met him. She had become pregnant with Thomas before Cullum had gone off to war. He had been to pilot school and did all his basic training just as the war was brewing. He had come home for a short leave before he had to report for his new assignment with the air force. She remembered the night she and he had made Thomas. They had a small apartment in San Francisco. After he shipped out, she moved back east. They had made love in the bathtub, candles lit, burning all around them in the darkened room. It was too short of a time together, but it always stayed etched in her memories. Nine months later, Thomas came along. He was born while Cullum was over in England getting ready to ship out to North Africa.

Cullum had kept the letters coming to her and Thomas the whole time he was gone. She cried when he wrote and told her about his crashing and walking through the desert of Algeria. He was vague about it, but she knew it had to have been a very horrible ordeal to go through. She was sure it had traumatized and scarred him for life. Now he was flying missions over Europe, enduring the pains and tribulations of this hellish war. She prayed that the war would end soon. All the papers and radio stations proclaimed the war was going great for the Allied forces, saying the end was in sight. She asked God to watch over Cullum and keep him out of harm's way.

Her nightmares had been occurring for quite a while now. As each night passed, they had gotten more vivid and terrifying. There was always death in the dreams; whether it was Cullum's, Thomas's, or hers, one of them had always died. At the beginning, the deaths had been mild or tame, as deaths go. As they progressed and wore on, they became more brutal and violent. Over time they tore at the fabric of Jane's stability. She kept telling herself that they were just dreams, but the realness and vividness of them made her doubt her mind and sanity. She hoped and prayed she wasn't letting craziness creep into her brain. Thomas needed her the most right now. She was his lifeline to a normal life. With Cullum's parents living in Washington State, she had moved to Boston to be by her mother. But a year after Thomas was born, her mom had had a major stroke that killed her. Less than a month later, both Cullum's parents had died in a car crash. With Cullum off to war, Jane was all he had left in this world.

"What about the bad ones? What are those like, Thomas?" Jane asked, but not really wanting to hear the truth. She knew he really didn't need to relive these traumatic things, over and over. She knew that every time he thought about them, it would tear him up just a little more each time. Her little boy was just too tiny and fragile right now in his young life.

Thomas lay there quiet for a long time, then finally spoke. "I see Daddy always running. He always looks scared, like I do when scary things happen to me. His eyes are big, and he's yelling. I think he's yelling for help." Thomas hugged his mother tight, trying to get as close as he could to her. Jane thought if he could, he would crawl inside her skin for safety. He nuzzled his head under her chin and continued, "I never could see what was chasing him. I didn't know why he was running. But now I do. It's a big ugly bird, Mommy. That's what he's running from. It has big wings and bright-colored eyes that look like fire. Every time I dream, the bird gets closer and closer to him. The last time I had the dream, Daddy was crying hard, because he was so scared of it. The big bird keeps getting closer and closer. I think soon it will get him. It really scares me, Mommy."

Jane could hear and feel his voice and chest heave and knew he was crying. She squeezed him tight with her arms. "Now, now, baby. Don't worry or be scared about that. It's just a bad dream, that's all it is. Your dad is safe and sound. I just got a letter from him today, and he says everything is okay." She stroked his hair gently and kissed the top of his head. "Now just relax and sleep with Mom tonight. Dream the happy dreams about you and your daddy."

Jane lay there a long time before she felt the crying tremors ease up and stop. She finally heard the steady and peaceful breathing from Thomas, knowing he had gone back to sleep. She felt her eyes get heavy and closed them. There were no more nightmares this night for either one of them.

*****

There was a knock at Jane's apartment door. It was about one o'clock in the afternoon. Thomas had fallen asleep on the area rug on the living room floor while playing with his toy trucks and listening to music on the radio. He loved his trucks, especially his fire truck. It was a massive thing made out of a heavy cast iron. Weighing close to two pounds, it could definitely do damage to someone if wielded the wrong way. Thomas liked holding it close to him when he went to sleep. Even at night, he would sneak it into bed with him. No matter how much she protested, he would plead and plead until she finally gave in.

Jane moved quickly to the door. She wanted to answer it before the knocking woke Thomas up. She pulled the door open to find Dillard Hines standing there. He also lived in the apartment building Jane and Thomas were in. His apartment was directly under theirs, on the floor below. He was a tall thin man in his late forties. A single man who stayed to himself, rarely talking to anyone else. He gave Jane the creeps, just by his demeanor and the way he handled himself. She felt he had problems bubbling just under the surface, problems that were not good for anyone, especially her. She had first caught him staring at her. A glance is one thing, but these stares seemed to be undressing her. Her skin always seemed to crawl when she saw him looking her up and down.

But now the uneasiness and creeps had escalated. He started trying to converse with her, she felt in a way trying to connect with her. It had started out with the occasional nod of the head as they passed each other in the halls or steps. But in the last week or so, he had started trying to converse with her. He would compliment her on the clothes she wore or how her hair was done up just right. She would thank him politely and try to move, but he would always try to extend the talk. He seemed to want to read her face and lips as she talked, to gorge on her every word. As they talked, he would move in close. She felt as if he wanted to bask and breathe in her aroma. She felt he just wanted to inhale every inch of smell on her body, to devour it. Most of the time he smelled of stale food or body sweat. He gave off the impression of a man who didn't care one iota about personal hygiene. His clothes were never ironed or crisp but seemed to have been pulled off a pile of them that had been lying on the floor in a heap.

"Well, hello, Jane." Dillard beamed a large smile from his pock-marked face, one that had waged a valiant war with acne, had won the battle, but in the long run lost the war and his good looks.

"Good afternoon, Mr. Hines. What can I do for you?"

She could tell Dillard was nervous. He fidgeted with his hands, rubbing them together and interlocking the fingers several times. He put one leg behind the other, shaking it mildly. But through the nerves and ticks, she saw and felt a cold, calculated evilness radiate from his eyes. He pushed a hand up and through his greasy black hair, fixing his part.

"I just thought maybe you'd like to come down to my apartment to spend some time with me. You know, talk…about things. We could have a drink. You do drink?" he asked Jane but never gave her time to answer. "I have several bottles of different things, booze wise, that is. If I don't have it, I can run out and get it for you. May I add, you look very fetching today."

"I really don't think so, Mr. Hines. It wouldn't be right." This had caught Jane off guard. They had talked in general about common things, but nothing like sitting down and conversing. Besides, she felt conversing was one thing he really didn't want to do with her. The dial on her creep meter pegged into the red.

"Aw…com'on now. I mean we could just sit and talk. I know with your man off to war and such… I don't see you with a lot of people. It's just you and your son. You have to be somewhat lonely. I know I am." He gained confidence as he talked, the nerves falling to the wayside. His eyes glimmered with carnal savageness and lust as he looked her body up and down.

Jane had on a modest dress but still felt on display. She quickly brought up the dish towel she was holding at her side and semicovered her breasts. "Now wait a second. You and I really don't know each other that well. I'm getting the impression that talking isn't the only thing you want. Like I said, Mr. Hines, it wouldn't be right. It wouldn't be proper. I'm not that type of person."

Dillard quickly interrupted her, "Now, now, honey. Jane…that's not what I'm getting at. You've got it all wrong. I just want to talk, get to know you better. Find out your likes and dislikes, maybe even find out we have the same interests or views about things. You know, get comfortable with each other. I am sorry if you're getting the wrong impression about what you think I'm thinking about." He reached out his hand and touched her forearm. Jane felt a cold clamminess in his touch on her skin as his fingers slowly caressed it.

"Mr. Hines, I'm sorry. I don't want to do that, and besides, I can't. Thomas is asleep here, and I don't want to wake him up, to take him to your apartment."

Dillard's grin changed to a more devious pose. "Oh, I don't want you to bring the boy down. No, sir, that wouldn't be good for him. I just wanted you to come so we could get to mingle better. If he's sleeping, let him sleep. He'll be fine in your place, till we're… done, you know…talking."

Jane read the expression on his face and knew she had the right take on the lines of bullshit he was spewing. The man wanted her and wanted her bad. She wanted no part of this man. The vibe coming off him was no good; she felt it in her bones.

"Stop it right there, Mr. Hines. I said no, and that's what it means. Good day, sir." Jane grabbed the door to close it, but Dillard now grabbed hold of her arm a little more firmly. She swung it with a little extra shove, helping to break his grasp on her. He jerked his arm out of the way so as not to get it pinned in the door. She brought her freed arm up and used both to slam the door.

"Mrs. Cullum, Jane. Aww, com'on, that's not what I meant," he returned loudly from the other side of the door.

Jane held her hands on the door, waiting. After a few seconds, she heard nothing else. Finally, she could make out his footfalls as he left and walked down the hallway to the staircase. She put her ear to the door, listening intently. Soon the sound of him descending the stairs, going back to his apartment, came to her. She breathed a small sigh of relief.

*****

Their dinner that night was spaghetti and meatballs. Jane felt like splurging a little with Thomas; this was his favorite meal. She had hoped fixing it would take her mind away from the incident with Dillard Hines. The look and expressions on his face permeated her head, making her feel anxiety.

While Thomas was still sleeping, she hand rolled the meatballs and seasoned them. He woke as she was just finishing them. "Well, Sleepyhead is up. Did you have a good sleep?"

"I saw birds again. They weren't chasing Dad though. They were just flying in a big group. The sky was dark, except for the big bright moon."

"We're not gonna even think about that. Just clear all that out of your head, darling. Tonight, I'm treating you to your favorite meal, spaghetti and meatballs. So get your eating shoes on."

Thomas looked at her oddly. "I've gotta wear shoes to eat?" A sheepish grin appeared on his face.

Jane burst out laughing, Thomas quickly followed. "No, you rascal. I just mean be ready to eat a lot."

Thomas ate ravenously, having second and third helping. He loved spaghetti but loved his mother more. Knowing she had treated him to this, he showed his appreciation this way. After dinner was done and cleared, they sat down and played Go Fish for a long time. Jane even threw in some games of War, just to change up the monotony.

It was close to seven o'clock when she told him it was time to take a bath and get ready for bed. She promised to read him a story before he went to sleep. Thomas lasted a good minute or two into the story from the fairy-tale book before he was sound asleep. Hansel and Gretel hadn't even made it to the gingerbread house and Thomas was snoring loudly. Jane lay in bed with him for close to an hour. His rhythmic breathing and snoring brought comfort to her. She gradually eased herself out of the bed, turned off the small lamp on the nightstand, and silently crept out of the room, closing the door on the way out.

Jane liked this time of the evening. It was her time to sit and relax, to just ponder. She had one guilty vice, cigarettes. Smoking them made her relax and throttle down. She could sit for hours and eventually, if she wanted to, smoke a whole pack. But that wasn't her game. In two or three hours she might go through four or five, at a very leisurely pace.

She would sit on the couch by the big window in the living room, staring out onto Boston's big bright city life, and let her mind float. She would always think about Cullum. What was going on with him, praying God would watch over him. Her chores and work for the next week would filter in to the floating images in her mind. Besides getting money from the military and Cullum, she did some sewing on the side, for everyone in her building and on the block. It wasn't much, but it helped pay the bills.

Tonight, she took to the luxury of her other lone vice. This one she didn't do nearly as often as her cigarettes. She pulled an ice-cold Coca-Cola out of the icebox and gingerly sipped from it. The evening was still hot. She ran the cold bottle across her forehead, getting an instant cooldown. She was in pure heaven. She wanted to turn on the radio but decided against it. No matter how low the volume was, it might still wake up Thomas.

Off in the distance, she saw small flashes of lightning. The radio announcer, on the afternoon report, had said a storm was brewing out over the ocean and might make its way inland, to the city. She couldn't make out any rumbling yet, but soon, she would begin to pick it out, she thought.

Her mind was snapped abruptly to attention from a pounding on her door. It started out as a double tap, then bloomed into a long tap of five or six raps. Jane quickly jumped up and ran to the door, hoping it hadn't woken Thomas. She took one last quick drag of her cigarette and inhaled deeply; then blowing it out, long and steady, she opened the door.

Jane's heart took an unexpected leap. In front of her stood Dillard Hines, all six feet of his lanky frame. He towered over her modest 5'4" build. She smelled him before he even spoke. It was the smell of bourbon. He was doing a slow wobble from side to side, a shit-eating grin on his face as he stared at her. The stare quickly became a leer as he looked at her body from head to toe.

She had a bathrobe on, but not cinched very tight. Underneath she wore one of Cullum's old T-shirts. On her, it hung long, but not as long as she would have wanted it to right now. It came to just below her crotch, showing a lot of leg. Her small breasts and pert nipples pointed out from the cotton fabric. Jane caught his gaze and quickly pulled the robe together with her one free hand, the other still holding the lit cigarette.

"Well, well, Janey my dear. Great to see you." Dillard brought his hand and arm around from behind his back, with what he had been concealing. It was an almost finished bottle of bourbon. It was a cheap brand from what she could pick out. "Thought maybe we could have that drinky now. You know, you and me." He winked a devilish wink of lust and drunkenness. The bottle held out in front of Jane, swinging back and forth, the brown liquid sloshing inside the bottled glass.

Jane's mind whirled, her heart beating fast. "No, Mr. Hines. I told you no. Now, you have to leave, and I mean right now." She emphasized "now" a little louder, but still trying not to yell for Thomas's sake.

"Ahh, com'on, baby. Just let me get a look at ya. Pleaseee…" His slurry words trailed off as his one free hand came forward, grabbing her robe, pulling it open.

Jane tried pushing his hand away, but it was to no avail. Dillard was a man, a strong man, even for his build. His hand gripped the robe tighter as he pulled her toward him, his mouth opening wide for a slobbery kiss. Even in her panic, she could pick out and count the fillings in his teeth as his lips parted, forming an *o* shape.

Jane reacted before she even thought. The hand holding the cigarette shot up to Dillard's face. She smashed its hot end into his left eye. It didn't catch him straight on but caught more of his bottom eyelid. The hot ash still made its way into his eye, causing him to yell out in pain. He dropped the bottle of bourbon on the hall floor, both his hands now going up to the injured eye. The bottle made a muted thud as it bounced and rolled around on the cheap carpet.

With her robe now free from his grip, Jane strode a step forward and with both hands pushed Dillard hard. It caught him off guard as the opened hands hit him in the chest, sending him backward. He danced awkwardly back, hitting the wall on the other side of the hall. His body made a loud thud on the plaster, as he slid down the wall, making another loud thump as he came to a rest on the floor. Jane wasted no time as she quickly stepped back inside her apartment and closed the door. She engaged the dead bolt as it made a metallic click. She turned and leaned her back on the door, bracing against it, waiting for a retaliatory attack. None ever came.

*****

Jane lay on her bed, awake, for a long time. It was late in the night, almost the witching hour. The pack of cigarettes was almost gone. The ordeal with Dillard Hines had put her in an agitated and tense state.

She had sat in her chair in the living room and waited for the heavy knock on her door, knowing it would be him. She figured he wouldn't go easily into that good night after what she had done to him. In one hand a cigarette, in the other a butcher's knife from the kitchen drawer. She waited and smoked, smoked and waited some more. Her fingers trembled as she put the cigarettes to her mouth.

She prayed Thomas didn't wake, especially after the loud struggle with the drunken creep. He didn't. He didn't even when the rumblings of the approaching storm grew louder. She was relieved for that.

Jane had finally calmed down enough to head for bed. If Dillard hadn't come back by now, she thought, he wasn't returning tonight at all. Her room was intense with heat and mugginess, common for the end of summer. She opened her window higher, letting in more of the cooling breeze from the storm that was now upon them.

The thunder boomed a mere second after the slash of lightning crossed the sky. She had been taught by Cullum that after a lightning strike, count the seconds between it and the first sound of thunder, and that would tell you how close the storm was. The calculation was a mile for every second between the two events.

As the force of the wind increased now, a little pitter-patter of raindrops began to fall. Her eyes stared up at the ceiling as she tried counting the drops. With every passing second, they increased in volume. They soon began playing a little metallic pattern on the fire escape outside her window. The hypnotic rhythm of it had her asleep in minutes.

Jane fell into a deep sleep. That's when the dream came to her. It was Cullum's B-17, flying in a terrible, lightning-infested storm. The bomber bounced and danced in the wind and rain. She could see Cullum in the captain's chair in the cockpit of the craft. He was all alone; not a single soul was with him on this flight. His face was tense. Sweat ran down his forehead and cheeks in streams. His hands clutched the steering wheel of the bomber with a whitened hardness. She could tell his whole intent was on flying the plane, keeping it on its designated course. Cullum's eyes seemed to peer into hers as she watched the massive bomber barrel toward her but never seeming to reach her. She could feel his heartbeat inside hers; it was beating horribly fast.

Jane's blood turned to ice as in the darkness behind Cullum's seat, two eyes, the color of orange and red, opened and blazed intently at her. She heard herself screaming at him to turn around, sensing the danger. The drone of the mighty engines wiped out her shouting voice. The eyes appeared closer with each passing moment, the glow of them becoming stronger and brighter as they moved toward Cullum. Out of the darkness below the eyes, two arms extended out. Long gaunt arms, still very toned and muscled, with long sharp talons on the hands, reached for him. Jane now screamed hysterically as the clawed appendixes were just inches from his neck and head. The talons opened and closed rhythmically as they closed on him.

Cullum never turned or looked around behind him. His gaze was intent on what was ahead of him. It seemed that his intent was her, that he was trying his hardest to reach her, to be with her. Jane began crying; the tears were running down her face. She could taste their saltiness on her lips and mouth. At this moment, she wanted him so bad, just to touch and feel him. To feel the blood coursing through his body, the warmth of it on her. She felt the love he had for her and prayed he felt the same love she had for him.

In the next instant, the clawed hands seized his throat, in a strangling gesture. Cullum's eyes seemed to almost pop out of his head as they widened in pain and shock. The creature's hands tightened on his neck as he tried to resist. His arms flailed out in an attempt to hit the thing but missed with every swing. The sharpened ends of the talons locked together, digging into his throat, popping veins that were bulging from the choking. Blood began flowing down onto his flight jacket. In seconds, it was covered in his life source. His mouth opened to scream, but nothing came out, just particles of spittle. He was being choked to death.

Jane's frantic screams at him seemed to fade also. She could feel herself trying to yell, but nothing was emanating from her throat. Her voice had completely escaped her. At the same instant, she felt pressure, a growing force pushing in on her throat and airway. The tightness kept increasing, seeming to take away all airflow to her lungs. She equated it to her holding her own breath, except this time, she wasn't doing it.

She saw Cullum's face go from a healthy blush to a dark blue. This creature was killing him, and she knew she couldn't save him. Hell, she felt like she couldn't save her own self from what was affecting her own throat and breathing. She felt a throbbing pain in her temples, like big gongs being beat upon. Her breath was leaving her fast. She put her hands to her neck, groping for whatever was inflicting this on her. Her fingers came to rest on flesh, human flesh that was not her own. The image of Cullum's thrashing body dissolved from her mind as she woke and opened her eyes from the dreammare.

In front of Jane, straddling over her body, was Dillard Hines. His face had a feverish, ghastly, maniacal look, as water dripped down his face and body from his rain-soaked hair. The open-armed white T-shirt he wore was also drenched in rainwater. His spindly arms rippled what muscle it had as his hands gripped her throat. He was choking her to death, and there was no talking him out of it. She tried to speak, but nothing coherent came out, just a gurgling, coughing wretch.

In her mind, panic was in full bloom. A large flash of lightning, followed by a roar of thunder, lit up the room. Jane looked out toward the window and saw it was raised to its fullest extent. Dillard had climbed up the fire escape and came through the unlocked and open portal. Rain was coming down in torrents as droplets crashed onto the fire escape and into her room. Nature was having her way with the world just as Dillard was doing the same with her.

Another flash of lightning and crack of thunder brought her mind racing back to the now. A large grin had formed on Dillard's lips, baring his gnarled, discolored teeth, as they snapped open and closed with his exertion of pressure.

"I'll teach you, to treat me like that. Yes, sireee, missy! No one does that to Dillard Hines and gets away with it!" His grip tightened harder on Jane's neck as he spoke. "When I'm done, you'll have wished that you had at least let me touch you!" he screamed in crazy glee.

The world seemed to darken even more around her. The sounds of the raging storm seemed distant, far away. The pounding in her head was still there, but seeming to recede in its intensity. Jane knew in the next few seconds she would be dead if she didn't move now. She brought her right arm up, hitting Dillard in the side of the head. The left came up and dug her nails into his cheek and eye. He screamed in pain as he released his grip on her throat and smacked her arms away.

"You bitch!" he bellowed as he swung his right fist out and into Jane's face. She felt her teeth crunch in a sickening wave of pain and a coppery taste of blood. For a brief respite, she sucked in air through her unrestricted throat, gasping and coughing through her damaged windpipe.

Dillard raised his arm back up to pummel her again, when something heavy and metallic connected with the side of his head. Jane heard the meaty splat of skin and bone being drastically abused. Dillard fell off her and rolled against the wall where the open window was, hitting it with a thud. The rain splattered his upper body, resoaking his wounded head. Blood began mingling with the water, running down his right temple to his chin, a reward of the unexpected blow.

"You leave my mom alone. You hear!" yelled Thomas, standing by the foot of Jane's bed, a heavy large toy fire truck still hanging in his hand, the weapon used on Dillard.

Jane rolled to the left side of the bed, away from Dillard, still gasping and trying to collect herself. She sat up on the side of it, reaching her arm out for Thomas. He seemed to be moving in slow motion to Jane as he stepped toward her. But on the other hand,

Dillard moved fast, with catlike reflexes. He was up and off the floor and around the bed before she and Thomas even touched. He yanked viciously on the boy's pajama collar, whipping Thomas around as the material of the top screamed in a tearing sound. Dillard pirouetted with the boy, flinging him back toward the open doorway. The fire truck flew out of his grasp, hitting the wall by the window, bouncing up in the air, flipping and landing perfectly on its tires on the wet floor. Thomas, on the other hand, didn't fare as well. His left shoulder and arm caught part of the framework of the doorway. There was a definite crunching sound made, indicating a bone somewhere on his body had broken. Thomas fell to the floor in a heap.

Jane had gulped in much-needed oxygen, and now her maternal engine roared to life. Like a woman possessed, she leaped from the bed onto the back of Dillard Hines. The nails of her hands tore into his face and dug deep, this time bringing blood. Dillard screamed in agony and pain, trying to reach around and hit her. Each time he did, she raked her nails harder across his face, causing it to turn into a furrowed mess of plowed skin and goo. Realizing he couldn't dislodge her quickly, not wanting to have his eyes clawed out, Dillard drove his body backward into the nearest wall. Jane was caught between, like a vise, as the two masses connected. The whole wall shook as a section of plaster gave way to Jane's body, exploding, sending pieces flying into the air. But it didn't give enough to keep her from having all the air taken out of her recently replenished lungs. The unexpected loss of oxygen sent her collapsing to the floor. She lay there, looking up at a ravaged Dillard, trying again to take in much-needed air, gasping between inhales.

Dillard looked down at her, blood dripping from ragged wounds. "Well, bitch! Now I'm gonna kill you and your little bastard of a boy. Then after I do that, I'm gonna fuck the shit out of you!"

When Dillard had climbed the fire escape to her apartment, he had done so without any shoes or socks; he had done it barefooted. Now, standing on the rain-soaked wooden-slated floor, his bare feet had become a liability. He made his move toward Jane, reaching out to grab her, as his feet slipped on the puddled liquid surface. Without traction, both feet and legs slid out from under him and kicked high into the air. His arms flailed, trying to grab anything to right himself. It was to no avail as he realized nothing was within reach to help him. All he could do was fall backward to meet the awaiting floor and the toy fire truck.

In the fire truck's journey of flying through the air, hitting the wall, and landing on the floor, it had landed perfectly facing up. Its long extension ladder, used by firemen to climb up and into burning buildings, had been freed from its neutral resting place and was now standing straight up at attention, as if waiting for said firemen to climb it and do their duty. Only this time no toy firemen would climb it. This time, it waited for the falling back of Dillard Hines. The hard metal piece caught his back, square between the shoulder blades. The velocity of him falling and his body weight was all that was needed. The ladder entered, impaling him, pushing through his body, tearing apart arteries and his cold, evil heart. As he hit the floor and the truck, the ladder broke through his chest and the T-shirt he was wearing. At first the material of the shirt refused to give but made an interestingly gruesome type of tent, held high in the air above his body. Then, with an eerie tearing of fabric, the bloody ladder popped through, exposing it, dripping with gore and pieces of his destroyed heart. Blood began pumping out of his ragged wound like an oil rig that had struck the mother lode.

Dillard looked up at Jane, who now stood over him. He tried reaching an arm out to her, panic and realization in his eyes. "Help… me…help…" With those last words, he ceased to exist. His arm flopped back to the floor, hitting the puddled water with a splat.

Jane stepped and fell back to the wall, resting against it, trying to get her breath and bearings fully back.

"Mommy?" The lone word came from the little body of Thomas, curled up on the floor.

Jane ran to him, rolling him over and bringing him up into her arms. Her eyes frantically searched his body for wounds or injuries.

"My…arm hurts…bad," he mumbled with pain in his tone.

"I know, sweetie. It's probably broke. We need to get you to a doctor right away." Tears ran from her eyes as her heart ached for him. She wrapped her arms around him in a loving and caring hug.

She thanked God that he was still alive. It would be her and Thomas against the world for a long time to come.

Way back in the recesses of her mind, she pictured Cullum. The feeling she got at this moment was different. She didn't know or couldn't define what it was. Or what to even call it. Most people would call it a premonition, a foreboding of things to come, or that were. It gnawed at the pit of her stomach, slashing into her body, her soul. Another type of heaviness hammered her heart, not just about everything that had happened to her and Thomas, but about Cullum. The things she had seen and felt in her dreams sent a message. It seemed now that it had sent a clear and defining message. Somewhere inside her it told her that she would never see Cullum Davis ever again.

Epilogue

(We're not in Kansas Anymore)

"Was that the last word you got from *Fallen Angel*?"

"Yes, sir. That was about twenty minutes ago," the radio operator at the control tower for Molesworth Airfield answered.

A B-17 came roaring over the tower, wheels in their down position, heading for the tarmac that was lined on both sides with large bright runway lights. Its wheels touched the landing strip. A screech of rubber on solid surface permeated the air, as it bounced slightly back into the air. It traveled a short distance and touched the ground a second time, this time to stay. The rear of the craft touched down on its single wheel, located below the tail section, as the bomber raced down the strip, slowly coming to a stop.

"That's the last one landing now, sir," a lieutenant announced as he approached the officer by the radio set.

"So *Fallen Angel* is the only plane still out there, Lieutenant Malby?"

"Yes, sir. The rest are all presumed lost."

"So what is that? We lost twelve out of forty-eight of this flight? Is that what the numbers state?"

"Yes, Major Sandersteen. Thirteen if you include *Fallen Angel*."

"Well, I'm not about to count her out yet. Cullum Davis is a good skipper. He still might bring her home." Major Sandersteen stood, arms behind his back, peering out into the dark gloom.

"Radar show anything on her?" Sandersteen yelled back to the radar operator, who was looking intently at his screen.

"Nothing, sir. She's not in range yet, still too far out."

RANDY STAN

"You said they sent a message?" Sandersteen asked Malby, looking very pensive.

"Yes. Benson, read the message back again." Malby looked back toward his radio operator.

Benson, the radioman, grabbed a sheet of paper from his desk. Looking it over, he slowly read it aloud, "They said, 'Plane damaged. We are under attack from harpies. They are...,' and that was the end of the transmission."

"What the hell, harpies?" Sandersteen asked inquisitively, looking around the tower room at everyone. His eyes settled back on Malby.

"Yes. Harpies. I'm like you, Major. Really, what does that mean? The term 'harpy,' does that refer to a type of aircraft the Nazis have? For one, I've never heard any of their planes ever called that. Is this some new one we don't know about?"

"Never heard of anything or aircraft with that name. The only harpies I know of are the ones from nature. You know, the giant bird or eagle-like things." Sandersteen stood closer to the large window of the tower, pondering.

"You know there are ones in Greek mythology, Major?"

Sandersteen looked at the lieutenant with eyes squinted in reproach, skeptical of what was just stated. "What are you talking about?"

"A harpy was some type of bird of prey. A rapacious monster, large, with the body of a bird, huge predator claws, but yet had the face of a female. Supposedly, Satan had control of them. They were his little helpers, so to speak. They would go out into the world, grab people, and take their souls back to hell, for the devil to devour. Yes, sir, that's the only ones I know about. But remember these are all just myths. Creature and things from ages long ago, when the world was rife with those stories," Malby returned, with a slight painful grin on his face.

"Well, for one I can't or won't even comprehend or believe that that's what's attacking our bomber. How in God's name could something like that be for real?" Sandersteen spun around from the window to face Malby.

232

"I'm just telling you what I know about, when the word 'harpy' was mentioned. That's all, sir." Malby's face turned a light shade of red, now realizing he had said the wrong thing to the wrong man.

"There is just no goddamn way something like that could ever exist. Not on this planet, not in this age. To say some kind of winged monster is attacking our bombers is just preposterous. I mean we kid about little gremlins screwing with our planes, fouling them up. But there has never been any proof of anything like that happening. It's just plain poppycock. Just like your myth, Malby, it's just an old wives' tale. If I were to go to the general staff and tell them this is what happened, they would want to put a straitjacket on me. I would wind up with them putting me in a padded cell and throwing away the key." Anger splashed across Sandersteen's face as he talked.

"Sir, I'm just stating the information. It doesn't mean I believe it at all." Malby felt fully embarrassed, his face a bright red as he looked around at the other soldiers in the tower.

"You brought it up, Malby, so I'm sure you're kind of thinking about it, thinking that just maybe that is really happening. Don't you?"

Malby scrambled inside, trying to right the ship, knowing he had put his foot in it, now trying to step out of it, without making a mess. "Not at all, sir. Maybe, just maybe, they might have been hit and torn up really bad. You know, shell-shocked. Sir, they might not know what they're saying or even seeing."

Sandersteen stood for a moment, fingers cupping his chin in thought. "We'll go with that, Malby. I can't or won't envision a modern-day bomber crew thinking they're doing battle with a creature from hell, something from hundreds of years ago."

Malby shook his head in agreement. Sandersteen looked around the room at all the soldiers in it. "Everyone is going with that logical answer. Does everyone get that?" The room was quiet. Not a sound came from anyone, just all the equipment making minor beeps or squawks. "Gentlemen, do you hear me? I want a response!" Sandersteen yelled out the last statement.

Every soldier in that room knew not to go against the major; he was the top dog in the outfit. You go against him and you were up shit's creek. "Yes, sir!" everyone returned in loud unison.

"Now, all we can do is wait and hope they come home." Sandersteen slowly walked over to the open door and stepped out onto the stair landing. He turned his head up to the starry night sky and stared. The bomber never returned.

Months later, when Allied forces made it to the last known area of where the *Fallen Angel* was last reported to have been at, they found a burned-out, destroyed hulk of a B-17. There were no bodies or any traces whatsoever of human remains. There was not a flight jacket, goggles, gloves, or shoes. It was as if the bomber had been swept and cleaned of any trace of a human being ever even being on it. Nor were there any remains of anything else, nonhuman, at the site. To everyone's belief and determination, the crew had bailed out of the disabled plane and were caught and probably killed by German soldiers. Their bodies were then taken away and buried in some mass grave, far from the plane. The United States Air Force signed off and marked the case closed on the downing of the B-17 bomber, numbered 5804, *Fallen Angel*.

Long years later, as he lay on his deathbed, blackish phlegm spitting out of his cancer-riddled body, and the edges of dementia settling into his brain, former major Samuel Sandersteen screamed out at loved ones around him. "Those things destroyed my bomber! Those damn demons killed my boys!"

The teary-eyed group gathered before him looked at each other, thinking it was just the ramblings of an old man at the end of his life.

About the Author

Randy Stan was born and raised in a small community in East Chicago, Indiana. He worked for many years in the steel mills of Northwest Indiana as a maintenance welder and safety advocate. After retiring from the mills, he worked as a jack-of-all-trades in a funeral home (the best job he ever had). These jobs plus his childhood experiences, and his ability to listen, have led to him writing all his different and eclectic stories.

CPSIA information can be obtained
at www.ICGtesting.com
Printed in the USA
LVHW030939260422
717217LV00006B/94

9 781638 816911